IMPACT

Book 3 of The Sunfall Series

D. GIDEON

IMPACT
Book 3 of The Sunfall Series
D. Gideon

Copyright © 2019 by D. Gideon
v. 12.18.19
Cover Art by Christian Bentulan
All rights reserved.
ISBN-13: 9781677245543

www.DrewGideon.com

For my husband, Mike.
Thank you for sharing our life with all
the characters living in my head. ;)

Necessity is the plea for every infringement of human freedom.
It is the argument of tyrants; it is the creed of slaves.

~ William Pitt

Any excuse will serve a tyrant.

~ Aesop

A patriot must always be ready to defend his country
against his government.

~ Edward Abbey

PROLOGUE

On the evening of Labor Day, an incredibly large solar flare caused a CME that impacted the Earth and destroyed the power grid.

At the University of Maryland, a group of students set off on foot to make it home to Snow Hill, Maryland...130 miles and one Chesapeake Bay away.

During their trip, they became separated. Corey and Melanie found bicycles to ease their travel, while Ripley and Marco continued on foot.

Back home in Snow Hill, Ripley's neighbor and grandmother-by-heart, Dotty Parker, watched her quiet little town be torn apart. Without electricity and running water, desperate residents and stranded tourists turned to riots and vandalism.

Snow Hill's Mayor offered to save the day: He'd open the local Recreational Center as a temporary shelter. Residents could find relief and safety there. The Center's bank of solar panels provided electricity, and the building conveniently gathered the townspeople together in one easily-controlled group.

The President declared the entire nation to be in a State of

Emergency. Martial Law was enacted. The National Guard was called forth to quell the rioting. The Governor of Maryland instituted a dusk to dawn curfew, and with the prisons running out of resources, he pardoned all prisoners within the state's boundaries.

With the federal prison warden MIA, former Warden and current Sheriff Simon Kane refused to release violent criminals onto unsuspecting townspeople. With help from some friends and a little creative thinking, he delivered the non-violent criminals in his charge to the Governor's doorstep in Annapolis. The violent criminals were given a party and set free...into a deep, dark pit from which they'd never rise. He and Father Bill Flannigan, a local pastor and leader of a congregation at the federal prison, chose a handful of deserving inmates to integrate into small-town life, naming it the New Hope program.

Feeling called to attend the New Hope meeting, Dotty Parker ended up adopting one of those inmates into her makeshift family: a heavily-muscled, heavily-tattooed beast of a man named Preacher.

On the seventh day after the sun fell down, Corey and Melanie made it home a few hours before Ripley and Marco. While they'd all been through harrowing situations and nearly lost their lives, they'd made it. They were safe now.

Or so they thought.

IMPACT starts ten days after the kids made it home.

PREACHER

The ragtag group pushed a wheelbarrow of weapons down the street, and the MRAP crept along behind them.

"I wish they'd hurry up and decide what they're gonna do," Ripley muttered.

"Stay cool," Preacher said. From the corner of his vision, he could see that the ruts in the sidewalk had caused the wheelbarrow's tarp to jostle out of place. The butt of Ripley's little rifle and the handle of his axe were showing. Nothing he could do about that; if he stopped to fix it, he'd just draw attention to it.

A small brown hand wrapped around his forearm and he smirked. To his left, Miss Dotty had stepped in close and taken his arm. It was nothing out of place for an older woman to do on an uneven sidewalk.

That it obscured the Guard's view into the wheelbarrow?

Damn shame, that. Really. Damn shame.

The MRAP's driver must have caught sight of the crowd gathering at the end of the street, because the vehicle accelerated past them in a loud rush. Dotty reached down and yanked the tarp back into place.

"I'm gettin' mighty tired of that," she said.

He nodded in agreement. "I'll lash it down next time."

"Not the tarp," she said, frowning. She waved a hand, indicating the MRAP at the end of the street. "That."

"The military on the street, or the extra scrutiny? Because you've got to expect some double-takes when someone like you is walking with someone like him," Ripley said.

"It's rude," Dotty sniffed.

"Inside or outside, all guards are the same," Preacher said.

Ripley gave him a sharp look. "You saying we're in a prison?"

He stared at the MRAP for a moment, then looked back at her, brows raised.

She sighed and frowned. "Point taken."

He caught her sideways glance at his hands; noticed her step further to the right. She was nearly off of the sidewalk now. The girl was a skittish kitten, always making sure she was out of arm's reach. He didn't think she even knew she was doing it. He scared her; he knew that. He scared just about everyone. So she'd surprised him this morning when she announced she was coming along. She was probably just doing it to make sure he didn't hurt Miss Dotty, but that was fine. There were full-grown men that would have refused to go into the woods alone with him, much less allow him to disarm them and hide their weapon out of reach. He'd heard Marco talking to Corey about what had happened to her on the way home. It hadn't been pretty. But here she was, head up and jaw set. The girl had grit.

"Looks like trouble," Dotty said, drawing his attention back to the corner. The members of the Guard were nearly yelling now, and men were climbing down from the top of the MRAP. The members of the group had spread out, giving each other room. The

MRAP's gunner swung his 50-cal around to face the small crowd. One of the civilians stepped in front of the others, his hands doing a "calm down" motion. A Guardsman shouldered his rifle and screamed for the man to get on his knees.

"Bill," Dotty gasped, and let go of Preacher's arm to hurry forward.

"Shit. Take this," he said, dropping the handles of the wheelbarrow.

"Got it. Go," Ripley said.

He passed Dotty in four long strides and spun to block her, holding his arms out. She nearly barreled into him.

"What-? Move," she said.

"No. Stay back here." He stepped off the curb when she tried to go around him.

"David, get out of my way. Bill could get hurt-"

"*You* could get hurt."

"Don't be a fool," she started, but jumped as a shrill WOOP WOOP sounded and a big engine accelerated behind them. Sheriff Kane's squad car went flying past, lights blazing.

"Warden's here," Preacher said, grabbing Dotty's hand. "He'll handle it."

She huffed in exasperation and shuffled her feet, but stopped trying to get around him.

"Next time, you've got permission to throw her over your shoulder," Ripley said, pushing the wheelbarrow up next to them. She set it down and came to stand behind Dotty, wrapping her arms around the little woman. Conscious of how close this put the girl to him, Preacher started to step away, but Dotty squeezed his hand and tugged him back. With her free hand, she stroked a small gold cross hanging from her necklace.

"I'm gettin' mighty tired of this," she said again.

The trio watched as Sheriff Kane exited his car and thrust

himself into the mess. His large frame dwarfed that of the soldiers, and holding his arms up, he looked even bigger.

"Put the guns down!" His voice carried in the town's quiet stillness, the only other sounds being those of his car and the MRAP's engine.

The man who'd been on the top of the MRAP barked a command. Sheriff Kane and the soldier, who Preacher assumed was a Sergeant, exchanged words. They weren't close enough to hear what was being said, but here and there a sharp word would ring out. Father Bill stepped forward, and Preacher heard the Sergeant's sharp voice tell him to step back. He thrust a finger in Bill's direction, and all of the men and women around Bill stiffened.

"Steady," Preacher said. "Not yet."

"What?" Ripley asked, her gaze snapping to him.

He gestured to the small crowd. "Prisoners," he said. "He shouldn't threaten Father Bill. They won't like it."

"Those people don't look like convicts," she said.

"They are," Dotty said. "I recognize a few of them."

The interaction between the Sheriff and the soldiers lasted another few tense minutes, and then the Sergeant took Bill aside to speak privately. The Sheriff looked back in their direction and nodded at Preacher. He hadn't forgotten they were there.

Preacher gave one short nod in return. *Warden doesn't forget anything*, he thought. The soldiers loaded themselves back up, hanging off of the sides of the MRAP like monkeys. The big vehicle turned and headed up through the center of town. The Sheriff waved Preacher and the ladies over.

"It ain't right," a tall, broad-shouldered white woman was saying as they joined the group. "The First Amendment says we can talk on this corner all day long if we're not bothering anyone or obstructing business."

"And it's past the curfew," said a lean man, a fine fuzz of blond hair beginning to cover his scalp.

"I know, Trench. Believe me, I know," Bill said. "But the Mayor and the Governor have given the Guard orders, and their job is to follow orders."

"What orders? And what were you doin' stepping out in front of all those guns? You trying to get yourself shot?" Dotty asked, hands on her hips.

"The Sergeant said they're supposed to break up any groups of more than three people," Bill said, stepping forward and pulling Dotty's hands free.

"The Mayor's calling it riot control," Sheriff Kane said.

"It ain't right, Warden," the tall woman said.

"Because of the declaration, it's a grey area," the Sheriff said. "I'm working on it."

Bill nodded and turned to the group, pulling Dotty to stand beside him. "Ladies and gentlemen, I'd like you to meet a friend of mine. This-" he stepped a bit to the side and waved his hand in a little flourish, "is Miss Dotty."

A hushed sound of wonder came from the assembled crowd, and the large woman stepped forward, hand extended.

"I am so honored to meet you, Miss Dotty," she said. "If it wasn't for those books you sent in each week, I swear I would've gone insane. Thank you so much for that."

Dotty shook the woman's hand and shrugged. "Well you're welcome, but it wasn't nothin'. They were just a quarter at yard sales-"

"They were a life saver," the big woman insisted. "The prison didn't have anything published after 1980, I swear. I'm Daisy."

"It's nice to meet you, Daisy. I've got more books at the house, if you want to come by-"

"I'll bring them tomorrow," Preacher said.

Dotty flashed him a look as Daisy backed up and a stocky, older black man took her place. Preacher raised an eyebrow at the little woman and shrugged. She'd probably get on him about it later, but he didn't want people just dropping by the house. It was already hard enough keeping track of all the people coming and going there.

"Miss Dotty I have to thank you," the stocky man said, taking one of Dotty's hands in both of his. "Father Bill told us about your trick, um, of putting fish heads in with tomato plants?"

"He did, did he?" Dotty said.

"Oh he told us all about your gardening tips," the man said, smiling broadly. "I used your tomato seeds, and I've, uh, been putting fish heads and egg shells from the kitchens in with my tomatoes every season for years now. My plants have the biggest and best-tasting tomatoes in the garden."

"Eugene was one of the men permitted to work in the prison garden," Sheriff Kane supplied.

Preacher looked around and swore under his breath. Ripley had left and he hadn't even noticed. He turned slowly, not wanting to worry Dotty, and saw the girl standing across the street. She'd taken her little rifle out of the wheelbarrow and was standing in the shade of a big elm tree close to the hardware store. The rifle was slung and at the ready. His eye caught a flash of metal, and he realized that she'd had her pistol on her the entire time. She'd covered it with a big button-down shirt that must have belonged to her father. She was wearing the shirt open, like an overshirt, and it was just enough to mask the pistol. He'd never have seen it if a breeze hadn't shifted the shirt to the side. No wonder she'd been okay with giving up her rifle. Clever girl.

The conversation continued, with more people wanting to meet Dotty, and Preacher stepped back from the crowd. He caught the Sheriff's eye and nodded towards Ripley. The Sheriff looked in that direction, then turned back and shrugged.

Preacher crossed the street and leaned against the other side of the tree. He scanned the sidewalks, but there was no one out this early. It was barely past daybreak. Normally, he'd have been in the woods by now. He caught his thoughts and nearly chuckled.

Guess I've got a new definition of normal.

Before Sunfall, as the townspeople were calling it, normal would've seen him running laps around the prison perimeter, outside of the recess yard but still within the fence. He was the only prisoner permitted out there, three times a day, for an hour each time. Warden Kane had extended him that privilege when his laps around the edge of the basketball court had made a deep rut. For some reason that he'd never figured out, the privilege had stuck even after Kane had left to become Sheriff.

For the past week, though, his routine had been to get up before daybreak, when all the nighttime trouble-makers were heading back to their rat holes, and bring the wheelbarrow down here to the woods. It was a routine he'd taken upon himself; a way to pay for his room and board. He was collecting dead wood out of the trees by the river to beef up Mr. Miller's woodpile. The family —meaning all nine of them living in the two houses—had decided that once it got cold enough, they'd all move into the Miller's house. It had a cast iron stove in the living room, while all the heat in Dotty's house was electric. But Seth hadn't had a chance to order another cord of wood for the winter; he'd planned to do it when he came home with the money from his seasonal work at the beach. They'd need more if they were going to make it through the winter without freezing.

Preacher tightened his fists to crack his knuckles, anxious to get to work. All this standing around, doing nothing, made him uneasy. At least the sky had stopped looking like it was bleeding. That shit had been creepy.

Ripley finally broke the silence. "You know that woman well? The big one?" she asked.

"Daisy? No," he said. "I only see her here, in the mornings."

"Yeah, I guess they wouldn't have let you fraternize with the women. It was a dumb question." She shuffled her feet and blew out a deep breath. He heard her ring tapping against the wood of her rifle and cocked an eyebrow.

"Problem?" he asked.

"She just reminds me of someone," Ripley said.

"A friend?"

"One of the women I killed."

He knew better than to say anything else. You didn't ask people about their kills. She'd talk about it if she wanted to.

"Why are they all fawning over Grams like that?"

"Father Bill talked about her a lot," he said.

"So she's like a prison celebrity?"

"Something like that."

They watched the crowd flowing around Dotty and Bill, each person stepping forward to make introductions and shake hands. Sheriff Kane leaned against his squad car, arms crossed, staring in the direction the MRAP had gone.

"Friggin' creepy," he heard Ripley mutter.

Truth be told, it was, but he understood it. Prisoners would latch on to anyone on the outside who showed them the smallest bit of kindness. Either to use them in some way, or just to remind the prisoner that there was someone out in the real world who still gave a shit. For years he'd been hearing stories from Father Bill about what Dotty had been up to, and the pastor had brought things from her every week. Books and magazines, seeds for the garden, even baked goods showed up now and then. The little woman had nearly reached the status of exalted saint among some of Bill's prison congregation, and she'd never even met any of them.

Creepy or not, he'd take it. If Dotty had a small army of adoring fans, that might make protecting her a little easier. He still didn't want people he didn't know coming by the house, though, and he didn't know *any* of the women in the group.

A tinkle of bells interrupted the silence, and an older man's voice called out. "Hey mister? You there, at the tree. Big fella."

Preacher and Ripley both turned. A skinny man, maybe in his early seventies, was leaning out of the hardware store and waving to them.

"That's Teddy," Ripley said, voice low. "He runs the hardware store. Grams used to work for him. Be nice."

Be nice?

Preacher frowned at her, and she fixed him with a scathing look.

"I'm serious," she said. "He gets cranky sometimes, but he's harmless. Don't kill him."

"Fine. But only because you said so."

Her eyes widened for a second before she realized he'd been joking, then narrowed into a glare.

"Come on over here," Teddy called. "I need to talk to you."

"Not. Funny," Ripley hissed.

Preacher smirked and stepped out from the tree, heading over to see what the little old man wanted.

PREACHER

Teddy kicked a worn wooden stop under the door and leaned against the frame, crossing his arms. He looked over the two of them with a critical eye as they approached.

"You Dotty's new prison stray that I heard about?" he asked.

Preacher bit back a response and looked at Ripley.

"Preacher, this is Teddy. Teddy, Preacher. He's come to live with us," Ripley said.

"So you *are* her new stray."

"She took me in," Preacher said, cautious.

Teddy scratched a short, patchy beard. "I've seen you, every mornin', heading off to the river. See ya heading back with a load of wood a while later. You gettin' that wood for her?"

"Need wood to make it through the winter," Preacher said.

Teddy nodded and looked towards the crowd at the corner. He pointed to the wheelbarrow.

"You've got a good work ethic, son, but all I ever see you with is a big axe and that wheelbarrow. That all you got?"

"It's all Dotty has."

"You could've asked my dad," Ripley said. "I thought you used that axe because you wanted to."

Preacher shook his head. "I work with what I've got."

Teddy clicked his tongue. "Hell of a thing, the Sheriff puttin' you out with nothing but the clothes on your back."

"The Sheriff did more than he needed to," Preacher said.

Teddy gave a little grunt that said he had his doubts, then nodded to himself and straightened.

"A man needs tools if he's gonna make a go of it. You know how to cut lumber? Build things? You good with a hammer? A wrench?"

"What do you need done?" Preacher asked.

"I ain't askin' you to *do* nothing," Teddy snapped. "I'm asking if you've got skills, son. I'm asking if you've got the capability to make yourself useful, besides usin' that brawn to bust up some old rotten trees."

"I do, but-" Preacher started, and Teddy interrupted him.

"Yeah? Well get on in here and pick yourself out some tools. I'll know whether to believe you by what you bring back."

Preacher shook his head. "I don't have money."

"Did I ask if you had money? Did I say you had to buy anything? You need tools. I've got tools. What the hell am I gonna do with two dozen hammers and another dozen saws? Build another case to hold my fifty thousand nails?"

Ripley gave a little snort and quickly cleared her throat, staring hard at the ground.

"What's the catch?" Preacher asked. Nothing ever came for free.

"There ain't no catch," Teddy said. "You use it to take care of that girl." He gestured towards Dotty. "She goes on about people not havin' no sense, then does fool stuff like bringin' home the biggest, baddest, meanest-lookin' sonofabitch she can find. She probably baked you *cookies*."

Preacher snorted and felt the edges of his mouth lift a bit. Dotty *had* baked cookies that first night, using the Miller's gas oven.

"They were oatmeal raisin," Ripley said, her smile wide. "She made them from scratch."

"See? That's what I thought. Fool woman." Teddy looked into the store, looked back at Preacher, and huffed. "You hard of hearing? I'm giving you tools. Go get 'em."

"He won't take no for an answer," Ripley said. "Grams calls him a stubborn old goat."

"Might be the only thing she's right about," Teddy said, stepping aside so Preacher could pass him.

Preacher didn't move. He definitely needed the tools, but life had taught him that everything came with a price. A steep, bloody price. And if you didn't acknowledge it up front, it would come back to bite you at the worst possible time. The old man seemed sincere, but Preacher was already walking a thin line. There wasn't room for trusting strangers.

"I don't mean to sound ungrateful, sir, but say I take some tools. What's to keep you from saying I stole them? The Sheriff's got a bullet waiting for me if I step out of line." He shook his head. "Thank you, but no. I'll make do with what I have. You have a good day."

He could hear Teddy cussing and griping as he walked back towards the crowd and Dotty's rusted garden wheelbarrow.

"Hold on," Teddy called. "What if I made you a trade for the tools?"

Preacher didn't even bother to turn. "I don't have anything to trade," he called back.

"You got those muscles, and you said you got skills, right? I do have a thing or two that you could work on."

That stopped him. A trade for labor, he could do. The Sheriff had thrust them out into this community and given them a couple of directives. The first had been to make themselves valuable to the community; integrate themselves. Use their skills as currency. That was part of why they met up each morning; for the Sheriff to keep tabs on what they all were doing and where they'd be, and to see if anyone had taken on a project that needed more hands. The other thing the Sheriff had them preparing for...well, hopefully that would never come to pass.

He walked back to the little man and saw that Ripley had gone inside the store. "What kind of work?"

Teddy huffed and made a face like he'd swallowed something sour. "Just to make sure we're clear, I ain't asking for help. I don't need help. This is a job offer."

"I'm listening."

Teddy studied Preacher's face for a moment, then nodded. "I can't stay here. Been sleeping here for days to keep them fools from breaking in at night. They ain't brazen enough to try during the day. *Yet*."

"What about your house?"

"That's the thing, ain't it? Can't be two places at once." Teddy scratched at his beard again; a motion that Preacher had caught himself doing often. A week of not shaving had covered his head and jaw in fuzz. It hadn't caught up to his goatee yet, but it was getting there. He'd thought about having Marco look for a straight razor on one of his clandestine scavenging trips, but then realized he'd fit in better if he left it alone. All of the male prisoners the Sheriff had brought out for the New Home program had been bald when they were released. It made them too easy to spot.

"So far they've been leaving my house alone. They're just

trying to loot out the stores. I gotta get what's here in my store moved to the workshop at my house. I got a truck you can use and some full gas cans in my shop. Should get you by if you're careful. You empty the store into my workshop, and I'll pay you in tools," Teddy said.

Preacher looked into the store, considering all the rows of shelving and bins. Ripley had pulled out a roll of chicken wire and was comparing it to a panel of heavier gauge stuff.

"That's not exactly a one-person job," Preacher said. "Not if you want it done fast."

"I don't necessarily need it done fast, I just need it *done*. And if it's going to take a while, someone needs to sleep here at night until it *is* done."

Preacher considered it. "What if I get help? Same deal? Pay in tools?"

Teddy crossed his arms. "Your guys, your deal. But you might want to put restrictions on it. Say, only as much as they can carry in their bare arms."

"If my pay is more, that could cause issues."

"Tell them to suck it up. A foreman gets paid more than a grunt," Teddy said. "And I ain't gonna stand here babysitting y'all. Both of these projects will be your responsibility."

"Both?"

"I need an outhouse, like what Seth Miller built. Close to the house, but far enough from the well that it don't get tainted. I've got an old barn at the back of my property that's been falling in for a while. Tear that down, use the wood for the outhouse."

"I want in on that," Ripley called. She stood, brushing her hands off on her cargo pants. "I need some wood for rabbit hutches."

"There's plenty to be had, if you ain't too picky," Teddy said.

"I've never been picky," she said, joining them at the door. She adjusted her rifle strap and thumbed back over her shoulder. "Me and the guys help Preacher out, and in return I get some wood and some of those 14 gauge wire mesh panels? The one-inch by half-inch stuff?"

Preacher checked the crowd and saw Dotty coming towards them. The sound of hammering started up inside the church; Seth Miller must have arrived to do more work. He heard a throat clear, and realized the old man was waiting for him to say something.

"What?" he said.

"I said it would be your responsibility," Teddy said. "You find the labor, you work out a fair deal."

"Why me? There's plenty of guys over there-"

"Because you're the only one I see busting his ass every morning. Because you wouldn't take a handout—I respect that. And because once I tell Dotty that we made a deal, she'll hold you to it while I'm gone." He grinned, a sly look on his face. "Insurance."

"Wait a minute. Gone?" Ripley said.

"My daughter and grand babies are up in Salisbury. They shoulda been here by now. I'm gonna go see why they ain't," Teddy said. "Bring 'em home."

"You do *not* want to do that," Ripley said. "You don't know what it's like out there-"

"Young lady, I've been to war. And I see these traitors toolin' around on our streets, harassing people while wearing our uniforms. I know *exactly* what it's like."

"Traitor is a harsh label, Teddy," Dotty said, coming up to put her hand on his shoulder.

"If they don't want the label, they shouldn't be actin' like it," Teddy said, shooing Ripley out of the way and closing the shop's front door. "I remember my oath. Enemies foreign *and* domestic."

"I agree that what they did earlier was a little over the line, but they're just trying to keep the peace," Dotty said.

Teddy snorted and pulled a folded paper from his back pocket. "I was back in the workshop yesterday getting Millie packed up. Heard some engines come and go. When I went back up to the house, I found this stuck in the door."

Ripley plucked the paper from his hand and opened it. Her brows furrowed. "FEMA Disaster Assistance?"

"There was a note with it saying I've got two days to fill it out and turn it in or they'll come back for a mandatory inspection," Teddy said. "That's not happening."

"Who's Millie?" Preacher asked.

"Not who, *what*," Dotty said. "It's his tank. And why are you packing it up?"

"How many times I gotta tell you? She's not a tank, she's a *track*. A personnel carrier. You gettin' memory loss already, woman?" Teddy said.

Dotty shook her head. "As far as I'm concerned, if it has those tread things, it's a tank." She looked back up at Preacher. "He went to at least a dozen government auctions before he found it and dragged it all the way back here."

"Millie kept me alive in Vietnam," Teddy said. "I wasn't gonna let her get turned to scrap. Brought her home and fixed her up right."

"He pulls it out every summer for the Fourth of July parade, and pulls people out of the ditches with it in the winter," Dotty continued. "In between I think the old fool rubs it with a diaper."

"It's a chamois," Teddy growled. "Keeps the water marks off."

Preacher pointed down the road where the soldiers had gone. "Like that thing? Big gun on top?"

"Nah, that's just a truck," Teddy said. "Millie's a one-one-three diesel. She *did* have a gun, originally, but it had been removed when I found her. Getting a replacement would've taken all kinds of extra paperwork and I didn't want to go through the trouble. Wish I had, now. But she'll keep me safe from small arms fire, and there ain't much that can stop her. I can even cross rivers if I have to."

Ripley had finished reading the paper, and was flipping it over repeatedly.

"The type is different," she muttered. Preacher held out a hand and she passed it over.

"See?" She pointed. "The typeface on the front isn't the same as on the back. Like...they printed it out, and then printed more stuff on the back from a different program or file. And what they're asking is just...ridiculous. They don't need to know all that."

"Damn right they don't," Teddy said, fishing through a ring of keys and locking the bolts on the door.

Preacher flipped it back to the front and scanned it. *Homeland Security* was printed across the top with *FEMA Disaster Assistance* right under it, and then a big block of small print about how the information would be used. The form on the front was relatively simple: name, address, date of birth, phone number and social security number. There was a little box to check certifying that the applicant was a US citizen. There was a place for a signature and date, and then a bunch of empty boxes for administrative use with a warning not to write there or the application would be delayed.

"You still haven't said why you're packing Millie," Dotty said.

"I'm going to Salisbury to get Bree and the kids," Teddy said. "And don't give me that look. My mind's made up. Save your breath."

Preacher knew that wasn't going to happen. As the two started arguing, he stepped away so he could concentrate on the back of the application. Ripley moved with him, although still out of arm's reach.

She was right. The letters on the back were smaller, and the print was different. He'd done some work in the computer room at his first prison when he'd been working on getting transferred, and if he had to guess, someone had whipped this up in Microsoft Word.

Ripley huffed and moved up next to him, so she could point out specific sections.

"First, they want every bit of info of *every* person staying in the house, their relationship to the applicant, and check this out: home address, if different than applicant's. They're specifically looking for out-of-towners."

"Or prisoners," he said. He pointed to a checkbox on the right. "Checkbox for convicted felons."

"And okay, I can understand the *are you in food distress* and the medical distress questions, but then to ask how many pounds of food are in the house? That can't be legit. It's like they're taking inventory."

The form also asked if anyone in the home had a medical condition, and if so, to list out each person's condition and the medications—including dosage and amounts—that they had on hand. That could be taking inventory, too. Then again, it could just be seeing if someone needed help. Preacher had to give them credit; the wording had been carefully done.

"And look here," Ripley said, moving her finger further down. He tried to ignore the yellowish-brown bruises on her knuckles. Seeing them made him want to teach someone some manners.

"They want you to list all the makes and models of your vehicles, whether they're gas or diesel, and how much fuel you have for each. Why would they need that?" she asked.

"Maybe they're planning on taking it." But the fuel question was followed up by something interesting: *Are you planning on evacuating the area? If so, on what date?* Beneath that was a space to leave a forwarding address.

He pointed to the address box. "What do you think about this?"

Ripley thought for a moment. "During the Great Depression, a lot of families lost their farms because they couldn't afford the annual property tax. Maybe they're planning on sending out tax bills so they can say there was no response, and then seize the properties?"

"Or handing out fuel to evacuate?"

She frowned. "I've never heard of disaster response teams doing things like that before. I've heard of them chartering buses, or even using military trucks to get people out of the disaster zone...but not handing out fuel for trips. For generators, maybe. But not trips."

Yeah. Both of these ideas were too convoluted. Occam's Razor said that the simplest solution was the most likely solution. That meant seizing the food, medicine, and fuel. Maybe even the vehicles, too.

The next questions pretty much sealed the deal.

Firearms On The Property: Make, Model, Caliber.

Ammunition On The Property: Caliber, Amount.

"Take Dotty home," he said. "Warden needs to see this."

MARCO

"You want me to scavenge garden hoses? You're sure you can't find a better way to get water to the house?" Marco asked, sitting on the closed toilet.

"Well, sure. A better way would be with real irrigation tubing. Even an inch in diameter would work. But without going to the Home Depot down in Pocomoke, that's out," Corey said, leaning against the bathroom door frame. "Garden hoses are more skinny than I'd like, but it's all we've got."

Marco frowned. "That's going to be a lot of hoses to scavenge. I'm not even sure there are enough vacated houses in town to do it."

"I've been thinking about that. Places like the prison should have longer hoses, and lots of them. 50, even 100 feet long. Maybe the churches, and the courthouse. Commercial businesses with landscaping. Places like that," Corey said.

"How do you even know you can get into the storm drains?" Mel said, snipping the scissors and laying the last rubber-banded lock of hair across the sink. She rubbed the stubbled remains on her head, sighed, and picked up the disposable razor.

"While you've been stuck inside the house for the past week, I've been out with a crowbar pulling up manhole covers," Corey said. "The storm drains give me a clear shot all the way down to the bridge. The exit drain to the river will be the tricky part."

"No. Getting all of those hoses will be the tricky part," Marco said. "It might even be worth a trip-"

"Too dangerous," Mel said. She whisked the razor in a mug of water and went back to her hairline.

"Just see what you can find around here first. If we come up short, we'll talk about going to Pocomoke City," Corey said. "It's about 25 miles there and back. We'd probably be able to scrounge up the gas for it, but I'd rather save it for the generator."

"Getting them sooner is better than trying to find them later, after everyone else has realized they need them," Marco said. He knew that line of thinking would be shot down, and sure enough, Corey snorted.

"I really doubt anyone else is building a hydraulic ram pump to push water," he said.

"Not now, but soon they will be," Marco said. "They'll be in the library looking up how to get water. I've seen it happen."

He couldn't get it through anyone's head. They were all trying to figure out how to adjust to this new "normal". But this was just the transition period between normal and chaos. They had to prepare for the chaos.

"Your turn, pretty boy," Mel said, holding the razor out to him so he could shave the parts she couldn't see. "And if you cut me..."

"You'll cut me worse, I know," Marco said, taking the razor. "Bend your head down."

Corey straightened from where he'd been leaning. "The sooner we get the stuff, the better. I know. I get it, Marco. But

Ripley's not ready. I've been catching her just staring off into space. I can say something and she won't even hear me. She's just... gone." He made a motion of something fluttering away from his head.

"Ripley doesn't have to go." Marco sloshed the razor in the cup. "I could go today, but *this one* told me we've got a scavenging trip planned."

"Because I'd bet money that you've been looking right over stuff that we need," Mel said. "Tampons, maxi pads, Pamprin. You need a female partner, and we need to be out there doing something. Just because we went through some shit-"

"We'll talk about it later," Corey said, cutting her off. "I've got more testing to do. Just get what you can in the meantime, all right?" He gave Marco a nod as he left. They heard the rear screen door bang shut a minute later.

"That's right, leave. Anytime I bring up what happened, or anytime I suggest that Rip and I need to stop sitting here stewing in our own brains, he just ends the conversation," Mel said.

"He can't forgive himself for not being there to protect Ripley. For not being able to protect you," Marco said.

"I didn't *need* him to protect me. I handled my shit." She huffed and scratched at a little stain on the edge of the sink. "He's treating us like fragile flowers. He thinks Rip is still upstairs in bed. If he knew she was in town, with Preacher? He'd be throwing a fit."

Marco pulled the razor up Melanie's head and frowned.

Corey could claim that he got it, but he didn't. None of them did. They should be covering the windows with wood, fortifying the doors...now, while they had time. The arrival of the National Guard had calmed things down, but in the end all it did was delay the inevitable. Sooner or later the Guard would run out of supplies or they'd leave. When that happened, it would be every man for himself. He'd seen it firsthand.

Which was why he'd taken Ripley's map of the town, the first night they'd gotten here, and gone for a walk. He'd marked off the houses that didn't seem to have anyone in them. No candlelight inside, no movement or sound. He'd continued doing that for the next two nights until he'd covered the entire town on the eastern side of the river. As the days had passed and he'd noticed more people leaving, he'd marked those houses, too.

Empty houses were full of abandoned, but useful things. Things that he knew the group would need later. And if he could get it and store it away before anyone else even thought to go looking for it, all the better.

"Done," he said, stepping back.

Mel lifted her head and eyed herself in the mirror. She rubbed a hand over her now-bald head, and to Marco, she looked a little shell-shocked. He'd never tell her that, though. He didn't need a razor in his eye.

She picked up the hair that she'd so carefully portioned out and secured with rubber bands. Thick braids, thin ones, locks of dark brown hair and locks of bright purple. All of it went into one of the brown grocery bags that Dotty had saved. Mel had said that one day she might tie the hair to barrettes and make extensions out of it, but he didn't think that's why she was keeping it. That hair had been her identity for years; her way of thumbing her nose at her mother and everything the Congresswoman's lifestyle signified. Giving it up was a huge change.

"Screw Preacher," she muttered, rolling the bag up.

"Preacher's not the problem," Marco said. "You know that."

"Save your psychology for someone that gives a shit," she said, handing him the bag and taking the cup from the sink. "I'll bitch at who I want, when I want. I'll dump this outside and then we can go."

She pushed past him, and he checked the sink and the floor for any leftover hair. It was important that if anyone ever came looking for Melanie Rhodes, infamous daughter of the Speaker of the House, there'd be no trace of her. They'd thought that in a small town like this, she wouldn't have to be so careful.

That had lasted all of one night.

Preacher had cornered Mel the day after meeting her and told her that he remembered where he'd seen her before...in the gossip magazines at the prison. One of the prisoners had even had a glossy full-page shot of her in a bikini on some rich playboy's yacht stuck under his bunkmate's mattress, but she'd had fire-engine red highlights then, not purple. The Speaker's wild child had been loved by the paparazzi and a constant burr in her mother's side.

Preacher had reasoned that if *he* could figure out who she was, then other people could, too. So had begun Mel's confinement, which Corey seemed to take as his personal mission. For the entire week they'd been here, she'd only gone outside in the daylight to rush to the outhouse and back, and then only with a cloth tied around her head and someone--many times, Corey--playing lookout. Sometime last night she'd decided she was tired of the whole situation. When he'd come into the Millers' house this morning to compare notes on everyone's plans for the day, she'd already been in the bathroom cutting her hair off and planning on coming with him.

"Not there," he said, stepping in to the kitchen to find her shoving the bag into the cabinet under the sink. She leveled a glare at him, and he held up a hand. "If you want to keep it, it can't be anywhere in this house. Get your pack, and make sure you've got water and a flashlight. I've been working on something, and it's time you saw it."

MARCO

Andrew Carnegie had once said that the wise man puts all his eggs in one basket, and watches the basket. Elon Musk said it's okay to have your eggs in one basket as long as you control what happens to that basket.

Living in Sarajevo as a young child when it was under siege and being bombed, Marco had learned that a man with just one basket was a fool. One who would soon be starving.

He didn't care how hard he had to work; he was never going to starve again.

He slid the silver key into the lock and checked back over his shoulder as he opened the door.

"Where the hell did you get a key to the back door?" Mel said, hurrying inside.

"It was in a little magnetic box stuck in the wheel well of the car in the garage," he said. He locked the door behind them and checked the window, triple-checking that no one had been watching them. Usually he made sure to only come in here at dawn or dusk, but Mel had delayed him today.

"So you broke into the garage?"

"No, they forgot to lock the door to the garage. But I would've broken in, if I'd had to."

Two days after he and Ripley had made it home, the couple in the house across the street had taken off. They'd packed up their dogs and their SUV, given Dotty a few tearful hugs, and had left. Marco had waited until near sunset—in case they changed their mind or realized they'd forgotten something—before he'd gone inside and started stripping the place of anything useful.

"The cache is in here, in the pantry," he said, crossing the kitchen.

"Cash?" Mel asked, following behind. "You're hiding money?"

It might as well be, he thought.

"Not c-a-s-h. C-a-c-h-e," he said. "You pull up the edge of the carpet here, under this curtain. Stick your finger in the hole, and pull."

The pantry was the size of a walk-in closet. It was lined with shelves on three sides and the bottom row had kitchen curtains stapled to them that just brushed the floor. The curtains hid large appliances that would look unsightly on the prim kitchen counters —or even on the pantry shelves—with all of their cords and accessory parts. Anyone coming in here would push the curtain aside, see a bunch of slow cookers, electric griddles, and waffle makers that they couldn't use, and move on. They wouldn't notice the precise cuts he'd made in the carpet.

That's what he hoped, anyway.

"I've glued the padding and carpet to the top of the door," he said, lifting it up. "If you close it from the inside, it'll lay back down and disappear." He motioned her to the steps. "Ladies first."

It had taken him nearly an hour of crawling and knocking on the floors to find the entrance. From being in Dotty's and Ripley's houses, which were old like this one, he guessed it would be built the same way...with a cellar. Walking around the outside of the house and pushing aside the knee-high grass, he'd found small metal air vents in the foundation. Those told him there was at least some kind of space down there; maybe nothing bigger than a crawl space. But there was no outside entrance. What he'd finally discovered was that the trap door to the cellar—in the very sensible spot of being in the pantry—had been carpeted over. Completely, as if someone had remodeled the place and simply decided that an old, dusty cellar was a relic not fit for their new, updated kitchen. Their lack of foresight was a huge benefit to him and the families.

"Holy shit, Romeo," Mel said from the bottom of the steps, swinging her flashlight around. "You've been busy. Or those people were preppers."

"I don't think there's been anyone but me and the spiders down here for years," he said. He climbed down and switched his own flashlight on. "When I found it, there was just the bare shelves and those old empty jars." He directed the light to a cluster of jars on the top of the shelves. He hadn't had the heart to touch those. They reminded him too much of his father's buried jars, hidden deep in the earth with their precious passports inside. Those jars had saved his and his parents' lives.

He shook the thought away and walked over to a little stool in the corner. It held a few candles and a handful of lighters. The little vents high in the walls provided some light, but not enough to actually see. Lighting a candle, he lifted the tarp on the floor.

"There's a mattress and sleeping bag under here," he said. "Bottled water and MREs from the Guard there on that shelf," he pointed, "and a bucket in the corner."

A twin-size mattress had been all he'd been able to squeeze through the trap door by himself, and even that had been a chore. Finding enough cardboard to line the bare dirt under it had been easy. He'd wanted something like mylar blankets to put under the cardboard, to block the cold from seeping through, but he hadn't been able to find any of those yet. Ripley had some in her pack, but it was important for those to stay there.

"You moving out?" Mel clicked her flashlight off and picked a paperback book off the shelf closest to the bed. "Planning on leaving us?"

"Well, I'm storing all these cans and stuff here as a backup cache. But the bed? The water? This is for you," Marco said.

Her head came up. "Excuse me?"

"If or when your mother makes Agent Perkins come looking for you, they'll tear Ripley's house down to the studs. Miss Dotty's, too. Just like at the school, your only choice is to not be there." He sat the paper bag with her shorn hair onto the shelf where the book had been. "So far there's only enough water for you for a week. The Guard stopped handing out bottles a couple days ago and it's bring-your-own-container now, but I'll keep looking-"

"You really think he'll come?"

"You really think your mother will just accept him not being able to find you? That she won't look for you?"

Mel snorted and tossed the paperback onto the tarp. "She'll probably be relieved."

Marco watched as she started to pace, hands on her hips. "No matter what her titles are, she's still your mother, Melanie. Mothers will raise heaven and earth to find their children."

Mel held up her hands. "Stop. Just stop. I know *your* mother did some incredible things to save your life, but she's not *my* mother." She pointed to her head. "I just shaved this so people wouldn't realize she *is* my mother. I just don't want to think about Mommy Dearest right now, k?"

"Okay."

Mel turned and started scanning the shelves. "I mean, don't

get me wrong, Romeo. I appreciate this. You just kinda hit me out of the blue with it."

"You're welcome," he said. "And you're right. I haven't been getting feminine things. When I go into the bathrooms, I'm looking for soap, bandages, and medicines. Prescription and over-the-counter."

"Looks like you found a shit-ton of those," she said. "There's even cough syrup."

Marco frowned. What she called a shit-ton, he called barely getting started. He needed help. More people could carry more things, make each trip more efficient. But more people also attracted more attention. He had two other spots in town where he was storing things, just so he could make shorter, faster trips and avoid being seen. Still, he worried daily that he'd open them up and find someone had come behind him to clean it all out. Going into houses in the daytime was tricky, because people were out and about. They walked to the Rec Center to get food and water from the National Guard. They stood on corners and chatted with neighbors. He'd even seen an idiot sitting in front of his house with his car running, charging a cellphone and a couple of bluetooth speakers on his dash. The longer this went on, the more people were getting cabin fever and coming outside, looking for something to amuse them.

Scavenging at night wasn't an option, because the flashlight waving around would catch attention even faster. It would be like a lighthouse beacon. He'd been trying to go out around dawn and dusk, because people paid less attention to what was around them when they were transitioning between daytime and nighttime activities. So far, he hadn't gotten caught. But it was all going so slowly, being alone.

And then there was the Guard. He'd been trying to time their patrol route, but either they didn't have a schedule or they were being random on purpose. Yesterday they'd stopped him and asked him where he lived and what he was doing. He'd given them Dotty's address and waved his empty bucket around, saying he was headed to the park to pick up sticks and branches to make a cooking fire. It was all "yes sir" and "no sir", with lots of smiling and acting like a clueless schlub. Anything to keep them from getting off of that MRAP and frisking him for weapons. They'd finally let him go, with a firm warning to be quick and get back home.

"I want you to talk to Corey," Mel said, pulling out a box of soap and sniffing it. She jerked her head back and made a face, dropping the soap back on the shelf like it was hot. "Cinnamon soap? Nasty."

Marco blinked and brought himself back to the present. "About what?"

"About crawling out of my ass. And Rip's. Someone needs to tell him, and he won't listen to me."

"I can try, but I don't know if it will help." He lowered himself onto the mattress. "How's she doing? I mean, really."

Mel turned to look at him and let out a huff of breath. "She's a little screwed in the head, okay? No way around it. But that's normal. It's a normal reaction to everything she went through. She had a guy try to rape her. She killed people. You don't just bounce back from that shit right away."

"You killed people. You seem to be doing fine," he countered.

"Yeah, well, I didn't grow up here in friggin' Mayberry, either," she said, waving a hand towards the ceiling. "She'll work through it. But he's got to *let* her work through it. He can't keep her caged up like he's tryin' to do. Either she'll crawl into a shell and never come back, or she'll go postal."

"Maybe we should leave it alone," he said. "She went out this morning-"

"She *snuck* out this morning. Not from Dad, but from Corey."
Mel called Ripley's parents "Mom" and "Dad". According to
Corey, she'd started it the first time Rip had brought her home
from college to visit with them.

"Mr. Miller was okay with it?" Marco asked.

"Well, he wasn't thrilled, but when she told him and Mom last
night that she was going, we all ended up talking about it. You
know, the buddy system, keep your head on a swivel, that kinda
thing. Then Dad just told us to be safe and go armed. Corey
would've flat-out told her no, he wasn't going to let her."

Marco had to agree. When Corey had stuck his head in the
bathroom this morning and learned that Mel was coming
scavenging today, the first thing he'd done was to catch Marco's eye
and shake his head no. Marco had ignored him.

Mel found an open pack of gum on a shelf and stuck a piece in
her mouth. She shoved the rest in her pocket. "He's gonna give her
hell for it when she gets back. Then I bet you ten to one he clamps
down even harder. He'll probably try to switch rooms with
Thomas to keep an eye on her."

"Mr. Miller won't let that happen."

The sleeping arrangements at the two houses had been...
difficult, those first few days. They'd started out with Ripley in her
own room and Mel in the Millers' guest room, but Ripley's
screaming nightmares had woken everyone up in the dense quiet
of a powerless night. Mel had switched to sleeping with Ripley,
and that seemed to improve things. At the least, she wasn't waking
the neighborhood up anymore. Thomas had moved back into the
Millers' guest room so that Corey and Marco could stop sharing a
bed. Marco had offered to be the one to move, but Mr. Miller had
put down a firm boot on either of the younger men sleeping in the
room next to the ladies. It would be interesting once winter came
and they were all under the same roof.

"Either way, he needs to back off. You can talk to him, or I can just shoot him in the ass. It's up to you," she said. "As thick as he's being, that still might not get his attention-"

"Shh," Marco said, cutting her off. He slipped off of the mattress and hurried to the stairs.

"What is it?" Mel stage-whispered.

He climbed up the stairs and grabbed the edge of the trap door, swinging it down and closing it gently above him.

He kept his voice to a whisper. "I thought I heard someth-"

Three hard booms reverberated through the silence. Shadows passed by the little vents, and they could hear boots moving through the high grass on all sides. Someone stomped up the back steps. There was a thumpa-thumpa-thumpa sound as whoever it was tried rattling the door open.

The booms sounded again.

"OPEN UP! SNOW HILL POLICE!"

PREACHER

Preacher briefly wondered if it was possible for two people to argue each other to death.

As Dotty and Teddy walked in front of him, bickering enough that he'd thought they would come to blows once or twice, he almost wished the Sheriff had asked him to ride along when he went to alert the others about the flyers. By the time he'd gotten done talking with the Sheriff and Father Bill, these two still hadn't moved from in front of Teddy's store. Ripley had given up and was sitting back underneath the tree, just watching the empty street. He'd been able to at least get them all moving towards home, but they'd continued their feisty exchange along the way.

"You are too damned old, and that's all there is to it, Theodore," Dotty said.

"Speak for yourself," Teddy snapped. "It's been months since you put in a full day's work."

"That's because you fired me!"

"I didn't have a choice!"

Preacher had another ring of keys in his pocket now, to both a store and a house he'd never set foot in. Teddy had just handed them to him as if they'd known each other for years, without so much as a threat about anything missing when he was done.

Dotty had given him her spare to the back door the night she'd brought him home, apologizing profusely that she didn't have one for the front. It had taken her a bit to realize that his silence wasn't from being offended that he didn't rate a front-door key, but shock that she'd given him one at all.

And now Teddy had handed his keys over after nothing more than sizing him up and bitching at him for ten minutes.

For a man who'd been in a cage a week ago, it was surreal.

The last time he'd had keys to a house was when he was sixteen. When his new step-father had moved in and kicked him out of his mother's home—there could be only one man in *his* house--he'd gone to the city and lived on the streets for months before one of the Brothers had taken him in. From that point on, he'd lived in a room in the old industrial building the Brothers used for their clubhouse. It was never locked; there was no need. Everyone knew better than to come through those doors if they weren't invited.

He'd even been the one to teach a few idiots that lesson.

Now here he was, set free by a lawman who thought Preacher would do the right thing. He was pushing a wheelbarrow behind two people old enough to be his grandparents, that fought like siblings and handed him the keys to their homes as if there was no question he was trustworthy.

It sure as hell made him *want* to do the right thing. But for a man who'd been caged for years, running out his life around the fence line like a wolf trapped in a zoo because once upon a time he *had* done the right thing...

"What's going on here?" Dotty asked, halting the group and breaking his reverie.

They were close enough now to see the tree line at the edge of the Millers' yard, and a couple of pickup trucks sitting in the road. There were men standing on the front steps of the house across the street—the one Preacher had seen Marco coming out of a few times. All of the men were armed, and one of them was beating on the front door of that house with a closed fist.

"That looks like the Undersheriff," Teddy said.

"Ripley," Preacher said, making a motion with his head indicating the wheelbarrow. "Gun."

"No. If they're armed, I want to be armed," she said.

"Use your head," Teddy said. "You don't go into something like this showing all your cards. You're out-gunned, and you need to find out what they want. *Then* you decide if it's time to shoot them."

Ripley glared at them both, but unslung her rifle and slipped it under the tarp. "With martial law being declared, that stupid *no open carry* law should be suspended, too," she said.

"Never shoulda been a law in the first place," Teddy said.

They passed the line of trees bordering the Millers' yard and found two more people standing on Dotty's porch, with another walking across the yards back towards them. There was a fourth in the double driveway between the houses, writing on a clipboard. From inside Dotty's, Preacher could hear Jax barking up a storm.

"This one seems to be empty too," the man coming from Ripley's house called out. "No answer, no dogs barking."

"Check the back yard," one of the women on Dotty's porch called back. "Verify the outbuilding. And we know there's another dog, so be careful."

The man nodded and jogged towards Ripley's back yard. Clipboard Man walked between the trucks, going out of sight.

There *was* another dog, Preacher knew. And he'd bet money

that dog was silently watching them right now, not giving away his presence. King was *scary* smart.

Across the street, one of the men with guns had started spray painting something on the front of the vacant house. Another was knelt down, fiddling with the door lock.

"Can I help you?" Dotty called, her voice sharp. The women on the porch turned, startled. One of them frowned, while the other quickly pasted on a smile.

Preacher recognized the one with the frown. She was Cathy, Dotty's next-door neighbor. He hadn't hit it off too well with her. She'd tried to talk to him when he was outside; if "talking" was leaning on the fence and asking a lot of nosy questions. He'd just not answered when she'd asked something she had no right to know. That must have given her the impression that he was either hard of hearing or mentally challenged, because she'd started loudly commenting on his physique as he worked to bust up the firewood. He hadn't been sure if she was flirting or just thought he didn't understand, so he'd just ignored her.

It had become almost routine. Every morning, a few minutes after he started chopping up the wood, she'd come out and lean on the fence to watch. She'd talk about how nice the scenery was these days, how strong he was, how she just loved to watch a man like him do his work. How there were all kinds of things around her house that she needed a *real* man's help with.

The fifth day she'd thrown those hints around, he'd stopped and looked her in the eye.

"Where's your husband?" He'd asked her.

"He's up at the roadblock with Thomas," she'd said, suddenly all smiles. "He won't be home for *hours*." She'd drawn the word out to emphasize it.

He had pointed at her wedding ring. "Go tell him you forgot what that means. Maybe he can remind you."

After staring at him for a minute with her mouth hanging open, she'd stormed off, and he hadn't seen her since. At the time, he'd thought it was a good thing.

Seeing her on Dotty's porch next to someone with a clipboard and an air of authority, he wasn't so sure.

"Miss Dotty! What a fortunate coincidence! We were just here to talk to you," Smiley-Face said. She didn't move from the top of the porch steps. Cathy leaned in and whispered something in the woman's ear. Smiley-face's gaze jerked to him and did a quick appraisal. She whispered something back to Cathy.

Yep. Pissing off Cathy definitely hadn't been a good thing.

"Mom should be in the house," Ripley said, her voice low. "She would've heard him knocking."

"Hush, child. Your momma's smart," Dotty murmured. She stopped walking a few feet from her mailbox and crossed her arms. "We can talk out here on the sidewalk, Cindy. Or should I say, Lieutenant Mayor?"

Cindy's face twitched but she didn't lose that red carpet smile. "There's no need to be so formal, Miss Dotty. We're all neighbors here."

"Then get those boys back up here where we can see 'em," Teddy said. "Neighbors don't go snooping in other neighbors' yards."

"They're just helping me follow up on some things for the City-" Cindy started, and Dotty cut her off.

"So you *are* here as Lieutenant Mayor," Dotty said.

"Well, yes, I am," Cindy said, and gestured with her clipboard. "The City's received some disturbing reports about numerous code violations on your property, and I'm here to get that straightened out."

"And you've got to fill out the survey," Cathy added, holding up a slim stack of papers. "Everyone has to fill out the survey or-"

Cindy jabbed her elbow into Cathy's arm and made a shushing noise. "So if you can just come up here Miss Dotty, we can discuss the matter in private," she said, her face as pleasant as if she was offering lemonade on a hot day.

"I prefer to discuss City business on public property," Dotty said, indicating the sidewalk. She put on a big, winning smile of her own. "We wouldn't want anyone to get the wrong idea that I'd invited you and your men to trespass on my private property, would we?"

The man who'd gone to the back of Ripley's house re-appeared. "Verified. They've built an outhouse back there. Some kind of animals on the back porch, too. Another structure with chickens in the yard behind that one, and big things like hot tubs full of water on both houses. Those might be attached." He followed Cindy's stiff gaze to the group and stopped.

"Yes, hello there," Teddy said, giving a little wave. "We're the people you'll be wanting to give your search warrant to. You've got one of those, don't ya?"

Cindy looked across the street to the group of men, still huddled around the front steps. "Frank? Frank! We've got a problem over here."

"Get that wheelbarrow off the sidewalk, son," Teddy murmured.

Preacher moved the wheelbarrow a few feet into Dotty's yard. Behind him, Ripley also stepped off of the sidewalk into the yard.

"Don't approach my men," Cindy warned. "You touch them and I'll have the officers arrest you for assault."

"What officers?" Teddy asked.

"Me," said a man crossing the road, one hand on the butt of his holstered pistol. "Me and the other officers here." He was well-built, but not too tall, in jeans and a t-shirt covered with an assault vest. He walked like a cop, stopped and stood in a pose like a cop, took them all in at a glance like a cop. Preacher hadn't ever seen the man inside the prison, but it would've been obvious even if he'd been standing at a grill flipping burgers.

"Correct me if I'm wrong," Teddy said, "but I recall the Sheriff firing you. Right in front of the whole town, even. You're not the Undersheriff anymore, Mister Stalls."

"It's *Chief* Stalls now, of the Snow Hill Police Department," The man said.

"Snow Hill doesn't have a police department," Teddy said.

"It does now. City Council made it all official three nights ago."

Teddy puffed up. "Funny...I don't recall voting on that."

Cindy spoke up from her spot on the porch. "Extenuating circumstances. Mayor Wilhelm saw a need, held an emergency session, and the Council took care of it. Now instead of relying on the Sheriff—whose forces are *obviously* stretched too thin to give us the kind of protection we need in these dangerous times—we have our own City Police Department."

Teddy's brows went up and he started to say something else, but Dotty silenced him with a hand on his arm. "It's good to have police officers here," she said, smiling at the Chief. "I came home to find these people on my property without my permission. I've asked them to leave and they won't. Will you please remove them?"

The Chief didn't even look towards the house. "We're all here on official business, Ma'am. I assure you, this is all above-board."

Dotty cocked her head. "I keep hearing that, but no one's given me a warrant. Surely you've got a warrant, Frank? Or perhaps your wife does? I'd just like to see it."

Frank frowned and glanced towards the porch, giving a little shake of his head. Cindy huffed and came down the stairs, her low heels tapping hard on the paved walk. Cathy stiffly followed her.

Frank waved a hand, and the man who had been in the backyard joined them.

"We're not here to start problems," Frank started, but Preacher cut in.

"The other one, too," he said.

Frank turned a hard glare at Preacher. "Did you miss the part where I was speak-"

"Behind the Beetle," Preacher said, pointing. "He goes, too."

"Beckett, get out here," Cindy snapped. The man stood from where he'd been crouching behind Ripley's Beetle, his face flushed red, and scurried to join everyone on the sidewalk.

"And whatever he was writing down about those vehicles can stay," Teddy said.

"What he was writing is official City business and it will *not* stay," Cindy said. She turned to Dotty, not bothering to hide her irritation. "Miss Dotty, we've received numerous reports of serious code violations on your property."

"If I've violated any codes, I had no idea I was doing it. Who gave a report?" Dotty asked.

"There were multiple reports, and they were anonymous," Cindy said smoothly. She looked down at her notes. "Let's see. New building structures without permits, altering the structure of a home in the historic district without approval, permits, inspections...all of that. Possible bypass of city sewage lines... which would not only violate code, but would be illegal on a state and federal level, and bring with it serious environmental fines. Also, livestock within City limits, at least one unlicensed dog— possibly more, and possibly classified as a 'dangerous breed', which are banned statewide. And finally: using a residential property as a commercial short-term rental in exchange for money, goods, or services; which the City banned years ago when that whole AirBnB mess got settled."

Cindy looked up from her paper. "The City needs to investigate these accusations, Mrs. Parker. These are serious charges that carry very heavy fines," she paused, and pasted on a fake sympathetic look. "And, I'm sorry to say, possible eviction from the property."

PREACHER

"That's bullshit, is what that is," Teddy said, pointing a finger at Cindy's clipboard. "Have you missed the part where all of the electricity is gone and the toilets don't flush?"

"You can't evict me," Dotty said, her voice firm. "Only my bank can do that."

"If you don't follow the regulations and restrictions for a historic home, we most certainly can, and *will*, evict you," Cindy said. She flipped through the papers on her clipboard. "And I don't recall seeing a property tax payment for that truck."

"Then you should be speakin' to your Treasurer, not me. My taxes are paid, and I've got receipts," Dotty said.

Across the street, a little cheer went up, and the front door swung open.

"Hey boss, we finally got it," one of the men called out.

"Good. Clear it, safeties off. Then start the inventory," Frank called back.

"Inventory?" Teddy said, pointing at the house across the

street. "Those men are breaking and entering, and you're telling them to take inventory?"

"They're my officers, and this isn't breaking and entering," the Chief said. "This is search and rescue; part and parcel of disaster recovery. The house appears to be abandoned, and it's our duty to verify there's no one inside in need of assistance."

"It's not abandoned. The Cobbs went on vacation," Dotty said. "They asked me to watch over their house while they were gone. You and your men have no right to go in there."

"FEMA directives say we do, Ma'am," the Chief said.

"Search and Rescue doesn't involve taking inventory," Teddy said.

"Mrs. Parker, we need to address these violations," Cindy said. "Please let the Chief do his job and allow me to do mine, so we can all get on with our day. I have many other houses to visit today."

"You mean you've got other law-abiding citizens to shake down," Teddy said.

"No, I mean we've already pulled six bodies out of houses in the last two days, and we need to get through the rest of the neighborhood before we find any more," Cindy snapped.

"Six bodies?" Dotty said, aghast. "How did they die?"

"Dehydration, medication, *lack* of medication, maybe," the Chief said. "A few were obviously killed, probably from a break-in. It doesn't really matter. We've got a job to do, we've got people to save, and you can either cooperate with us or get the hell out of the way. I don't want to bury any more of my townspeople."

"Going into people's houses just ain't right," Teddy said.

"Even if it's to save their lives? You need to check your principles, Teddy," the Chief said.

"I know exactly what my principles are, and what my rights are. And law or not, FEMA or not, this ain't right." Teddy's face was flushed red and his fists were clenched.

"Teddy, maybe he's right. If people are dying," Dotty said, "we need to get them help."

"But you *know* there's no one in that house," Teddy said.

"And regardless of what you tell me, I still have to check or it's my ass on the line," the Chief said.

Preacher watched as the little man chewed on his thoughts for a moment, and then gave a curt nod. "These folks that died, who were they? What did you do with the bodies?"

"We've started a list at the Rec Center for family members and friends. We'll be in contact with the local church leaders at the end of the day and determine where they need to be buried," Cindy said.

"So are you going to cooperate? Can I go oversee my disaster recovery?" The Chief said.

"There's nothing to cooperate with," Dotty said. "My taxes are paid, and we're in an emergency. I reject any violations the city wishes to bring against me."

The Chief rolled his eyes and held his hands up. "I've got a house to go through. Yell if you need me." He crossed the street and entered the Cobb's house.

Cindy huffed and pulled two papers from her clipboard, holding them out to Dotty. "This is a survey you need to fill out and turn in, and a list of the violations you've been accused of. Consider this your only warning. We'll be back in 48 hours to inspect the property, and if it is not in compliance with city codes and regulations, as well as federal codes and regulations, we will start measures to seize the property."

"Aren't townspeople dying a little more important than my backed up toilet?" Dotty said, not taking the papers.

Cindy knelt and placed the papers on the ground at Dotty's feet. She stood back up and made a hand gesture to the people with her. "Fortunately, Mrs. Parker, not all of the townspeople are so selfishly interested in their own well-being," Cindy said. "We have a lot of volunteers willing to help us with the mountain of things that we need to get done. Now if you'll excuse us..." she stepped into the street and walked around the truck. Cathy and the three men followed her without comment.

Teddy stepped on the edge of the papers to pin them before they blew away and cocked his head, looking at Dotty. "What do you plan to do about this?"

Dotty glared at the papers fluttering under Teddy's toe, then stooped and picked them up. "I guess I'll just have to fight it once they start the proceedings," she said. "We need the outhouse, we need the water troughs, and they're not permanent. A judge should agree with me on that."

Teddy snorted. "If they can even *find* a judge," he said.

"I don't like them being on the property," Preacher said. "Someone should have been here."

"My mom should be home," Ripley said. "I'm going to go see why she didn't come out."

"You leave her be," Teddy said. "If she's home, layin' low was the right thing to do. It's obvious these two houses ain't vacant. They ain't gonna kick in *those* doors."

They all looked across the street, where a few men, and the group following Cathy, were huddled in discussion in the front lawn.

"Well, forewarned is forearmed," Dotty said. She gestured to the wheelbarrow. "Get that thing out of sight and let's see if there's some way that we can hide what we're doing from people walking by on the street. The less they can see, the less complaints there will be."

"Those complaints weren't anonymous," Preacher said, lifting the handles of the wheelbarrow and starting up through the yard.

"I know," Dotty said. "There's no way to hide what we're

doing from Cathy, but if we can block the view from the street, it still might help the next time they come."

"I'm gonna head home and get the truck ready," Teddy said. "Preacher, you comin'?"

"I need a few minutes," Preacher said, tipping his head towards the house across the street.

Teddy glanced in that direction and nodded. "I hear ya. I'd stay too, 'cept I need to get stuff ready."

Preacher took the wheelbarrow to the back of the house.

He could see the sense in checking houses for people that might need help. But the Chief had specifically said "inventory", and that didn't sit well. There had been too much tension and too many people around to make a fuss about it. He really should stay and see if they took anything out of the house, but there was too much to do.

The back door of Ripley's house opened and Lily stepped out onto the deck, followed by a giant of a dog. Ripley was right behind them.

"I'm not going to open the door and risk having them make an excuse to come in when I'm the only one here," Lily said. "If your father had been home or one of the boys had been around, I'd have come out and told them to get out of the yard." She nodded to Preacher as she stepped down onto the grass.

King jumped off of the deck and headed straight for Preacher. Preacher froze, one hand still on the wheelbarrow handle. The dog hadn't warmed up to him yet, but he hadn't given Preacher any trouble, either. King just didn't take kindly to him being within a few feet of Ripley. That was fine. Ripley didn't take kindly to it either, so he made sure to leave room.

The big dog loped near him, sniffed the air, and ran for the tall pine tree at the back of Dotty's yard. That pine was taller than the gum trees surrounding it, and anytime the wind blew and it started swaying, Preacher thought about trying to climb it and lop it off. If that sucker ever came down, it was tall enough to reach the house. It was King's favorite place to cock his leg; almost as if by conquering the *tallest* tree, he conquered *all* of them.

Preacher could relate. It had been his habit to go straight for the biggest guy in the bar, too.

"They should have checked before leaving," Ripley said. "You shouldn't have been here alone."

"I had a gun, and King was right beside me the whole time. I was fine. I just needed to pee."

They didn't give him so much as a glance on their way to the outhouse—other than Lily's initial greeting—not bothering to check and see where he was or if he was watching them. It hadn't been that way the first few days. They were starting to trust him. It was slow progress, but it was still progress.

He'd take it.

MARCO

Marco crouched in the darkness under the cellar stairs. Mel squatted beside him. Above them, booted feet walked all through the house and made dust sprinkle down from the cellar's ceiling.

"What if they find us?" Mel whispered.

"They've been inside for more than ten minutes and haven't found us so far. They won't," he whispered back.

"But what if they do?"

"Then we go with them. *Quietly*," he stressed, seeing her glare.

A shrill voice cut through the muffled talk of the men who were searching the house.

"Frank? Frank! Where are you? I need a word with you," a woman called. She didn't sound happy.

Almost right above them, there were heavy steps, and a man spoke. "Are you about finished in here?"

"Yes sir," someone responded. "I was just checking for a can opener. Looks like they took all of the food with them."

"Okay. Give me some room, then. Let the others know," the

man said. After a moment with more steps above them, he spoke up a little louder. "I'm in the kitchen."

The woman's heels struck the floor as if she were trying to leave marks. She stopped directly overhead; she must have been standing right next to the pantry door. "What the hell was that out there?" she demanded.

"That was you getting caught trespassing in broad daylight."

"So?"

"So, what was I supposed to do?"

"You're *supposed* to back me up," she said.

"I backed you up as much as I could. You want me to put a couple of seniors in cuffs where anyone watching could see they hadn't done anything wrong?" The two were both silent for a moment. "That was sloppy, Cindy," he said. "You should have just left the notice and the survey, and come back later to inspect the place. Above board."

She started pacing, right above their heads. More ancient dust rained down. Mel covered her nose and hunched her head down between her shoulders. Marco pulled the neck of his t-shirt over his nose.

"That will take too long. This was the perfect opportunity to get Dotty Parker out of that house and you didn't take it," Cindy said.

Beside him, Mel gave a little gasp. He squeezed her shoulder, hoping she wouldn't get pissed enough to start yelling.

"There were too many witnesses and you don't have solid proof of anything yet," Frank said.

"I do have solid proof! You can see the water catchment from the damn sidewalk! You can see that big man going in and out of her house like he's living there."

"Fine. But you don't have a paperwork trail. There's steps you have to follow-"

"We're on a tight schedule, Frank," Cindy said, her words sharp and punctuated. "You read the Governor's message. Michael's headed here. We need these FEMA forms filled out and every resource in town inventoried, at *least*."

Frank made a snorting noise. "I still don't buy that. Michael's gonna travel from Texas all the way up here to Maryland? I think your friend the governor is lying. Push the towns to round up all the food in one spot. Makes it easier for his goons to come through and pick it all up."

Mel looked up. "Who's Michael?" she whispered.

Marco shrugged. "The head of your FEMA agency, maybe?"

"I don't need your conspiracy theories, Frank. I need her out of that house," Cindy said. "All the other streets have 75% compliance with our suggestion that they evacuate their homes and come to the Rec Center. This street? Complete opposite. Only 25% vacancy."

"And you think that's her fault?" Frank countered.

"That little busybody's keeping everyone's spirits up. The little old lady down the street, the one that caused such a fuss a few years back cutting down that tree in her yard? She told me Dotty had been by to check on her just yesterday. And Seth Miller's promised to get her *another* tree she can cut up with that chainsaw of hers. They need to be removed. If the other residents see Dotty and her dysfunctional clan evacuate, they'll do it too."

"Why not just tell them Michael's coming?"

"And cause another panic? Hell Frank, they'd leave the Rec Center and go back to their houses to put everything somewhere safe."

"Don't do the air quotes thing, Cindy. Kenny does that shit. You know how I hate it."

Cindy kept going as if Frank hadn't even spoken. "We'd never find the stuff then, and good luck getting those people back to the shelter before Michael gets here. That would make the Mayor look bad, Frank. That would make *me* look bad."

"Oh, god forbid you look bad to the Governor, who's all the way across the Bay. I've got people shooting at me, Cindy. They see us pull up in the truck and out come the guns."

"So talk to the Guard! The Governor sent them here to help us," she said. "Get one of their bullet-proof trucks they're driving all over town."

"You think I haven't tried that? It didn't fly. *They* can commandeer *our* stuff, but not the other way around."

They were both quiet for a minute. The thumps of boots in the rest of the house had all but stopped. Marco could hear the sounds of people milling around and talking outside.

"So *you* commandeer something. You're the Chief of Police," Cindy said. "Solve the problem. Then work on getting that woman out of her house. We need results, Frank. We do this for the Governor and we'll be set for life."

She started across the floor, then stopped. "If we don't, we'll be out of a job and starving like the rest of them. We *can't* let that happen."

Frank said something in reply, but Marco didn't catch it over the sound of Cindy's heels leaving the house. After a moment, Frank left, too. The front door slammed and Frank started shouting to round everyone up. Engines started up, and pulled away. Within minutes, all was quiet outside.

"They're trying to push Grams out? What the hell?" Mel said, her voice still barely above a whisper.

"I'm not sure," Marco said. "But if they're taking inventory and gathering stuff up, that means we've got to work faster." He moved out from under the stairs and looked up at the trap door, thankful it hadn't been found. He made a mental note to rig up some way it could be locked from underneath.

Mel came out and grabbed the stool next to the mattress. She moved it underneath a vent and climbed up, peeking through the screen.

"Looks like the street's all clear," she said. "We've got to warn Grams."

Marco adjusted the pack on his back and nodded. "Let's go."

DOTTY

Dotty stood on her back porch, watching the chickens scratch through the grass inside of their run. Her eyes traveled over to the fence surrounding her yard, and from there into Cathy's backyard.

Everything we do here is in full view of that woman, she thought. *There's no way to hide anything from her.*

It was too late to build a taller fence. There wasn't anywhere to get the materials now, and even if there was, there wasn't money to buy them.

Maybe we could string up some tarps?

No, that would just bring more complaints about things being unsightly and not fitting in with the historical code. With one hand, she brought a glass of Bill's iced tea to her lips and took a sip. With her other, she rubbed at the cross hanging from her necklace.

There had to be a way out of this. She couldn't let Cindy kick her out of her own home, codes or no. She couldn't let a vindictive, bigoted neighbor get the better of her.

If only her late husband Nate had been here. He'd have talked everyone down, smoothed everything over, and they'd all have walked away happy. He wouldn't have made things worse, the way she had.

"What do you think, Grams? Does Michael ring a bell for you?" Mel asked from the kitchen doorway.

The question yanked her out of her thoughts and brought her back to the present. Her kitchen was full of people, all trying to talk at once. The noise was what had driven her out here to the porch in the first place. She loved having a full house, and these people were her family, but when everyone was on edge like this, it got to be too much.

"I've got no idea, sweetheart," Dotty said, not turning around. "You're probably right. It's probably the head of FEMA. Who else would be coming here and have the City people in such a tizzy?"

Lily stepped out past Mel and dropped into a chair. "I don't like this. They're brazen enough to come here in broad daylight and just walk right through our yards like they own the place. What are they going to do next?"

"It's not what they're going to do next, it's what we're going to do to prepare for it," Marco said from further inside. Dotty saw Lily raise an eyebrow, and Marco quickly added, "with all due respect, Miss Miller."

"No, you're right," Lily said. "I just don't want this happening again. I don't think they'd have done it if one of the men had been here. A man's just more intimidating than a woman is, even if she does have a shotgun."

Ripley moved up beside Mel. "Dad's gonna shit a brick when he finds out."

"He'll be mad at himself for not being here, and then he'll feel guilty for thinking he should've left Father Bill high and dry," Lily said. She made a disgusted noise. "There's just so much to do."

"Well we've got lots of hands to get it all done, honey. We'll find a way," Dotty said.

"Are you going to go up the Rec Center and complain about Cindy and those men?" Ripley asked.

Dotty shook her head. "I thought about it, but I don't think it would help. It might make things worse. If I talk to the Mayor and get Cindy in trouble, she'll come up with more things to fine us for. Maybe get your Mom and Dad involved, too."

"The Mayor might be the one telling her to do all this," Lily said. "He's not the cleanest politician around."

"Sounds like he and my mom would get along great," Mel said. "The only way to deal with people like that is to dig up dirt on them. We could maybe go up to the Rec Center and nose around-"

"No," Dotty said, setting her tea down. "We're not going to stoop to their level."

"So we just sit here on our hands and hope Cindy doesn't follow through?" Ripley waved an arm towards her house. "We've been doing that for a week and it didn't stop them from targeting us."

"They're targeting *me*," Dotty said. "And if I can keep it from spreading to the rest of you, that's what I'll do. You are not to get involved."

Ripley made a frustrated noise and disappeared back into the house.

"I'm not going to lock myself in the house again," Mel said. "I won't do it."

"You can help me," Preacher said, stepping up where Ripley had been. "The sooner it's done, the sooner I'm here." He nodded to Lily. "For intimidation."

"She needs to be helping me," Marco called from his spot at the kitchen table. "We need to scavenge. We need to find boards we can put over the windows, so those men can't see inside, or maybe throw things inside."

"Teddy's got plywood," Dotty said. "His inventory's not much, but there'd be at least enough to do the front windows."

Preacher shook his head. "It's spoken for. Gotta cover the shop windows."

"Then I'll get some blankets and cover the windows-" Dotty started.

"That won't stop something from coming through," Marco called. "Rocks, tear gas, molotov cocktails-"

"It will have to do for now. You said Teddy offered the wood from his old barn. Maybe we can cover it with that later, if we need to," Dotty said.

"And tools for whoever helps," Preacher added.

"I'll help with the shop stuff," Mel said. "Marco, too. That way you won't be gone for days. We get it done and you're back here to growl at people while we go scavenge."

"I've got things to do-" Marco started.

"And you can't do them in the daylight, Romeo, so quit arguing," Mel shot back.

"I'll go too," Ripley called. "And we should find Corey. With all of us, we could maybe knock it out by tomorrow night."

Mel snorted. "If we track him down and try to get him to come with us, he'll spend the entire time bitching at us for being out of the house."

"Not in front of me, he won't." Preacher said.

"So we're just going to leave Miss Dotty and Miss Lily unprotected?" Marco asked. "There are all kinds of problems with this plan."

They all fell silent, thinking.

Dotty snapped her fingers. "If Cindy's going to accuse me of raising an army, then that's what I'll do. I can't go to the Mayor, but I can go to the people. I'll talk to Bill and see if he can talk to the congregation. I'll visit with the people still on the street and see if there's anything we can do to help them. With a little goodwill, maybe the neighbors will step up and raise a fuss if the City comes here again."

"That's a good idea," Lily said. "That census form says 48 hours, so they *shouldn't* be back today or tomorrow. That gives us a little time. We cover the windows so they can't tell if anyone's home. We leave the dogs in the houses to discourage them from coming in, and maybe make them think someone's hiding inside."

"Lily, I don't want you dragged into my mess," Dotty said.

"They were stomping through my yard too, Dotty. I'm already involved. I'm going with you," Lily said.

"Find the Warden. Tell him what happened," Preacher said.

Lily nodded and stood. "We will. I'll go find blankets to cover the windows. You think we should do just the front, or the whole first floor?"

"The whole floor," Marco said, squeezing past Mel and stepping out onto the porch. "Might be good if we could block sight to the porches, too." He pointed to Cathy's house and raised his eyebrows.

Dotty huffed a breath and clapped her hands together. "Okay then. Lots of blankets for us, and lots of work for you kids. Y'all be careful."

Preacher shook a set of keys. "Whoever's with me, let's move."

PREACHER

"I still can't believe that woman next to Teddy's shop nearly shot you," Mel said. "Although, you *do* look like you'd be robbing the place." She pushed a box into his waiting arms. "As big as those muscles are, do you think bird shot would just bounce off?"

The sound of an engine and a flash of lights pulled Preacher's attention from Mel's teasing. He looked towards Teddy's house and saw headlights coming in through the driveway, stopping in front.

"Heads up," he called to Teddy, and when the old man swung around, he pointed.

Teddy peered through the drizzle and spat out a string of sound that was probably curses.

"Girls, get down out of the truck. Close it up," he said. "Hurry now. Get on down here."

Preacher tossed the box he was holding back into the truck and dodged as Ripley's foot swung by him. She pulled on the truck's door strap, swinging her legs out for leverage. The door came rolling down with a loud crash.

Voices sounded from the front yard, and a flashlight swung around the house. "He's back there!" a voice called out.

"Shit," Teddy spat, then raised his voice. "Boys, get those doors closed." The old man started shuffling towards the big outbuilding, and Preacher overtook him in a few steps.

"People here. Close it up," he called, and grabbed one of the two big doors. Marco and Corey scrambled to him, and together they got the big doors shut just as Teddy caught up. An engine revved, and Preacher stepped around the building to find a pickup truck barreling down the long drive towards them.

"Let me do the talking," Teddy called out. "Stay calm. It might be friends."

"Friends would announce themselves," Marco said. "We need the guns."

"Not where they can see 'em," Teddy said. "Girls, with me. You boys get out of sight."

"Mine's inside," Corey said. "I'll stay in the back partition." He slipped through the smaller door set to the side of the outbuilding.

Marco and Preacher held back as Teddy stepped out to the front of the building, directly into the glow of the headlights.

"I don't like this," Marco said as they watched the girls join the old man. He jogged over to where his shotgun lay on top of a burn barrel and hurried back.

Preacher didn't have a gun with him. Dotty had shown him the shotgun she kept at the house, but he'd left it there. He knew the girls each had a pistol, and Corey had Ripley's little Ruger 10/22 with him inside. Teddy's outbuilding looked like a big barn with doors in the center, but was split into three sections with partitions inside, like his old chicken house back on his mother's farm. They'd been offloading the truck into the far left partition. The center was something of a workshop, or what Mel had called a "man cave", and in the right section--closest to the house--was

Millie, Teddy's old APC. Each of the end partitions had big swing-out double doors on the ends of the building, with a smaller, normal door on the long side.

"I'm going for higher ground," Marco said, and started climbing a multi-level stack of big 50-gallon barrels Teddy had piled on the corner.

A pickup truck pulled up and stopped in front of the workshop doors, bathing Teddy and the girls in blinding headlights. The old man held a hand to shade his eyes, and Preacher could see by the silhouettes that each of the girls had their hands on their pistols.

The engine shut off and the truck's door opened, but the headlights stayed on. "Teddy," a man's voice called out. "Just the man I've been looking for."

"Yeah?" Teddy called back. "Well, you found me. Why don't you come out here where I can see who I'm talkin' to?"

"There's more men getting out of the back of the truck," Marco hissed from his perch on top of the barrels.

"Have your ladies take your hands off of those weapons and I'd be happy to," the man said. "My officers and I have been shot at enough these past few days."

Teddy grunted and stood a little straighter, hands on his hips. "Well Frank, if you're coming on people's properties uninvited like you did just now, I can see why," he said. He turned and looked at the girls, then back towards the truck. "Kill those damn headlights and tell those men I hear to stay in the truck. Then you can come out here and tell me whatever it is you think is so damn important you can just drive through my property."

The headlights clicked off. Frank Stalls stepped around the door and came to the front of the truck, hands raised.

"I'm here on official City business," Frank said.

"That's the second time today I've heard that," Teddy said.

"What is it this time? You here to inventory my house too? If so, you can go home."

"Like I said, my men and I have been taking a lot of fire the past few days. We need more protection. Seeing you this morning reminded me that you've got that APC from the war. I'm here to see about it."

Teddy's stance didn't change. He just stood, staring at Frank, not saying a word.

Everyone waited, the sound of crickets and bugs from the trees at the back of the property seeming over-loud. Frank slowly dropped his hands, resting one on the hood of the truck. Preacher looked up at Marco, who caught the movement and shrugged.

Finally, after at least a full minute of no response, Frank cocked his head. "Well?" he said.

"Well what?" Teddy said.

"I said I'm here to see the APC," Frank said.

"I heard you."

Frank took a deep breath and blew it out slowly. "Annnnd?"

"And now I'm waiting for you to leave," Teddy said, shrugging. "I didn't invite you here to look at my property, and I've got no reason to show it to you." The old man crossed his arms over his chest. "So you, and all those men there, can go on home."

"Teddy I don't think you understand the situation," Frank started.

"I understand just fine. You want my property. You ain't got a warrant, you ain't got a valid badge of office, and you ain't got a pile of cash to buy it, not that I'm willing to sell it. That sound about right?"

"The City made me an officer, Teddy, and as an officer I have the right to commandeer property as the need arises. The City will compensate you-"

"No."

"Excuse me?"

"I said no. You can't have it. I'm not giving it up without a valid warrant from a valid judge and due process. You remember due process?"

Frank sighed and looked towards the back of the truck. Preacher couldn't make out the details, but he could see the shadow of a man sitting in the cab, and darker lumps towards the back that looked to be about five men.

"Fellas-" Frank started.

"Is this where we pull out the guns?" Mel asked. "I'm ready to pull out the guns."

"Same here," Ripley said.

"You keep your men in the truck, Frank. We don't want things escalating," Teddy said.

"I'm not leaving without that APC, Teddy. I need it, and by law-"

"It don't run, anyway," Teddy interrupted. "Starter's broke. I never got around to ordering another one."

"Bullshit," Frank said. "You keep that thing running like brand new."

Teddy held up his hands in a *what can you do* gesture. "I got busy."

"Show me."

"Excuse me?"

"I said show me. You see, Teddy, I don't believe you. You've got some kind of burr up your ass about this whole situation, and you've made it clear that no matter what the City says, or what the law says, you're not going to cooperate. So when you tell me that your APC, that always looks like it just rolled off the showroom floor and purrs like a kitten in all of the parades, *isn't running*, I find that a little hard to believe."

"I don't care what you believe," Teddy said. "Without a warrant, I ain't showing you a damn thing."

"I've got six men with me that can force the issue," Frank said.

"And I've got men with guns trained on you and your boys," Teddy said. "I give a signal, and they start shooting."

"Like hell you do, old man. These girls-"

"Boys, say hello!" Teddy called.

"Hello," Corey yelled.

"Aimed and ready," Marco called out.

Preacher took a deep breath. "*LEAVE,*" he bellowed.

Frank flinched. There was muttering from the back of the truck.

Teddy stood silent for a few moments and crossed his arms again.

"I think it's time you turned that truck around and get off of my land," Teddy said. "And just so you know, I'll be up at the Rec Center filing a formal complaint about how you're out here harassing US Veterans."

"And young women," Mel said.

"Senior citizen," Ripley added.

Frank shook his head. "Why you gotta make things hard, old man? A little cooperation-"

"You took an oath!" Teddy jabbed his finger towards Frank. "The same oath I took 'fore you was even born! And you're out here spitting on it! All of ya! I ain't cooperating! Not now, not ever! I *remember* my oath! Enemies foreign *and* domestic!"

"Is that a threat?" Frank said, his voice suddenly cool.

"You bet your ass it is," Teddy said. "Now get the hell off my property."

"Frank, let's go," a man called from the cab. "We'll get it later."

"You ain't gettin' shit," Teddy called back.

Frank held his hands up and backed up. Preacher watched as

the man climbed back in the truck, still wishing he had his own weapon. He had to fix that, sooner rather than later.

The truck started and Frank turned it around in a wide arc, then rolled it slowly back up the drive. Everyone seemed to hold their breath until the sound of the engine faded away beneath the light rain. One by one, they came out of their hiding spots and gathered around the old man.

"They're not going to stay away," Ripley said.

"And lying about the starter won't keep them from trying," Marco said.

"That wasn't a lie," Teddy said, slipping his hand into a pocket and coming out with a fist-sized hunk of metal. "Without this solenoid, it won't start until I want it to."

"Smart," Preacher said.

Teddy looked in the direction the truck had gone and scowled. "Sometimes being smart only buys you a little time." He jabbed a thumb at the truck. "You kids get back to that truck. I've got some things to take care of."

Preacher stepped aside as the little man hurried off towards his house, his steps sure on the slick ooze of the oyster shell drive.

"What do you think he's up to?" Ripley asked.

"Guess we're about to find out," Preacher answered.

DOTTY

Dotty leaned one hand on the back of a kitchen chair, the other holding a cotton hand towel at her hip. Candles lit the space, adding to the muggy heat. Even with both the doors and all of the back windows open, it still felt like a sauna inside.

She took a deep breath through her nose, blew it out slowly, and looked at the kids seated around the table. "So he just left?"

"He put the part back in his tank, had a talk with Preacher, and then he was gone," Ripley said. "He wanted to get out of town before Frank came back with more men."

Mel straightened up and put her arms on her hips, then said with a bad imitation of Teddy, "Frank's showed me twice today how far he's willing to go. Someone shows you who they are, you believe 'em."

Dotty looked to the porch doorway, where Corey leaned against the frame with his arms crossed. "He didn't say where he was going, exactly? What route he was taking?"

Corey shook his head and jutted his chin towards the table. "Just gave us those."

Dotty regarded the fat brown envelope on the table. It had a sticker from a legal firm in Salisbury, and her name typed on it. She wasn't ready to open it. It looked too official. What had that old coot been planning?

"What about Preacher?" she asked.

"He's spending the night in the hardware store," Ripley said.

"Even though you've emptied it?"

Ripley nodded. "He said he'll put the plywood up over the windows tomorrow and then it'll be done. The guys are supposed to take turns keeping watch on your house tonight."

"But we can't, so Thomas will have to stay up," Corey said.

"Or you can sleep next door," Marco offered.

Dotty huffed and dropped the towel on the table. "I'm a grown woman in my own home. I've been doing just fine sleeping here for years. I think I can handle one night without you men keeping watch." She pointed at Corey. "But you...this ain't no time to be headed down to Pocomoke in the middle of the night."

"We need plywood, or hoses and tubing, Grams," Corey said. "We don't have time to find them piece by piece."

"Teddy was right," Marco added. "We saw them taking things this morning. We need to prepare for that now. Cover the windows. Maybe build something in the living room to catch bullets."

"Catch bullets?" Dotty gasped. "Isn't that a little much?"

"If someone's firing into the house, we want to be able to get down behind something," Marco said. He gestured with his arms. "We can build something to make the bottom two feet of the room safe. That's enough to crawl and get out."

"Maybe we can find some more Quickcrete," Corey said. "We grabbed everything Teddy had, but it wasn't much."

"You *really* think someone's going to be shooting at our *house?*" Dotty asked. "With all the people in here? They'd have to be-"

"Desperate," Ripley said, her voice flat. "Desperate, or just angry. On the way home, people were shooting up stuff just because they could. If the City thinks we've got something they want, who knows what they'll do?"

"Show up with a bunch of men and guns, judging by tonight," Mel said.

The room fell quiet. Dotty picked her towel up, tucked it in her waist apron, and moved to the living room doorway. There was barely any moonlight coming in through the windows with all of the cloud cover, and no candles. No reason wasting a candle if no one was going to be in the room. She took in her pretty lace curtains, her antique writing desk in front of the windows, and her worn area rug.

It was a place of comfort for her. The big overstuffed chair in the corner by the desk was her favorite spot to sit and read when she couldn't sit on the porch. The light coming in through the windows was perfect right there. The old couch was worn but still comfortable, and the boys had always loved to take naps on it. Her little paintings on the wall of old fishing boats and fishermen, that she'd bought from local painters back in Baltimore at the harbor, reminded her of times with Nate. His father's flag, folded and in its special case on the wall, was a family heirloom. There was a framed photo of her daughter, Corey and Thomas' mother, in her uniform.

What was left of her life was here. The thought of someone standing outside and shooting into this house, into her sanctuary, riddling her furniture with bullets and destroying her beloved things...

She rubbed her fingers across the cross at her neck and tried to calm her anger. Nate would tell her not to worry herself over it; it could all be replaced. It was just material things.

"Not all of it," she whispered. The flag, the little clay dog that

Thomas had made for her in grade school, her photographs - these things were priceless. When they'd moved her valuables down into the cellar, they hadn't taken these, because they didn't look like they were worth stealing. A burglar would pass them by, looking for electronics or things he could pawn.

She moved through the living room by memory, and picked up the little clay figurine. Maybe it was time to move these things, too. After what she'd seen this morning, she couldn't put anything past the Stalls. Those men had been armed.

In the kitchen, Marco started talking, low and hushed. He was arguing with Ripley, trying to convince her that he and Corey needed to go, *had* to go, tonight. Tomorrow night might be too late; there wouldn't be time to put plywood over the windows before daylight. The census had said forty-eight hours.

Would Frank really have those men fire into the house?

The kids said he'd threatened Teddy. There was no reason for them to exaggerate. Things were bad enough as they were. Frank had threatened Teddy--a known military veteran--with men and firepower. And the kids had been there, so he'd been threatening them, too. To think he wouldn't do the same to her and anyone with her would just be wishful thinking.

It would be foolish.

She had to protect the family.

She set the figurine back down and walked back to the kitchen.

"We'll take a dolly, and we'll grab another if we see it. Even if the truck can't make it back, we can put the stuff on the dolly and make it back before daylight," Marco said. "It's less than 15 miles."

"After the stunt you pulled this morning, you've really got no room to talk, Rip," Corey said. He'd moved to a chair at the table.

"Oh, here we go," Mel said.

"Don't even," Ripley said. "Me walking down to the corner and intending to help with firewood is in no way comparable to you heading off to the city."

"I'm just saying, we don't need your permission," Corey said.

Ripley's volume went up a few notches. "You think this is about permission? I should've asked you for *permission* to leave my own house?"

"We're supposed to be a team. I just think it would be considerate of you to let the rest of the team know when you're planning on doing something stupid."

"Stupid? Getting firewood is stupid?"

They were practically screaming now. Corey was half-standing, slamming a finger down into the table with his words.

"Quit playing dumb. Going off to the woods with a friggin' inmate was stupid. He could have done anything to you and none of us would have even known where to find the body!"

"I'd have known," Dotty said.

The kids stiffened. Ripley looked down at the table and Corey lowered himself back into the chair.

"If you two are going to be yelling at each other, you'll take it outside," Dotty said. "I won't have that kind of discord in my house."

"Sorry Grams," Ripley said.

"Sorry," Corey echoed.

Dotty took a deep breath and blew it out. "You want plywood to cover the windows, yes? You can't get that from Teddy?"

"The hunters cleaned him out to make their blinds. Everything he has left, Preacher's going to use to cover the shop windows," Marco said.

"And these hoses...we'll have fresh water here at the house?"

"I've got the ram pump put together and in the river," Corey said. "I just need more hoses to get it here. It won't be much, with the hose being so small, but it'll add up."

Dotty nodded. "Fine. But concrete won't work. It'll take too long to set up, and you'd need too many hands to keep stirring it. Besides, it would be too heavy to move. A cubic foot of concrete is 150 pounds, and a cubic foot of dirt is only 40."

Marco grinned at her. "You're a surprising woman, Miss Dotty."

She gave a dismissive snort. "I worked in a hardware store for years. It was either learn or get fired. Now," she pointed to the boys. "If you're going to make a wall under my windows, you'll use a frame and dirt, and it'll be lined with plastic. I won't have dirt and bugs spilling out all over my living room."

"We can do that," Marco said.

"Yes ma'am," Corey said, nodding.

"Good. Get going. I want you back here by daylight. And if either of you comes back with more holes than you had when you left, I am *not* going to be happy."

"You wouldn't like her when she's angry," Mel said, grinning.

Corey got up and wrapped her in a hug. "Thanks, Grams. We'll be back before you know it."

"You'd better be," she said. "You do what you have to do to get home. We'll worry about the consequences later." She let go of Corey and pulled a surprised Marco into a hug. "That goes for you, too. You be careful."

"I'll try, ma'am," Marco said.

"Go on now, before I change my mind."

The boys moved around her and headed for the front door.

"Be careful," Ripley called to them. Then quieter, she muttered "even if you are an asshole sometimes."

"Sometimes?" Mel said, getting up. "That's been his default state all week long."

"We're all under a lot of pressure," Dotty said. "It's times like these when we need to remember to show a little grace."

"I don't think I've ever had any," Mel said. She walked over to the sink and dipped her hands into the bowl of soapy wash water. After rubbing down her hands and face, she moved to the bowl of rinse water and did the same. Toweling off, she sighed. "I miss having a working shower."

"You're doing fine without one," Dotty said. "I'd imagine that's a big change for you. And you *are* handling it all with grace."

"Well, I haven't cut anyone yet, so there's that," Mel said. She waved to get Ripley's attention. "Are we staying here tonight?"

"Dad would kill me, even with Preacher and Marco gone," Ripley said. "They could come back while I'm asleep...and that's too much of a risk for him. It was enough that he let me go this morning. I don't want to push it." She moved her chair back and stood up. "Sorry, Grams."

"You don't need to apologize, child," Dotty said. "Thomas is upstairs, even if he could sleep through y'all yelling like that. And I've got my shotgun. I'll be fine."

"I'll stay until Thomas gets up," Mel offered.

"That'll work," Ripley said. "I'll send Jax over, too. Love ya, Grams." She leaned down and gave Dotty a kiss on the cheek.

"Love you too, sweetheart. I'll see you in the morning."

The screen door on the back porch banged as Ripley left, and Mel shuffled into the living room and started fussing with the pillows on the couch. Dotty folded up the kitchen towel and started to pull off her apron, then remembered she hadn't checked the coop for eggs tonight. She'd been shooing the birds back into the coop when the kids had come around the back of the house looking for her.

"Mel, I'll be right back. I'm gonna see if we've got any eggs."

"K Grams."

The night air outside was cooler than in the house. Not by much, but enough to notice. If her back wouldn't punish her for it, she'd consider sleeping on the screened-in porch tonight.

The grass back here was still knee-high and wet, but there were clear paths worn to the outhouse, the chicken tractor, and over to the Millers' back porch. Even so, her pants would be soaked by the time she got back inside.

"I need to get the boys to move this thing tomorrow," she said, pulling a little flashlight from her apron and aiming it at the coop's back door.

It hung open.

"I know I latched that...I had to have latched that," she said. She ran over the memory in her mind. She'd been inside the run, and had just gotten the little rooster to follow his girls up the ramp. The kids came around the corner, arguing, and she'd just had time to shut the ramp door before they'd started calling for her. She'd gotten out of the run as quickly as she could, and pushed it shut behind her.

She swung the flashlight over to the door over the ramp. It was closed, and latched.

Then what had she done?

She couldn't remember clearly. The kids had been crowding around her, all talking at once, and shoving that dang envelope at her. Teddy was gone. Frank had threatened them. They were worried and wanting to batten down the hatches.

I wouldn't have had that back door open, she thought. *Not when I was trying to get the chickens back in there. They'd have gone in one door and out the other. So there'd have been no reason for me to make sure it was closed.*

Still, she couldn't remember for sure. She braced herself for tragedy and opened the door. The chickens were on their roost, grumbling and restless. They should've been sleeping by now. Passing her flashlight over them, she quickly counted. Then she counted again. One by one, she looked them over.

The little rooster was missing.

PREACHER

Preacher lifted the panel of plywood into place and braced it with his thigh. He'd nearly gotten doing this by himself down to a science, now. Having some help would have been nice, but everyone had something important to do. He reached back and grabbed the drill from the top of the shopping cart he was using as a mobile sawhorse, and aimed it at his face.

This was the tricky part; getting the screw in his mouth to match up with the bit, all while staring cross-eyed down his nose. He wiggled his lips back and forth until he heard a click, then carefully let go of the screw.

It held. Now he just had to hope the hole was still lined up. Teddy had holes pre-drilled in these panels, and each one was marked with which window they were supposed to cover. It had been easy to match up the panels with the windows, but figuring out how to get them up—and keep them there—by himself while wrangling the drill and screws had taken most of an hour.

The street was quiet, and the overcast sky cast a depressing gloom on everything. There was no wind, but storm clouds in the distance said that wouldn't be the case later. This had to get done now.

Besides, as soon as he had this done, he could go home.

He *needed* to get home.

Home.

It still rattled him, whenever that word crossed his mind. It broke his concentration.

I've got a home now.

And wasn't it his luck, that he'd survived prison, he'd survived the prison culling, and he'd found a home...and now the powers that be were trying to take it away.

He was going to do his best to make sure that wouldn't happen.

The screws across the bottom finished, he held the panel flat while maneuvering one of his two ladders into place. This one would brace the panel tight against the window frame, the other was for standing on.

He had just gotten the first top screw into place when the consignment shop door opened and the same woman who'd aimed a shotgun at him yesterday stepped out. Her bright pink hair was spiked up today, and her cat's-eye glasses were perched on her head. She was somewhere in her forties, white with a bit of a tan, and thin. Too thin. There were women who weren't ever able to gain weight, and the slightest bit of stress ripped away whatever progress they'd made. His mom had been one of those. This lady looked like a strong wind would knock her over.

She pointed at her wrist. "You got a minute?"

It was obvious he didn't have a minute. He fired the drill up and screwed the top corner in place.

"Look, I'm sorry for pointing that shotgun at you," she said when the drill went quiet. "It was bothering me all night long. My dad taught me to never point a gun at something I wasn't willing to shoot."

He snapped the next screw into place and lined it up with the hole.

"Wait a minute! Please?"

Preacher sighed and regarded her with raised eyebrows.

"When you're done with that window, can you come over here? Just come right on in the shop. I put together a little something...an apology gift."

"Not necessary," Preacher said. He pulled the trigger and watched the screw sink in.

When he finished, she was still standing there, but now with her arms crossed.

"Teddy told me you're staying with Dotty. If you want, I can just go there and wait, and make a big deal out of this. You know, lots of people, maybe some squealing, lots of attention." She cocked her head. "You don't strike me as the type that likes attention."

He frowned at her.

"That's what I thought," she said. "You come over when that window's done and let me off-load this guilt. Otherwise, I show up at your house and make a scene. Sound good? Good."

She didn't wait for an answer. She was back inside her shop before he'd figured out that she'd just threatened him...with squealing.

He growled and put the next screw into place.

A PLEASANT LITTLE tune sounded when he stepped into the annoying woman's shop. It was so out of place that he stopped and looked up at the top of the door.

"Battery operated. Hasn't worn out yet. It's not like there's been any customers to give it a workout." She got up from an overstuffed chair next to an antique full-length mirror and strode forward, hand out.

"I'm Lisa," she said. She waited, raising her eyebrows and jiggling her hand a bit when he hesitated.

He shook her hand. She had a good grip. "Preacher," he said.

"Good. See? We can do this. Just two friendly people having a conversation without killing each other," she said. She stepped back and motioned her head towards the back. "I've got your stuff on the counter. C'mon."

The store smelled like an old closet mixed with vanilla. Circular racks were heavy with clothing, and cheerful signs on top advertised a different type of sale every day. Bookcases lined the wall, and all sorts of nic-nacs, teddy bears, and appliances sat on the shelves, waiting for their new home.

"I was just working on getting all of my Halloween outfits hung and put out when the lights went out," she said, tapping a mostly-empty rack of costumes as she went by. "Guess there won't be any trick-or-treating this year, eh? Blessing in disguise, if you ask me. We won't be subjected to Cathy Riggs' latest *sexy* costume. She's been talking all summer about how she was going to be a *sexy* Bob Ross this year. You know, that painter with the afro? She was in here buying the shortest, tightest blue jean shorts she could find. God help us."

Preacher snorted.

Lisa moved around the sales counter and gave him a serious look. "You laugh, but I'm dead serious. Each year, it's worse than the one before. Last Halloween she was a sexy Twizzler candy. A red catsuit with some swooshy stripes." She moved her hands around her torso. "It was ridiculous. Anyway, here's what I came up with."

She stepped further down the counter to a number of neatly-folded stacks of clothing and raised her hands in a Vanna White impression. "Ta-da!"

"Clothes?" he asked.

"Clothes!" she said, nodding vigorously. "You're wearing the same clothes today you had on yesterday. So I figured you must not have too many clothes, right? A guy your size...it's not like you can just borrow a pair of pants."

Preacher had been wearing the same pants nearly every day since the Warden had let him out. Corey had given him a pair of cut-off sweatpants and a couple of stretchy tank tops, but everything else he had was too skinny. He tried to rinse his shirt out every night and hang it up on the porch to dry, but the jeans took too long to do that.

He moved down to the piles and picked up the first shirt.

"See, the thing is, we've got a lot of guys around here that are way too wide for their height, if you get me. But that means some of these might fit you. They might be a little tight in the shoulders, but if you get 'em wet and you're careful, you can stretch them out."

She was right. The two dress shirts looked like they'd fit him around the chest, which was rare enough, but the shoulders would be a little small. He wasn't sure if that material would be able to stretch, but he was willing to try. Under the dress shirts was a stack of t-shirts, with garish designs on them of old rock bands or weird cartoon characters, but they all looked like they'd fit.

"Like I said, wide guys," she said. "Here's a couple of sweatshirts that might work, and this sweater is *really* nice. I live next to Sheriff Kane's mom—really sweet woman—and she knitted this for him for Christmas last year. He can't wear it. The wool in it makes him break out. She brought it in about six months ago, but with it being so hot out this summer, no one's even taken it off the shelf."

The sweater was thick and heavy, with a cable-knit design. He held it up to his shoulders and shook his head in wonder. It was damn near perfect.

"And here's for your other half," she said, pushing another stack at him. "I mean, except for the underwear. I don't do underwear here. But do you know I've had people ask? Used underwear. Blech."

He reached for the pair of sweatpants on top and checked the size. They'd fit his waist. He pulled them off of the stack and held them up.

"I hope you're not too picky. I know the waists will fit you, but the length is hit or miss," she said. "It's not so bad with sweatpants, most people wear 'em scrunched up over their calves anyway. The jeans are where we'll have to get creative."

He shifted the pile to the first pair of jeans and checked inside the waist.

"How'd you guess my waist size?"

Lisa actually looked offended. "I've had this shop for ten years. This is what I *do*. This is my *art*. The day I can't guess the waist size on a fit man is the day I need to lock my doors."

The jeans fell about halfway down his calves.

Damnit.

He must have broadcast that thought with his expression, because Lisa fluttered her hands. "Don't get discouraged! The waist and hips are what's most important. The length we can fix. Look here."

She reached under the counter and came up with a laundry basket full of denim. She thrust her hands into the basket and lifted them up, letting the cloth fall down like rain.

"I pick up a lot of men's jeans at yard sales with little holes in the crotch," she said. "I don't know what it is, men digging at their junk all day or something, but it seems like the crotch is always the first to go. Anyway, I cut those up, and make my Denny Bears."

Lisa pointed to the denim teddy bears on the shelves. "Aren't they adorable? They sell like hotcakes at the holiday craft fair. Well, they *did*. Don't guess we'll be having one this year."

He pulled a piece of denim off of the pile and turned it over.

"We find some leg pieces in there that are the same width as those jeans, and we add them on as extensions. It might look a little different, but it's better than nothing, right?"

Anything was better than nothing. Then again, nothing was ever free.

"I don't have money," he said.

She put her hands flat on the counter, leaned forward, and spoke sternly. "I. Almost. *Killed* you yesterday." She straightened. "Let me make it up to you. *Please*. It's not like I can wear this stuff, it's all way too big for me. And no one else is walking in here wanting new clothes. They've all got closets stuffed full and more in boxes out in their sheds. They're drowning in clothes. Take the stuff. Please?"

When he hesitated, she held a finger up and hurried around the counter, plucked a bear from the shelf, and hustled back. She thrust it at him.

"I'll even throw in a Denny Bear. This one looks like it was made for you," she said. " Look at him. You can't say no to that cute little demonic face."

He took the bear from her. It was a faded blue, like an old favorite pair of jeans. Its four paws ended in patches of soft black leather, and the insides of his ear tabs were leather, too. It had dark red buttons for eyes, and some black thread for a nose. He turned it over, and found a little skull and crossbones design on its back.

It looked like a little hell raiser. It was perfect.

"Look at that, he *can* smile," Lisa said.

The little chime sounded and they both turned to the door. Ripley stuck her head and shoulders in, squinting as her eyes adjusted.

"Oh, thank god," she said. "Preacher...I need you."

PREACHER

Preacher followed Ripley up the road, both of them walking straight up the center as if cars didn't exist. It was no matter to step to the side when the Guard came barreling through; they could see for hundreds of feet in each direction. It wasn't like the big diesel engines could sneak up on them, anyway.

"You were my only option," Ripley was saying. "It was nearly daylight when the guys got home, so they're still asleep. Thomas is helping my Dad put up the plywood they brought back--and how they can sleep through that, I have no idea--and I can't take Mel up there and have someone recognize her."

The sun was merciless, and he felt like he was going to sweat through the long-sleeved button down Ripley had made him put on. *Better if we can hide the tattoos*, she'd said. *Then you'll be less recognizable later on.*

He wasn't quite sure what she expected to happen *later on*, but trying to keep as low a profile as possible made sense.

Walking straight past all the Guard in their tents on the Rec

Center grounds and presenting themselves at the front doors was the opposite of low-profile.

A dark-skinned, female Guardsman stood next to a table, holding a clipboard. There was a short line of people waiting to get inside; she seemed to be questioning them. A few other Guardsmen stood nearby, rifles at the ready, and a tall skinny kid whose uniform was about to slip off of him was wanding each person that made it past the clipboard lady. The extra Guardsmen hadn't even glanced at anyone else since *he'd* gotten in line. Their suspicious stares were nothing new. He pasted on his neutral expression and stared over their heads.

"State your purpose for admittance," Clipboard Queen said when they finally made it to the table.

"We're just here to get a couple meals and take them home," Ripley said.

Clipboard Queen, whose name tag read *Wilson*, shook her head. "The rules changed. Only one meal per person, and you gotta eat it here."

According to what Marco had told them, that was different.

"Really? Why?" Ripley asked.

"The Lieutenant Mayor said so. Something about people hoarding the MREs, and maybe selling them. Black market kind of thing. I dunno, not my problem. We're just here to provide support, we don't get to make the rules. Name, street, and ID?"

"Jennifer Miller and Thomas Winters," Ripley responded. She flipped her wallet open and handed over her driver's license. "We're over on Washington Street."

Clipboard Queen flipped through the papers on her clipboard, read for a moment, then marked something off. She handed back Ripley's license and held out her hand, wiggling her fingers at him.

"His wallet was stolen," Ripley said.

"I've got this piece of mail," he said, pulling a crumpled and slightly damp envelope from his pocket and handing it over.

In truth, his wallet was under the counter in Teddy's shop, along with the clothes and the little Denny Bear Lisa had forced on him. Ripley had made him leave it, and had shoved the envelope at him. It was a reminder from the DMV to renew the license plates on Thomas' truck.

Letter from the state, can't get more official than that, she'd said.

"Uh-huh," Wilson said, checking the name on the envelope and then leafing through the papers on her clipboard. Her brows drew together. "Says here on the voter registration form that you're black."

He blinked. "It was a phase."

Wilson's brows flew up. "A phase?"

"Everyone was identifying as something they're not. I convinced the lady at the DMV that I come from a black family, so I identify as black," he said, shrugging.

Ripley caught on. "I still can't believe you had her thinking you'd use the Civil Rights Act to get her fired if she discriminated against your identity."

"I can be intimidating sometimes," he deadpanned.

Wilson stood looking from one to the other, her eyebrows still sky high. "Uh-huh," she said again. "I'm supposed to believe that *you* got your wallet stolen. You. A man big enough to knock over a horse?"

"Well I wasn't gonna hit a woman," he said.

"A *woman* robbed you?"

"*Mean* slip of a girl. Held a gun on me," he said. He held his hand up even with the top of Ripley's head. "About yea high, brown hair."

Wilson blinked at him, her mouth hanging open a little. Okay, maybe he'd pushed it a little too far, but he was flying by the seat of his pants here.

"Look, you've verified I'm a resident, and I vouch for him; isn't that enough?" Ripley asked.

Wilson shook her head. "I'd love to let you in, big boy. I haven't been entertained this much since we got called up for this shit post. But I can't let in unidentified people or guests of residents. Y'all would have to be married or something-"

Ripley held up her left hand and wiggled her fingers. She was still wearing Mel's diamond. "Does fiancé count?"

"You're shitting me," Wilson said.

"He proposed right before I went back to school," Ripley said with a smile.

"Wedding's April first," he added.

Wilson blinked at them some more, then shook her head. "Girl, you like to live dangerously," she finally said. She thrust the envelope back at Preacher. "You know what? I think the bullshit's getting too high out here. I'm getting the vapors." She put her clipboard down on the table and pointed at the skinny guy with the wand. "You two get past him, and you can do whatever the hell you want. I'm taking a break." She motioned to one of the extra Guardsmen. "Sisson, get over here and relieve me. I'm going for a walk."

"Go, go," Ripley whispered, pushing him from behind.

He went.

They made it through the wanding and into the building's lobby before Ripley spun on him and punched him in the arm.

"You nearly blew this!" she hissed.

He held his hand up to the top of her forehead. "*Mean* girl," he said. "Yea high."

"I didn't steal your wallet, I just made you leave it behind."

"Engaged for ten minutes, already broke."

"Ha. Ha."

"There's no loitering in the lobby," A woman called out. Preacher looked up to find a middle-aged woman, pasty and plump, standing behind a big curved counter.

Ripley faked a concerned look and spun around. "I haven't been in here before. I'm not sure where to go."

The lobby was a big open area, with a polished floor and a few groupings of furniture. There were only three ways to go; the doors they'd come through and two wide hallways on either side of the reception desk.

The woman pointed to the hall on their right as they walked to the big counter. "Meals and registration for the shelter are down that hall," she pointed to the opposite opening. "The City's temporary offices are down that one. What are you here for?"

"I...need to report an attempted assault," Ripley said, leaning her elbows on the counter. "Yesterday a bunch of men in a pickup truck threatened to shoot me and another girl if we didn't tell them what food we had"

"Oh dear," the woman said. "Things have gotten so bad out there. You'll be wanting the county clerk's office. She's handling the police reports until they can find someone else. First door on the right."

The clerk was a harried-looking woman with lots of freckles and reddish hair in a tiny office. A wide filing cabinet behind her held stacks of paper at varying heights, and plastic bins lined the walls stacked up in twos and threes. When Ripley repeated her story to her, she sighed and took a sheet of paper off of a stack behind her and handed it over.

"Fill this out with as much detail as you can remember," she said. "Be sure to put the location, too. I'll be honest with you, though: it's not likely that they'll be found. We've got so many reports coming in daily of vandalism and robbery that we'll be backed up for months trying to follow-up on them all."

"Well these guys were pretending to be police officers," Ripley said. "Wouldn't that mark it as urgent?"

The woman made a disgusted noise. "There's been people in neon yellow vests pretending to be power workers to gain entry to houses, and people dressed like those Mormon people—you know, the ones that ride the bikes—telling residents they were taking donations for the church. I guess it's just the next step for them to start dressing like police men."

"Plain clothed," Preacher said.

Ripley nodded. "Yeah, they didn't have on uniforms. That's what made us suspicious. But they had these forms they wanted us to fill out."

The woman perked up. "Oh sweetie, do you mean the census? Here." She leaned over to a plastic bin under the window with a stack of papers on it nearly a foot high. She pulled off the top sheet and handed it to Ripley. "Did it look like this?"

Preacher leaned over Ripley's shoulder and looked. It was the same form they'd been given, only this one was completely filled out.

"This is it," Ripley said, nodding. "You mean it's legit? The City really wants to know all this stuff?"

The woman nodded. "The City *has* to get this information. The Governor wants every resource accounted for."

Ripley's voice was full of doubt. "The Governor wants to know how much food we have? Seriously?"

"Honest to God."

"And those men, they weren't pretending to be police officers?"

"That was most likely our new Police Chief, Frank Stalls. He's deputized some men as officers to work with him. You don't remember him being Deputy Sheriff?"

"I've been away at college for more than a year, and I just made it home yesterday," Ripley lied, handing the census form back. "I don't even know who's who anymore. The Sheriff, the Mayor-"

"Oh it's still Kenny Wilhelm," the clerk said, putting the form back onto its pile. "But he's not just the Mayor anymore. He's also *Judge* Wilhelm, *and* the Governor has appointed him Civil Officer, at least until all this is over. As for Sheriff, we've still got Simon Kane, not that he's doing any good."

"What's he doing?" Preacher asked.

"He made this big scene at a town hall," the clerk said. "Tried to get a lot of people in trouble. Even nearly got the Mayor killed out at the park during another town hall because he wouldn't provide enough security."

"Sounds pretty bad," Preacher said. Dotty had told him what had happened at those two town halls, and from what she'd said, any rioting had been the Mayor's fault.

The clerk nodded. "He's been useless." She leaned one elbow on her desk and started ticking off things on her fingers. "Won't do a thing the City Council tells him to do. Wouldn't assign his deputies to protect the government here in town. Isn't using his deputies to protect the people now. He's the biggest part of the reason we've had to move the town operations here to the Rec Center."

"God. Can't he be recalled or something?" Ripley asked.

"We're trying. Problem is, it can't just be a town vote, like the emergency one we held to make the Mayor a judge. Sheriff is a county position, and the whole county has to be involved in a recall vote. The Mayor's working on it, but without phones and email it's slow going. And it's just getting more and more dangerous out there the longer the Sheriff's refusing to do his job."

"Sounds like hell," Preacher said.

The clerk nodded. "There's just so much to get done and no one's willing to help. The Mayor's just swamped, bless his heart. He's working himself to death for this town." She sighed, shaking her head. "I'm sorry. I don't mean to unload on you, or seem like I'm gossiping."

"Don't apologize," Ripley said, leaning forward in her chair. "I'm thankful for the information. I didn't know any of this. I mean, I didn't even know you guys were here at the Rec Center until I went to City Hall today and saw the sign."

"See?" The clerk said. "The Sheriff needs to be getting that info out. Notices on all the doors or something. Ugh. But you two really should get some things together and move here, into the Rec center. At least until the Guard can get things under control. It's a lot safer than being out there with all the vandals and druggies running around."

Ripley looked up at him as if looking for his agreement. "We could do that, honey. Get the dog, some stuff, and come back this afternoon."

The clerk shook her head. "You can't bring any pets. Just yourselves."

Ripley looked genuinely confused now. "How are we supposed to keep our dog safe and healthy if we don't bring him?"

"Just put him in an indoor room, leave him some food and water. Pets are resilient. He'll be fine."

"It's not safe enough for me to be out there, but it's safe enough for my dog-" Ripley started, and Preacher hopped in before she pissed the clerk off.

"Is there anything special we have to do to get into the shelter? Pay money?"

"Oh goodness no. It's free. You just have to bring your clothes, and toiletries...here, let me see." She stood and crossed the room to a filing cabinet, and leafed through some papers there. "Here we go. Here's a full set of the rules and what you need to bring." She handed the paper to him. "The Guard is providing two meals a day, and cots in the gym. Everything else is your responsibility."

Preacher pretended to scan over the list and handed it to Ripley. "If it'll be safer in here..."

"Yeah," Ripley said. "Maybe we should."

"Oh you really should," the clerk said. "A pretty young girl like you? Young people like yourselves, out there alone? I shudder to think what could happen."

"Could we...see the facilities?" Ripley asked.

"Well we don't allow anyone who isn't signed in to go back there, but I could take a few minutes and give you a tour, if you want?"

Anything that would allow them to gather more info that might be useful against the City was something both he and Ripley wanted.

"That sounds like just what we need," Preacher said.

DOTTY

The next morning was cool, with a thick fog hanging in the air. Preacher had gone to the corner and returned, with Sheriff Kane in tow. Dotty had sat with them on the front porch, enjoying the cooler weather, as everyone else was waking up and doing their morning routines. Dotty and Preacher filled Simon in on everything he and Ripley had learned the day before at the Rec Center, including the clerk's personal opinion about the job he was doing.

"If they make me out to be the scape goat, they can justify a lot of things," Simon said. "There's not much I can do about the rumor mill."

He'd gone back to looking out over the fog, silently swinging the porch chair back and forth.

The waiting was driving Dotty crazy. They'd made all the preparations they could, and discussed what reaction they'd have if Cindy and her goons actually showed up today.

The houses both had their front first-floor windows covered in plywood. Thick blankets covered the other windows. The doors were being kept locked, and everyone had to use their keys when they wanted to go in or out. Seth's reasoning was that if a door was unlocked, the City could say it was open, and that was a clear invitation to come inside.

Marco had wanted to line both porches with people and guns, but Dotty had nixed that idea. She didn't want anyone getting shot. Besides, they had no idea how many people Cindy would bring with her. It might just be the few she had last time. Maybe Frank and his new officers would come with her. Maybe they'd bring the Guard.

It was just too risky.

Over the past two days, she'd personally visited every remaining neighbor on the street. She'd asked them to keep an eye on her house, and if they saw any activity, to come and be a witness.

If the City showed up and both she and Seth refused to allow them to enter the houses, having witnesses here might keep the City from doing something rash and lying about what led up to it.

Most everyone had said they'd come if they saw anything.

And now the fog's so thick you can't see past the neighbor's yard, Dotty thought. *Murphy's law.*

She rubbed her cross pendant between her fingers and prayed for a peaceful outcome.

Marco came jogging across the street from the Cobbs' house. He thumped up the porch stairs, causing Jax to go nuts barking inside.

"I've got Thomas' cellphone recording in that upper window," he said, pointing. "Both houses are in the picture. Lily has a phone over there, and I've got one here. Whatever happens, we'll have video proof."

"I'm supposed to sit here and pretend I didn't just see you

come from that house, which isn't yours, and hear you admit to being inside?" Simon said.

"They gave Miss Dotty a key," Marco said, holding up a silver key. He handed it to Dotty. "Said if she needs anything, to feel free."

Dotty pocketed the key in her apron and glared at him, but didn't say anything.

More lies by omission, she thought. *I'm starting early today.*

"Mm-hmm," Simon said. "That's certainly...convenient."

The front door opened at the Miller's, and Mel stepped outside. She stood fanning the door open and closed, trying to get some air into the house.

"It's hot as balls in there," she called. "We could have all the windows open and have this cool air moving through if it wasn't for this twunt and her crusade."

"Twunt?" Dotty said.

Marco started to speak but the Sheriff sat forward suddenly, making a loud buzzer noise.

"It means *nasty woman,*" Simon said, raising his eyebrows and looking at Marco.

Marco nodded. "Nasty woman," he repeated.

She looked back and forth between them. They obviously weren't telling her the whole truth.

It must be the day for that, she thought, gave a mock glare to them both, and let it go.

"I hear an engine," Marco said.

The Sheriff straightened and turned, looking into the fog.

"I hear more than one," he said.

"Guys? Guys! Someone's coming!" Mel shouted into the Miller's house. Footsteps pounded in both houses and people emptied out onto the porches. Dotty stood as everyone jostled for a good view, locked the big door, and pulled it shut. Next door, Seth was doing the same thing.

Dotty moved to her front steps and scooted over when Simon moved up beside her.

"I appreciate you being here today, Sheriff," she said. "No matter what happens, I want you to know that."

"Let's just hope my presence is enough to make them turn around and leave," Simon said.

Marco leaned against the railing and held up a phone. "Start recording!" he called out.

"Already started," Lily called back.

Pickup trucks rolled through the fog and lined up in the street.

Dotty's heart sank. They'd come in force.

The trucks emptied out, with so many people milling about that Dotty couldn't keep count. All of them had rifles or shotguns. Frank Stalls started calling out orders, splitting the group into two.

"Group 1 at that house, Group 2 at that one," Frank said, pointing. "No use of force without my order. You've all got your zip ties?"

"I guess that's my cue," Simon muttered, and moved to the bottom of the steps.

"Lord God, watch over us and protect us," Dotty whispered. "Watch over Sheriff Kane as he stands up for us. Watch over the men that have come here today to trespass against us, for we know not what lies they've been told."

Marco had heard her. "It doesn't matter what they were told," he said. "What matters is that they're choosing to come here prepared to shoot us, without proof. Without trial. They don't deserve your prayers."

"Everyone deserves a prayer now and then," Dotty said. She looked back over her shoulder, past Thomas. "David, sit down.

You'll make them nervous looming over them like that. You too, Corey. Dang tall men."

Preacher lowered himself onto the porch swing and crossed his arms. Corey scowled at her, and when she raised her eyebrows, he grumbled and took her chair.

In the street, one of the men patted Frank on the shoulder and pointed. Frank looked up and frowned.

"Didn't expect to see you here, *Sheriff*," he called out.

"I heard there's been some trespassing going on," Simon said. "I came by to make sure it doesn't happen again. These people don't want strangers on their properties."

Frank's face broke into a wild grin and he shook his head. "So you're gonna cowboy up against the big evil posse, is that it?"

"Is that what this is?" Simon said. "I see a bunch of town residents, armed, preparing to illegally trespass. I can't speak to your motivations, but if you want to call yourselves evil, well..."

"I'm not calling-" Frank stopped and took a deep breath. He scanned the two porches, his eyebrows drawing down.

"Mr. Seth Miller, Ms. Dorothy Parker," he called out. "I have here in my possession two warrants giving my men and I authority to search these residences. If you, your family members, or anyone on your property attempt to obstruct our *lawful* search-" he plucked some folded papers from his shirt pocket-"those people will be arrested and charged." He held up the papers.

Warrants? Dotty's heart raced. *Where did they get warrants?*

Next door, Seth strode across the yard towards Frank. "Let me see that," he said, holding out his hand.

Dotty was down the steps and across the grass before she realized she'd taken the first step. Frank turned from handing a paper to Seth, checked the remaining piece, and handed it to her.

"You'll find everything's in order," he said. "Men, pro-."

"Now you hold on," Dotty said. "I haven't agreed to this yet."

"You don't have to agree, Ms. Parker," Frank said. "You just have to stay out of our way. Are you going to comply, or not?"

"Give her a damn minute to read the warrant at least, Frank," Simon said from right behind her. "I don't know how you managed it, but if this is legal, it doesn't give you cause to be a pompous ass."

"I'm not being an ass, I'm doing my *job*," Frank said. "Maybe that concept is something you should re-acquaint yourself with."

Dotty scanned down the paper. There was her name and address, a lot of mumbo-jumbo, and Judge Kenneth Wilhelm's signature at the bottom.

"It's signed," she said. "*Judge* Wilhelm signed it."

"Same on mine," Seth said.

"Now that we've established that," Frank said, "men, proceed."

Seth handed his paper to Simon. "We've got no recourse, Sheriff?"

The two groups of men split and approached the houses, weapons drawn.

Ripley stood on her porch stairs, holding her arms wide.

"Wait, wait!" she shouted. "There are dogs inside. Let us get the dogs!"

"Not my problem-" Frank started.

"Oh for christ's sake, let them get the dogs, Stalls," Simon said. "You're being recorded. You want video going around of men shooting dogs on your orders?"

"Hold up," Frank yelled. He glared at Simon. "Secure your dogs and bring them outside," he called out. "Keep them away from my men. You've got one minute."

Dotty watched both Ripley and Corey disappear inside the houses. She looked around. Next door, Cathy had come out onto her steps and was watching, arms crossed and a large smile on her face. It occurred to Dotty that someone was missing.

"Where's Cindy?" she asked.

PREACHER

Preacher leaned forward in the swing, tapping his foot.

He didn't like this. At all.

"Pardon me?" Frank asked.

"I want to know where Cindy is," Dotty said. "This is her show, isn't it? Shouldn't she be here?"

"The Lieutenant Mayor's whereabouts are none of your concern," Frank said.

Dotty pointed at the neighbor's house. "You're here, her *assistant* is here watching, but she-"

The rest of her words were drowned out by Corey banging through the door, Jax in his arms. He rushed to Preacher and held the dog out.

"Hold her," he said. "I can't find a leash. I gotta go back in for it."

Preacher grunted a bit as the big dog's weight landed on him, and he scrambled to keep hold of her as she saw all the strangers and started barking. Corey was back inside in a flash.

Jax pushed against the swing and nearly launched herself out of his arms, so he hoisted her up and stood. Her feet scrabbling in the air for purchase, she continued to bark and growl. When those men started to come up on the porch, he wouldn't be able to keep hold of her. He moved down the steps to put some distance between the dog and the so-called officers. The movement caused Jax to shut up and start wagging her tail. She must have thought he was taking her to Dotty.

"Jesus christ," he heard one of the men say. "Look at that frickin' thing."

He looked around Jax's head to see Ripley coming down her porch steps, leading King with a skinny joke of a leash. King was walking against her leg, lips drawn back and a low growl rolling out of his chest.

"That leash ain't gonna hold him if he tries to come after us," the same man said.

Ripley gestured to Preacher and pointed to her Beetle. "Over here," she called. "We'll put them in my car." She unlocked the passenger door and coaxed King inside, shut him in and ran around to the driver's side.

"Here, I'll get the door," she said. As she opened it up, heat rolled out.

"Too hot," he said, stepping back. He wasn't going to cook the dogs just to keep that damn cop happy.

"I've got it," she said, and cranked the window down about a third of the way. "That'll be enough. If they're here too long, I'll start it up. It's got air. It's not the greatest, but it's got it."

He deposited Jax on the driver's seat and slipped out of the way as Ripley shut the door.

"I don't like this," Ripley muttered. "It wasn't supposed to go down like this."

"He's got warrants," Preacher said.

"Those warrants wouldn't have meant shit if he didn't have all these men," she said.

"Okay folks, I want everyone down off of the porches. Let's give these people room," Sheriff Kane called out.

Translation, Preacher thought. *Get everyone out of arm's reach so they can't say someone was being aggressive.*

The two families emptied off the porches and gravitated to the driveway between the houses.

"This is some bullshit," Mel said, stomping to the Bug and leaning on it.

"Keep recording, Marco," Lily said.

"Yes ma'am," Marco said.

There must have been some agreement, because Dotty and Seth both went up onto the porches and unlocked the front doors. When they got back to where Frank and the Sheriff were standing, the Sheriff made an *after you* gesture.

Stalls blew a piercing whistle and circled his finger in the air, then pointed forward.

"What's he think he is, a war general?" Mel asked as the two groups surged forward.

"Keep it down. Don't give them a reason to come over here and arrest you, *Leandra,*" Thomas said, using the fake identity Mel had been hiding behind. He raised his eyebrows and made a pushing motion with his hand. Behind him, the groups pushed through the front doors at the same time, clipboard-holders bringing up the rear.

Jax was whining, wanting to be outside with her humans. Preacher stuck his arm in through the window and scratched her behind the ears.

Ripley made a frustrated sound of anger, and then started waving her arm in an exaggerated gesture.

"Hi Miss Cathy!" she yelled. "Nice to see you out here this morning! Enjoying the show?"

"Jennifer!" Lily hissed. "Stop it!"

"Grams said there's people waiting to show up if they saw something, but how are they going to see?" Ripley said. "Maybe they'll hear me yelling."

"Well find another way to yell," Lily said. "Don't give that bitch more reasons to hate us. When this is all over you'll go back to the University, but your father and I will have to put up with her."

Ripley put her arm down and looked out at the fog in desperation.

Preacher had an idea. He reached out to touch Ripley on the shoulder, then thought better of it and snapped his fingers. When she turned around, he moved his hand from Jax's head and pointed.

Her eyes widened.

"Yes," she whispered, and spun back around.

"Sheriff Kane, do those warrants let these men search our vehicles?" she called out.

The Sheriff cocked an eyebrow at her, then consulted Dotty's paper. After a moment, he shook his head.

"No. The houses and structures only. And they can't take anything with them. Just search and inventory," he said.

Officer Stalls didn't look happy.

Join the crowd, Preacher thought.

"So they can't touch my Bug?" Ripley said.

"No. If you'd feel safer inside it you can-"

Ripley turned, pushed her arm through the window, and slammed her hand onto the horn.

Preacher was watching Officer Stalls. When the Bug's horn started blaring, his face went from unhappy to pissed off in an instant. Preacher nearly grinned.

Dotty turned and gaped. Seth's shoulders started shaking, and he covered his mouth and turned to face the street.

Ripley kept hitting the horn. Mel slapped her hands over her ears and started cheering. Corey scowled and shook his head.

Officer Stalls was shouting something and pointing at them.

Preacher waved his hand in front of Ripley's face and pointed into the car.

She lifted her hand off of the horn. "What?"

"Get *in* the car. Hurry," he said. "Out here he'll arrest you."

"But he can't open the car door," she said. He nodded, and she got inside, pushing Jax into the back seat. He shut the door and turned around, bracing his feet and crossing his arms.

They'd have to get through him, first.

"Tell her to stop that right this-" Frank yelled.

The horn started blaring again. Officer Stalls took a step forward and the Sheriff moved in front of him. Preacher couldn't hear a damn thing other than the horn, but it was obvious by their faces and wild gesturing, they were arguing something fierce.

Another horn joined in, and Preacher looked over to see Thomas sitting in his little truck with the door open, jabbing his steering wheel in opposite time to Ripley's blasts.

Boooop. Beeeep. Booop. Beeeep.

One of the 'officers' came out on Dotty's porch and waved at him. Preacher waved back. The man shook his head and made a cutting motion across his throat, then pointed to his ear. Preacher shook his head.

You want her to stop blowing that horn? Come over here and try to make her, he thought.

Something tugged on his sleeve, and he looked down to find Mel. She was pointing back across the driveway and mouthing something. He caught movement out of the corner of his eye. Two more men, this time from Seth's house, strode across the yard towards them.

Preacher banged his hand on the roof of the Bug and Ripley stopped. Corey got Thomas to stop.

"Keep your distance," Preacher called out. "Warrant don't cover the cars."

One of the men stopped, but the other kept coming. "Is she gonna keep doing that shit? Our team can't communicate."

"Not our problem," Preacher said.

"It's gonna be your problem," the man said. "I can arrest her ass for interfering." His partner said something, but the man held up a hand to silence him, and kept coming.

"Miss Lily, move this way," Preacher said.

Lily cast a look back over her shoulder, then backed up around the hood of the Bug. Preacher let her pass him, then stepped in front of the car.

The man stomping towards them froze when Preacher moved out where he could be fully seen.

"Sheriff," Preacher called. "This one's making threats."

"Call your boy off, Stalls," the Sheriff said.

"She's interfering with our execution of the warrant," Frank said.

"Warrant says nothing about the vehicles," the Sheriff said. "Anyone touches that car and I'll arrest them for an illegal search and attempted assault."

"What about this one?" The man in front of Preacher called out. "He's not in a car, and he's being aggressive."

"I'm just standing here," Preacher said.

"You're standing there *aggressively*," the man said. "Your posture is threatening."

"You can't arrest a man for standing still in his own driveway," Father Bill called out. "We can *all* see that he's not threatening you."

PREACHER

Preacher looked over to find Father Bill, all of Sheriff Kane's inmates, and a small crowd of people he didn't recognize. They must've been townspeople. They spread out on the road and sidewalk, one or two holding up cellphones of their own. They probably didn't even have a charge on the battery, but if Chief Stalls thought they were recording, that would be good enough.

"It's nice to see you, Bill," Seth called out.

"We heard the commotion and came down to see if anyone needed help," Bill said, crossing over and shaking Seth's hand. Finished with that, he wrapped an arm around Dotty's shoulders.

"So you just decided to bring half the town with you?" Frank practically snarled.

"We were having an outdoor revival on the church lawn," Bill said, shrugging. "It was cooler outside than in. And of course, with those horns blowing, we all came as quick as we could. That much noise, there could've been someone hurt."

"Chief?" The man in front of Preacher called.

"Stand down," Frank said. "Get back inside and get back to

work. I'll handle things out here."

"But you said to arrest-"

"*I said stand down!*" Frank yelled.

The man turned and jogged back to the house, his partner giving Preacher a glare and then joining him. Preacher let out a breath and nodded to the crowd on the street. Trench gave him a thumbs-up.

"Looks like it's a good thing we came," Bill said, his voice overly cheerful. "Seems this situation is in need of some impartial witnesses."

"You're busy, Frank. I'll handle the crowd," the Sheriff said with a wide smile.

"Screw you, Kane," Frank said as the Sheriff passed. "You had this planned."

"No, *Chief* Stalls, this was all me," Bill said. "It's my job to look after my congregation. Besides, isn't it better to be out-planned, than out-gunned?"

Frank turned his back to the old preacher and spit into the grass.

"Folks, if you could stay back, out of the *officers'* way, we'd appreciate it," the Sheriff called out. "It's best if you all move to the sidewalk, though. Wouldn't want anyone to get arrested for blocking the road."

"What's going on?" Daisy asked. "Is Miss Dotty being evicted?" There was a chorus of mumbling and objections from the crowd.

"The new Police Chief and his men have warrants to search these two properties. Just the houses, not the vehicles, and they're not permitted to remove anything from the premises," the Sheriff said. "I'm here to make sure the warrants are executed to the letter."

Preacher heard a car door shut and Ripley stepped up beside

him. "That horn idea was quick thinking," she said, keeping her voice low. "Thank you."

"Welcome," he said, and turned and leaned against Seth's truck. He was pretty sure if he sat on the Bug, he'd dent it.

"He would have tried to arrest me."

"*Tried* to," Preacher said. "Would've had to come through me."

"Yeah well, that was kinda stupid," she said. "You can't afford to get arrested. I can."

"Ain't that the truth," Mel said, sitting down on the Bug. "Pretty college girl? She'd be out in an hour or two. But you?"

"You gotta be more careful," Ripley said. When he frowned, she raised an eyebrow. "What do you think Grams would have done if you got arrested?"

"Been thankful it wasn't you."

"No," Ripley said. "You're not cannon fodder. It's not like that."

"Not what I meant," he said. He knew Dotty didn't think of him that way. The rest of them might, though. He was fine with that.

"You might be a monster, but you're *our* monster," Mel said. "You're not allowed to get your ass dragged off by the bad guys."

"Your monster?" he asked.

"Yep. Like that big blue guy from *Monsters, Inc*," she said. "All scary and mean-looking to the bad guys, but a big fluff-ball to the good guys."

Preacher rubbed his face. Him, a fluff-ball. He just didn't have a come-back for that.

"So I guess now we just wait?" Corey asked.

"We wait, we record, we don't give them a reason to come near us," Lily said. "Now that we've got witnesses, we're a little safer, and they probably won't take anything, but it's not a sure bet. Just keep quiet and still."

The very idea of that went against everything Preacher knew. Prey kept quiet and still. He wasn't prey. He wanted to take action. To do something, anything, to make this stop.

But he had other people to think about. People to protect. And the wolves were circling.

A crash sounded from inside the Millers' house. Then another. As if in response, there was a noise of something falling in Dotty's house, like someone had dumped out the silverware drawer.

"Sheriff Kane?" Lily called. "Can they do...whatever they're doing?"

"Everyone just keep calm," the Sheriff said. "Mr. Miller? Dorothy? If I could have you move over to the vehicles...that's good. Thank you. You can keep recording."

He made motions for everyone to gather around him next to Seth's truck. Father Bill kept hold of Dotty's hand. Seth ruffled Ripley's hair and then kissed her on the head.

"Good job, kid," he said. "Quick thinking."

Ripley pointed her thumb at Preacher.

"He gets the credit. It was his idea."

Seth reached up and clapped Preacher on the shoulder. "Thanks, man. You brought the calvary."

The crashes and thumps kept coming from the two houses.

"Listen to me. I suspect they've been told to instigate a response from you," Simon said, keeping his voice low. "So I need you all to just stand here, and *not react*. Got it?"

"It sounds like they're destroying my home," Dotty said. "This ain't right, Sheriff."

"It's just material things, Dotty," Bill said.

"But they're *our* things. Things we need to get by," Dotty said.

"And you can bill the City for anything damaged," the Sheriff said.

"Like they'll pay a dime," Mel snorted.

"They might not. But what's important is that you stay calm, and don't give them a reason to escalate this. Understand?"

There were a lot of sighs and some mumbling. Everyone seemed to be agreeing, though.

"Okay then. It's a plan. We just settle in, and wait. I'll be the go-between. You got a problem, you come to me first. Bill, you go over there and keep your people happy. I'm gonna glue myself to Frank's ass and make him as uncomfortable as possible. We'll get through this, people. Just stay calm."

Bill and the Sheriff moved off, and Corey stepped in to wrap his arms around Dotty's shoulders.

"It'll be okay, Grams," he said.

"Ripley, honey, can you take this?" Lily asked, holding the phone out. "Feels like my arm's gonna fall off."

"Same here," Marco said.

"I've got it, Romeo," Mel said, taking the camera. "You just stand there and look pretty."

Ripley took the phone from her mother, and Lily moved into Seth's arms. There was some jostling around as they all settled in.

The crashing and thumps continued. With each noise, Dotty flinched and winced.

"You think they'll find the cellar doors?" Thomas asked.

Corey shrugged. "I've got the rug over it, and the patio table. They might move that, though."

"Our is covered, too," Seth said. "We'll just have to keep our fingers crossed."

A door thumped, and a voice called out. "Are these fricking rabbits? Are we supposed to count the rabbits?"

Dotty turned and leaned her forehead into Corey's chest. Preacher heard sniffling.

He sighed and tried to tamp down his anger.

There had better be a reckoning for this.

DOTTY

In the end, it took hours.

The officers didn't find the cellars, but it was a near thing. While counting the rabbits on the Millers' porch, one of them got loose. The resulting chase disturbed the rug enough that had they paid a little more attention, they'd have seen the cut in the deck plank cover Seth had made for the cellar entrance. Finding that probably would have caused them to look on Dotty's porch for the same thing.

It was a small blessing, Dotty told herself as she looked out over her front yard, now full of blankets covered in food, spices, band-aids, toilet paper, and anything else the officers had deemed important. Even her and Marco's shotguns were laid out for all to see.

We need room to spread it out so that we can properly inventory it, Frank had told her.

She knew better. It was spread out so that everyone passing by could see exactly what they had, and how much of it.

The Millers' yard looked the same.

Next door, Cathy paced back and forth along the bushes at the very edge of her yard. It was as close as Simon would permit. She scowled, walked down the sidewalk to scan over what was in the Miller's yard, and stomped back.

"That's not all of it, Frank," she said.

"This is all of it. We've pulled out every bit of food in the house," he said.

"I'm telling you, there's way more food than that. They've got it hidden somewhere."

"No, Cathy, there's not. Now if you'd let me-"

"Where are all the canning jars?" Cathy called to Dotty. "I've been in your house. I've seen the big cupboard in the kitchen filled with meat and stuff you've canned. Where is it?"

"It's been used," Dotty said.

"Then where are the empty jars? You don't just throw those away," Cathy said. "We could use those jars up at the Rec Center. The canners, too."

Dotty tried to keep from glaring. The jars were down in the cellar, and if Cathy kept prodding, Frank and his men might look harder.

"The jars are at the church," Bill said. "Dotty canned chicken meat for the people who didn't have food."

It was the truth, at least partially.

"Then we want that chicken," Cathy said. "Frank, you need to inventory the church."

"What's your title?" Dotty asked.

"What do you mean?"

"Well you're out here sticking your nose in this, and giving Frank orders. You must have been given some kind of job, some title, to justify your interest in this,"

"I don't need a title. This community needs food, and you're hiding it away so you don't have to share," Cathy said.

"Miss Cathy, Dotty gladly shared what she had with the church. You were invited to come down and participate in the dinners if you had a need-" Bill started.

Cathy flushed deep red. "I don't *need* the church's help. I don't *need* the food. But other people do, and Miss Dotty here has tons of it. She's being selfish."

"Selfish is demanding what someone else has," Dotty started, but Simon cut her off.

"That's enough," the Sheriff said, moving to break the women's line of sight with each other. "Miss Cathy, if you can't stay quiet, I'm going to have to ask you to go back inside your house."

"You can't tell me to do anything," Cathy said. "I'm on my own property and I've got freedom of speech."

"Freedom of speech doesn't include the ability to actively disrupt execution of a lawful warrant," Simon said. "Would you rather spend the day down at my jail?"

"Frank are you going to let him threaten me like that?"

Frank, talking low with one of the women manning the clipboards, ignored her.

"Frank!" she yelled. When he sighed and looked her way, she pointed at Simon. "He's threatening me!"

Frank looked over at Simon and the two shared a suffering look. He rolled his eyes and looked back to the clipboard. "Go inside, Cathy. You saw what you came to see."

"Cindy told me to make sure you got a *full* inventory!"

"And I've done that. Now please-"

"You haven't! She's got more food! How do you think she's feeding *all* of these people with that piddly bit of food?"

Frank made a growling noise and stomped over to Cathy. Dotty couldn't hear what was being said, but by his gestures and the stiff-armed way he pointed to Cathy's front door, it looked like Miss Nosy was getting taken out to the woodshed.

"Cindy's going to hear about this!" Cathy snapped, stepping back.

"I'm sure the entire town's going to hear about it," Frank said, turning and coming back. Cathy stomped away and went through her door with a resounding *slam*.

"I don't know how you do it, Frank. I gotta give you credit," Simon said.

"Trust me, if she didn't have herself shoved so far up Cindy's ass that she can't see daylight, I'd have arrested her myself," Frank said.

"Might still be worth it...get some peace and quiet for a few days," Simon said. "'Cept, where would you put her? This new Chief of Police position doesn't come with access to the Sheriff department's jail."

Frank shook his head and waved a hand. "Don't need it. We're using one of the office bathrooms at the Rec Center. Couple of cots from the Guard, there's toilets with bags in 'em...it's good enough."

"That's all they need," Simon agreed. "You been arresting people?"

"Nah," Frank said. "Just some troublemakers in the shelter. Stick 'em in there for a few hours and they straighten up."

"You remember that one guy, that drunk from Ocean City? Shit on his bed and tried to sleep on the toilet?" Simon said.

"Yeah, that guy was something else," Frank said, grinning. Then his brows knitted together and he scowled. "But that was back before you fired me. What is this, Simon? Old memories day? What are you playing?"

Simon held his hands up. "Just trying to lighten the mood, that's all. It's been a stressful day for everyone."

"Well go lighten it somewhere else," Frank said. "You and me, we're not buddies. We're not even co-workers anymore. So I'd appreciate it if you just stayed in your lane and let me do my job."

A skinny woman with light brown skin and her curly hair pulled back into a bun came around the front of the driveway, holding a clipboard. "Chief Stalls?" she called.

Dotty blinked. She hadn't noticed when all this started, but this was Stella. She went to Father Bill's church and sang in the choir. She and Dotty had worked together on a lot of outreach projects.

Simon was still standing with his hands up, frowning. Frank was staring him down. Simon dropped his hands, shook his head, and walked out towards the street.

"Chief Stalls?" Stella called again. "I'm finished with the inventory and need you to come and take a look."

Frank sighed and tilted his head back. He took a deep breath, let it out, and turned to her. "I'll be over there when I'm finished here," he said. "Just give me a few minutes."

"But sir, there's a lot of firearms over here. Should I leave them laying out, or...?"

"Is there someone guarding them?"

"Yes-"

"Then leave them until I get *finished here*." He didn't even bother to look over his shoulder.

Stella huffed and rolled her eyes. She leaned back against Thomas' truck and wiped her arm across her forehead.

Watching Frank out of the corner of her eye, Dotty walked up the driveway. Stella's eyes were closed, but when Dotty got close she opened them and paled.

"Miss Dotty," she said.

"Miss Stella," Dotty echoed. "What a shock, seeing you here." Dotty gestured to the clipboard. "Doing...this."

"I didn't want to," Stella said, her words quick. "Really, I didn't. I don't agree with this at all."

"But here you are," Dotty said, "going through my things for strangers."

"Not *your* things," Stella said. "I made them promise me I wouldn't be going through your things."

"So it's all right, as long as you're not pulling *my* things out onto the grass for everyone to see? How is that Christian of you?"

"You don't understand," Stella said. "I *have* to do this. I *have* to be here. I've got no choice."

"There's always a choice," Dotty said. "I'm so disappointed in the one you've made."

"I didn't—look, they made us a deal. If we volunteer as officers-"

"Stella!" Frank barked, and both of the women jumped.

"Yes sir?" Stella asked.

"Go wait with your inventory," Frank said, pointing.

"Yes, sir," Stella said. She turned and hurried off without even giving Dotty another glance.

Dotty leaned back against the truck and crossed her arms. Frank watched her for a minute, maybe waiting for her to say something, but she stayed silent. Finally, he turned back to his work.

Well wasn't that something? Dotty thought. *She had no choice?*

And apparently Frank didn't want her to know about whatever was going on.

She watched Bill until she was able to get his attention, and motioned her head for him to come over. He immediately started her way.

We'll just see about what you do and don't want me to know, Chief Stalls.

Bill leaned on the truck next to her and bumped her shoulder with his. "I was wondering if you'd seen Stella. Are you okay?"

Dotty made a face and lowered her voice. "Can you get into the Rec Center?"

SIMON

Simon leaned against the wall of the Rec Center's gym and wiped his face with a handkerchief. It was hot enough in here to be criminal, despite the second day of cooler air outside. It was raining again today, and the wind had picked up. The doors at the end of the gym were propped open, but the breeze outside wasn't helping things in here much at all.

Probably blowing the wrong way, Simon thought. *Too bad it can't get in here and clear some of this smell out.*

The gym reeked of unwashed bodies, and the effect was nearly enough to make a person choke.

The National Guard had set up porta-potties, halfway between their makeshift camp and the gym doors. The entire thing was walled in by one of those instant fence contraptions that they'd erected all the way around the property. Shelter residents could step outside of the gym and walk around on the grounds or use the temporary facilities, but they couldn't leave the Rec Center grounds from there.

If what Father Bill had found out was true, they couldn't leave at all. Not without special permission, and that was hard to come by.

Getting kicked out, however, didn't take nearly as much work.

He checked on Father Bill again—praying now with an older couple that must have been from his congregation—and moved closer to the outside doors. He didn't want to get too far from the little man, but he needed more air.

That, and the looks he was getting from the shelter residents were making him feel heavily outnumbered.

He'd told Dotty that if there were rumors being spread about him there wasn't much he could do, but hearing it was different than *seeing* the effects those rumors had had. There were more than a couple hundred townspeople crammed into this gymnasium, and he could've counted the number of friendly smiles he'd received on just one hand.

He pulled out his cellphone and checked it again. Marco had given him a power brick to take home with him last night so he could charge the thing up. It was set on camera and ready to go.

"Hey, you getting a signal?" A sickly-looking pale girl, about Ripley's age, said from beside him. "Could I-?" She reached for the phone.

"No," he said, moving it out of her reach.

"No what? No, I can't make a call, or no, you're not getting a signal?"

"Both," he said, pocketing the phone. "I was just checking the time."

"Yeah right," the girl said. "Your watch isn't good enough?"

"It's slowing down. Needs a new battery."

She gave him a flat look. Then her eyes lighted on his chest pocket and she pointed. "Then how about that? Can I have that?"

He looked at the Clif bar—one of the last from his stash in his office desk—and shook his head.

"Sorry, no to that, too," he said. "It's probably the only thing I'll eat today."

"Yeah right," the girl said again. She snorted. "Guess it's right, what they're saying about you."

"What are they saying?"

"They're saying you're living high on the hog out there, not doing your job. Say you're holed up with some friends and a bunch of food that you refuse to donate to us here at the shelter."

"That's not true. Not a word of it."

"And here you are, looking all nice and clean, with a working phone and so much food you're carrying it around in your pocket. Sure, it's not true." She flipped him the bird and walked past, heading out into the rain.

He scanned the crowd and found a few people nearby regarding him with disgusted looks. When he caught them looking, they turned away and leaned close together, whispering.

I've had about enough of this, he thought. He pulled the pocket flap out from where he'd had it tucked in, and buttoned it in place. Now his Clif bar would be hidden, at least.

He hadn't been lying. It probably *would* be the only food he'd have today. He had taken everything he had over to his mother's house, and they were running low. He'd been eating as little as he could get away with, so it would last longer for her.

This apocalypse situation had taught him all kinds of things he'd never wanted to learn. For instance, if you're used to eating three meals a day and suddenly go down to less than half a meal, the hunger pains can be enough to make you double over. He thought it might be better to just stop eating all together. Then the constant gnawing, burning pain in his stomach might finally give up and go away completely.

"Lost in thought?"

Simon blinked and found Father Bill standing at his elbow. That was something else: lack of food meant a lack of focus.

"Yeah, sorry," he said.

"No need to apologize. We've all got a lot to think about. Are you ready for stage two?"

"Ready as I'll ever be. Those doors over there lead to the side of the building with the offices, but they're probably locked. We might have to go back around through the lobby."

"They *are* locked," Bill said. "The Johnsons just told me that King Kenny has kept them locked since the first night the shelter opened up. Let's work our way around and get this over with."

Moving back into the hallway was such a relief. The air conditioner was running in this part of the building.

"I'm surprised Wilhelm let the air stay on in this hallway," he said. "Being that the shelter residents use it to get to the cafeteria."

"I'm sure he'd shut it off if he could, but it keeps the Guard happy," Bill said. They moved to the side as a few children ran by them, heading back to the gym. "As it is, the shelter residents are only allowed a half hour in the cafeteria. Twice per day if they volunteer, once per day if they don't."

They made their way through the lobby, Bill smiling and raising a hand to the receptionist. "The congregation's doing well. We'll be seeing about those patrols now," he said.

"Clerk's office is the first door on the right," the receptionist said. She gave Bill a big smile in return, then glared at Simon once Bill passed by.

Can't catch a break, he thought. *Kinda makes what's about to happen worth it.*

Bill slipped into the clerk's office with a big hello and lots of friendly chatter. Simon leaned against the doorframe and tried to look like nothing more than a dumb, bored bodyguard.

Don't mind the Sheriff's outfit. Nothing to see here.

Bill was telling the clerk about his congregation members outside of the shelter having trouble with vandalism, and asking when the new police chief was going to start patrols. The clerk was trying her best to dodge the question, focusing instead on getting him to fill out a police report on any crime he had specifics about.

"Could I get a handful of those?" Bill asked. "I know of at least ten different crimes that have taken place, but I'm not sure of the specifics. I could have my church members fill out the forms and then I could bring them all in at once."

"Sure honey, that'll work," the clerk said, counting off forms. "What kind of crimes are we talking about?"

"One lady on the very same street as the church got up this morning to find two of her chickens missing," Bill said. "That's the third one to disappear. She's getting very worried."

Simon frowned. Dotty was missing more chickens? She'd thought the first one might have gotten out through carelessness, but it looked like that wasn't the case.

Down the hall, Cindy Stalls came out of one of the offices and walked away from him, turning through an office door on the other side. Simon heard Mayor Wilhelm's voice.

The clerk handed a bundle of forms to Bill.

That was his cue.

Simon straightened up, rolled his shoulders a bit, and stepped away from the doorway. When there was no objection by the clerk, he started down the hall.

There was another door on the right with a nerdy-looking fellow in glasses going over some maps, muttering to himself. He didn't even look up as Simon passed by. The next doors were on the left, directly next to each other. The restrooms. Both had shiny, heavy-duty clasps installed on them, and pins to keep the doors locked. Those must be the new ad-hoc jail cells.

He knocked softly on each door. There wasn't a response.

Next he stopped and peered around the office Cindy had come out of. Unlike the clerk's office, this one was larger and more well-appointed. There weren't any stacks out at all, much less out of place, and a laptop sat open on the desk.

There were a number of additional doors dotting the length of the hall, but his target was here. He slipped the cellphone from his pocket and checked it again.

Ready to roll.

The door to the office Cindy had gone into was slightly ajar. He could hear the two of them talking. He pushed the door open silently, held the phone up, and started snapping pictures.

The digital shutter noise fired off rapidly and both of them looked up.

"Say cheese," Simon said, tapping the *video* button.

"What the hell are you doing?" Cindy said, while Wilhelm took a more congenial approach.

"Sheriff. Are we missing some kind of joke?"

"No joke," Simon said. "Just getting some good mug shots of you both. That way when I file a report to the FBI about what's going on in this city, I'll have great photos to go with the names."

"The FBI?" Wilhelm sputtered. His big hands curled into fists. "Exactly what are you accusing us of?"

"Give me that goddamned phone," Cindy said, starting around the desk.

"Don't approach me *aggressively*, Lieutenant Mayor. My jail isn't air conditioned like the ones you've got set up here."

Cindy pulled up short. "I'm not aggressing upon you, Sheriff. I'm *requesting* that you delete those photos. I did not give you permission to photograph me."

"I don't need your permission," Simon said. He turned to Wilhelm. "Yesterday, officers of this city spoke like that to your registered constituents. Officers who had *your* signature on a search warrant. These people were accused of no crime, they weren't resisting, and yet your officers treated them with disrespect and accused them of being aggressive. Do your officers' actions reflect the way you feel about your citizens, Mayor Wilhelm?"

"What the hell is this about, Simon?" Wilhelm said. "What are you trying to pull here? You want an apology? You won't get it. We *lawfully* sent out those census forms and those families refused to cooperate. We *lawfully* followed up on the census and took our own inventory." Wilhelm's voice rose as he spoke.

"By what law?" Simon asked. "Only the federal government has the authority to conduct a census. If you want to do one, it has to be voluntary."

"By the title granted to me by the Governor," Wilhelm said. "You don't like it? Take it up with him. Good luck getting across the Bay Bridge. Now get out of my office!"

That last was shouted. Simon nearly smiled.

"Not before he deletes those photos," Cindy said. She held out her hand. "Hand it over."

"No," he said. "*You* have no right to take *my* personal property. Not unless you get your *conveniently-elected* pocket judge here to write a warrant out for it. Seems you like that whole chain of command-"

"Give me the goddamn phone!" Cindy yelled, swiping for it. Simon stepped back into the hall and held the phone in the air. A quick glance over his shoulder showed him the muttering nerd sticking his head into the hall, and further down, Bill doing the same.

"Oh dear," Bill said. "I think you'd better go help."

"I'd like to thank you both for your time and service to this county," Simon started.

"Give it to me! Simon! Kenny, call Frank! Tell him to get down here immediately!"

The clerk rushed up next to him and made calming motions with her hands. "Okay everyone, settle down. I'm sure there's a *peaceful* way to solve all this, yes?"

"I am being peaceful," Simon said. "It's the Lieutenant Mayor here who's escalating the situation."

Simon flicked his eyes towards the end of the hall. Bill slipped out of the clerk's doorway, holding a very thick stack of papers. The little man hustled out into the lobby and around the corner.

"I'm not escalating anything, you're the one who came in here uninvited and started taking our pictures without permission!" Cindy yelled.

"Well this *is* public property," the clerk said. "Technically, he doesn't need your permission. And being the Sheriff and all-"

"Not for long." Cindy nearly spat. "Not if I've got anything to do with it."

"Well, I can tell where I'm not welcome," Simon said, faking a frown. "I guess I'll go lick my wounds. And like I said, Mrs. Stalls, if you'd like these photos, just get a warrant."

He turned and tipped an imaginary hat at the clerk, and set off down the hall. Cindy was barking orders at Wilhelm, who was bitching that he couldn't get the radio to work.

No one tried to stop him.

The rain had let up again outside, and the weary Guardsmen nodded at him as he strode past. He made it to his car with no objections, and had the key in the engine before the door was even shut.

"Did you get them?" he asked, turning the wheel hard and weaving around the cones exiting the parking lot.

Bill patted the pile of sheets in his lap and smiled.

"They were right where Ripley said they were. I got every last one of them," he said.

PREACHER

Preacher pushed the wheelbarrow to the edge of Dotty's yard and sat it down beside the burn barrel. None of the neighbors had shown up yet, but they'd be here within the hour. The census forms that Bill had nicked from the Rec Center wouldn't be enough to keep the fire going, so he'd had to donate some wood to the effort. He'd picked the worst pieces he could find, but it still bugged him that this would mean less wood for the stove this winter.

I'll just have to work harder to get some more. With all that's been going on, been slacking on that anyway.

Thomas opened up his truck and sat inside for a moment, then music filled the air. After a second it cut off, and various levels of static shushed through the speakers as he flipped channels on the radio.

When Thomas finally gave up, the sound of hammering caught Preacher's attention. He looked down the street to see Corey just on the other side of the trees at the far end of the

Millers' yard. He was hammering some two-by-fours together, while a hose barely trickled water at his feet.

"Guess I'll have to go through my CDs," Thomas said. "Hope they like nineties hip hop." He got out of the truck and shut the door. "Too bad we can't have some barbecue for this block party."

"Too bad," Preacher agreed. He tossed a couple of pieces of half-rotten wood into the barrel. Corey's banging stopped with a muttered curse. Preacher looked back up to see Corey sucking his thumb and thumping his heel on the ground.

Preacher brushed his hands off on his too-short jeans and walked down to see what was up.

"You okay?" he asked.

Corey made a disgusted face and held his thumb out. "Damn hammer glanced off of the nail and banged my thumb, is all. Hurts like a mother."

Preacher nodded and looked everything over. The hose snaked up out of the storm drain, looped around the bottom of the frame, and then lay on the ground between the frame's supports.

He didn't understand it.

"What's the frame for?" he asked.

Corey pointed with the hammer. "The hose is supposed to come up on top of the frame, and I'm gonna clamp it down so it doesn't slide off. Then I'll attach that tub-" he pointed over to the sidewalk where a big plastic tub for christmas paper sat waiting-"to the bottom of the frame so people can't walk off with it. The hose fills up the tub so we can dip containers in and take the water out, instead of waiting for the hose to fill our container."

"It's not much flow," Preacher said. "Would take forever to fill."

"Yeah, that's why the tub, you know? I'll put a couple boards across it so folks can set their jugs under the stream and wait, if they want to. But with just these skinny garden hoses instead of irrigation piping, this dribble is as good as it's going to get."

"What about winter? Will it freeze?"

"I've been thinking about that," Corey said. "Maybe I'll box in the frame and stuff some insulation in it. Paint it black. Maybe use rocks instead of insulation; they'll hold the heat and weight it down. The storm drains are below the frost line, so it should be okay there. And the water's moving; that will help keep it from freezing. Guess we'll just have to see."

Corey bent over and started hammering again. Preacher scanned the street. Still quiet. Dotty and Bill were up on the porch swing talking, with Marco at the other end of the porch leafing through the stack of census forms. Last Preacher had seen, Marco was busy blacking out the names with a big marker. Now that Corey had brought the storm drain to his attention, he noticed them dotted here and there along the sidewalk's edge. There was one just on the far edge of Cathy's yard.

Hmm.

"Corey."

"Yeah?"

"You got enough hose to exit there?" Preacher pointed.

Corey straightened up and cocked his head. He nodded. "Yeah, definitely. Why?"

He pointed at Cathy's house. "She says Dotty's selfish. We're *all* selfish."

"Yeah well, she's a stuck-up idiot."

Preacher pointed down. "Here, looks like it's just for us." He pointed at the drain by Cathy's. "There, looks like it's for everyone."

"Putting it there makes it easier for her to get water than us. I'm not that nice, Preacher."

"Easier for *everyone* to get water. At *her* yard."

Corey thought about it for a minute, then his eyes widened. "That would drive her nuts. All those strangers coming to the edge of her yard? She'd flip." His grin was a mile wide.

Preacher nodded and smiled a little himself. "You need help doing it?"

"I don't *need* help, but it'll go a lot quicker."

"Tell me what to do."

NIGHT HAD FINALLY FALLEN, but this time it was anything but quiet.

Thomas' truck pumped out music. People milled around, some talking by the burn barrel, others sitting on the grass in little clumps here and there. Once the first few had showed up and saw the water contraption, then gone hurrying home to get their own containers, the crowd had steadily grown. There were milk jugs and soda bottles lined up waiting to be filled by the hose's new outlet at the edge of Cathy's yard. One woman had brought a little radio flyer wagon with six milk jugs in it.

A strong, warm breeze was blowing through, catching the sparks from the fire and raining them out onto the sidewalk now and then. Dotty and Bill walked among the crowd, chatting people up and thanking them for coming out. There wasn't any food, but there was plenty of good will and camaraderie.

Preacher sat on the sidewalk across the street, well out of the glow of the fire. From here, he could see both houses, all of the people, and the street in both directions.

He wondered if any of the people here tonight making nice had enjoyed a fresh chicken dinner back at their home. No one had seemed to be paying attention to the backyard, or had made any moves to go back there. But it was possible that one of the people here had been the one to take three of Dotty's chickens.

They won't be taking another one.

The latest song ended and Thomas stuck his head into the truck to pause the CD. Preacher wondered how much longer the truck battery would last. It wasn't like they had the extra fuel to let the truck idle and build that charge back up. He sighed.

Not my truck, not my problem. Worry about what you can control.

Bill made his way to the burn barrel, the stack of census forms in his hand. He held them high and called for everyone to gather around him. As people came near, he handed them each a few of the forms. There was lots of murmuring and shuffling around as they waited for everyone to get close.

A slim figure walked out of the dark and lowered herself to the sidewalk beside him. She pulled her hair from her ponytail and bent her head forward, ruffling the locks free with her hands. When it was all fluffed out she flipped it back, tilted her head back to the sky, and sighed.

"Not joining in?" he asked.

"Nah," Ripley said. "Too many people. Besides, I'm sore. All that going up and down stairs last night wore me out."

"At least we got finished."

She nodded and leaned forward, propping her elbows on her knees. "You think anyone saw us moving the food?"

"Not in the rain." After Frank and his posse had left, they'd all scrambled to get the stuff in the yards back into the houses. The rest of the day had been spent putting the houses back together. The assholes had pulled out drawers and dumped them on the floor, flipped the mattresses off of the beds, pulled clothes out of the closet and dropped them in piles. Then they'd walked on those piles. Furniture had been moved, pictures pulled off the wall…it had been horrible, watching Dotty walk through it.

When she'd finally finished picking her way through the destruction and they'd uprighted the kitchen table, she'd told them she wanted every scrap of food out of the house.

They'll be back, she said. *And they'll look harder. We can't leave anything for them to find.*

Once night had fallen, he and his team of college kids had started the leg-killing chore of bringing the food up out of the cellars, sneaking it across the street, and tucking it away in the cellar of the Cobbs' house.

"I'd like to thank you all for coming this evening," Bill called out. "When a community comes together, good things happen. We're living in dangerous times. We've got tyranny right on our doorstep. How we choose to handle that will determine how much more tyranny we're subjected to. What we allow is what will continue."

Preacher heard a door shut. He squinted down the street, but couldn't see far. The cloud cover was too heavy. After the past few days, he was surprised it wasn't raining again.

"What I did today, some may consider a crime," Bill continued. "I don't see it that way. As far as I'm concerned, these papers that we hold in our hands were filled out and handed in under duress, and are a severe invasion of privacy. And as you may have seen yesterday, some of them were filled out by force." He held up a sheaf of papers paper-clipped together. Preacher had seen it. It was Dotty's census sheet, with multiple pages of inventory listing attached. The Millers had one just like it.

"Dan's in his yard," Ripley said, straightening. "I don't see Cathy."

"She left this morning. Haven't seen her come back," Preacher said. Now that Ripley had pointed it out, he could see the man standing by the bushes bordering Dotty's yard. All last week, Dan had been meeting up with Thomas right about the same time Preacher was leaving to get firewood. But since the Sheriff had called off the roadblock a couple days ago, Preacher hadn't seen hide nor hair of the man. Ripley unfolded herself and got up; Preacher stood up with her. Marco was in an upstairs bedroom watching over the gathering with some firepower, but if trouble happened, he'd have a hard time getting a clear shot.

"Like many of you, I took an oath once upon a time: to defend and uphold the Constitution of the United States," Bill said. "And beyond that, I took an oath to a higher power to guide, protect, and defend my fellow brothers and sisters. Taking this information back for all of you from the hands of tyrants fulfills both of those oaths."

The two of them crossed the street and wove through the crowd as there was some scattered applause. Ripley headed towards her parents; Preacher took up a position right behind Bill and Dotty.

"Now I could have just burned these myself, but you know how we church men are about symbolism and rituals," Bill said, smiling. There were chuckles from the crowd. "I thought it might help for everyone to be involved; for us each to do a little part in taking back some of our power and declaring our dissatisfaction with how things have been here lately. Maybe give us an opportunity to speak, and be heard, so that we know we're not alone. Would anyone like to say a few words?"

"I would," Seth said, holding up a hand. He stepped closer to the light of the fire. "I just want to say thank you to everyone who came out yesterday and stood witness while the city's new police force tore apart our house. Without you there, things probably would have been a lot worse for myself and my family. Thanks to all of you, we're not sitting in jail...or worse. So from the bottom of my heart, thank you."

The crowd shifted around a bit and a man Preacher didn't recognize, that looked to be in his mid-fifties, stepped forward. "I took an oath, too," he said. "And I've had to watch every year as this state stripped more and more of our rights away. There was nothing I could do about it. Voting sure as hell didn't help; all our votes are erased by the DC rats living across the bridge." This got a lot of murmured agreement and a few calls of *damn straight* and *no kidding.* He continued on. "But this is happening right here, in our town. If any of you here ever took an oath, I want you to please think about that. Think about it long and hard. And if you decide you've had enough, come talk with me. I'm at the big brown house up there-" he pointed up the street-"with the white fence. Even if you didn't take an oath but you're of a like mind. Stop by anytime. Anytime. I mean it."

Preacher looked over the crowd, watching Dan. As this last fellow finished his statement, Dan moved forward into Dotty's yard and crossed to the edge of the crowd.

"Heads up," Preacher said to Bill, and both the little man and Dotty looked up.

"Dan?" Dotty said as Dan wove his way through the crowd. When he stepped into the firelight, Dotty gasped.

Dan sported one hell of a black eye. It was all puffed up and multi-colored. He looked down at the burn barrel, then back up at Dotty and Bill.

"I'd like a couple of those," Dan said, and his voice came out a bit raspy. "I know what's been going on and I don't support any of it. I want to help."

Bill pulled some sheets out of the clipped inventory and handed them to Dan. When he spoke, his voice was soft. "You can definitely join in. Looks like you might need some help yourself."

Dan made a noise halfway between a chuckle and a snort, and then visibly winced in pain. "Let's just say not everyone agrees that what's going on has been bad."

"Did Cathy do this to you?" Dotty asked. "Do you need help? Someone to stay with you tonight?"

"I wouldn't subject anyone else to this," Dan said. "If she finds someone at the house...no. I could maybe use some new locks for my doors, if anyone has an extra laying around." He looked around, blushing furiously but seeming determined. "The house is in my name. She can be the one to leave, if she hasn't already."

"I know where there's some locks," Preacher said. "I can bring them tomorrow." There were at least a dozen different door locks tucked away in Teddy's storage barn.

The man who'd pointed out his house put a hand on Dan's shoulder. "I'm Wade. My kids moved out years ago and I've got two extra rooms. You come stay at my place tonight. Tomorrow I'll come down here with you and we'll get those locks changed."

"I'll help," Preacher said.

Dan blew out a breath and wiped a hand across his good eye. "Thanks guys. I really appreciate it."

"Okay," Bill raised his voice and looked out over the crowd. "We're all in this together. Come on up and let's get this done. A revolution starts with just one spark, and we're going to have a lot of sparks tonight."

With that, he dropped his handful of papers into the burn barrel. A cheer went up. Seth leaned forward and dropped in the thick stack inventorying his family's life. The applause kept going. Dan crumpled each of his pages into a ball and tossed them in, one by one.

"That didn't go the way I expected," Corey said behind him.

Preacher looked over his shoulder and stepped back. At the

barrel, people were moving aside to let others come up and make their contribution to the fire.

"It's good, though," Preacher said. "Takes a lot to ask for help."

Corey nodded. "Yeah man, I get that. I'm just thinking now we won't get to see the crazy woman have a royal fit on her front lawn over the water." He grinned.

Preacher cracked a smile.

A heavy engine sounded at the end of the street and rumbled their way. The crowd's applause died down more the closer it got. After a minute, the Guard's familiar MRAP pulled to a stop in front of them and a stern-looking man--the same Sergeant who had harassed them earlier in the week--leaned an elbow out of the window.

"Curfew is at sundown, and the City has an emergency rule about people gathering in groups larger than three," he said. "Do you people realize how much trouble you're in?"

DOTTY

Dotty grabbed Bill's arm as he stepped in front of her.

"Sergeant, we've had this conversation before. The Constitution says that we the people have the right to assemble."

"And we're on private property," Dotty said. "*My* private property. These people are my guests."

The Sergeant killed the engine on the big MRAP and got out. He waved a hand at his men and the two that were hanging off of the back got down to join him.

Bill went to the edge of the yard to meet them; Dotty followed close behind. She wasn't about to let him do something as foolish as she'd seen before. Preacher started to step forward, but she shook her head at him. He settled back against Thomas' truck with a grim expression. Seth separated from the group and shadowed her.

"There's veterans in this group," Wade called out. "Whatever you're about to do, you're doing it to your brothers in uniform."

"You're not doing yourself any favors, bud," the Sergeant said.

"We've been having more trouble from the vets than from the civilians lately."

"Well I'm one of those veterans," Bill said, "and I'm the church leader for this group. I assure you, sir, that we mean no harm."

Dotty couldn't help but notice that the man behind the big gun on the top of the MRAP had turned that long barrel to point towards her yard, and all the people standing there. Her grandkids were in its line of fire.

The thought made her blood run cold.

The Sergeant took off his little hat, crumpled it in his hands, and stuffed it into a pocket. Behind him, the two men who'd jumped off the back stared over his shoulders, weapons ready.

At least they're *not aiming at anyone. Yet.*

"Sir, by law I'm required to follow the Governor's orders. He's set down a curfew from dusk 'till dawn for the duration of this recovery effort."

"And just how long is that supposed to last?" Dotty said. "We all know this isn't going to be fixed anytime soon. We know the power grid's down across the country. We could be at this for years."

The Sergeant's eyebrows shot up and he glanced back at one of his men. "If you got that information from any of the National Guardsmen that have been supporting this town, I'd like to know what their name was," he said. "That's privileged information."

Dotty huffed. "We knew that before you and your men ever arrived. The whole town did. The regional head of Dominion Power announced it at a town hall more than a week ago."

Bill nodded. "It's the truth. Everyone standing here knows. Everyone up at the Rec Center knows, or has at least heard. Whether or not they believe it is another story."

The Sergeant rubbed his hand over his face and let out a deep breath. He turned back to his fellow soldier again. "You believe this shit? The Mayor's had us prancing around like we're sitting on some big secret, and the whole town already knew."

The soldier behind him shrugged. "Seems about par for the course," he said. "Guy's a dirtbag." He paused a mere second, then added "Sir."

The Sergeant turned back. "Okay, level with me. What else do you know?"

Dotty and Bill looked at each other. Dotty shrugged. She couldn't think of anything she shouldn't know.

"I know that a large amount of forms, containing the City's unconstitutional search information and 'census' info given under duress, has gone missing," Bill said.

Dotty squeezed Bill's arm. He reached over and patted her hand. Foolish man. He was going to get himself court-martialed, or jailed, or whatever it was they did to military people.

"Is that so?" The Sergeant said, and this time he grinned. "Couldn't have happened to a nicer tyrant. Err...guy. Couldn't have happened to a nicer guy." He looked over the crowd and thought for a moment.

"Let me get this straight. You all are a group of civilians and former military, who claim to be peacefully assembling, past curfew and despite the ban on assemblies, is that correct?"

"Correct," Bill and Seth said at the same time.

"On private property as guests," Dotty put in.

The Sergeant nodded. "And as a whole, the group of you are refusing to disperse as ordered?"

"Yes," Bill said.

"Damn straight," Seth said. There were various sounds of agreement from the crowd.

"My grandkids are in that crowd, Sergeant," Dotty said. "Are you going to fire upon them?"

The Sergeant frowned at her. She jutted her chin out and

stood her ground. It was the elephant in the room--or in the street, she supposed--and she wasn't going to ignore it. If it was going to happen, she wanted the kids warned enough so they could try to run.

"No ma'am," he said. "I've been given orders to do so, as have all of my men. But we've discussed it, and we came to the conclusion that we have a duty to disobey unlawful orders. We are *not* willing to fire upon civilians."

"Oh thank God," Dotty said, bowing her head. Her knees felt weak. Behind her, she heard sounds of relief from the crowd.

"So it seems we're at an impasse," Bill said, smiling and spreading his hands. "We refuse to leave and you refuse to take action. If we had any beer, I'd offer it to you, but all we've got is some boiled river water."

The Sergeant scratched the back of his head and rubbed the top of his crew cut. He was sporting a bit of a smirk again.

"I'll have to get a rain check on that beer," he said. "Maybe some other time we can sit down and trade war stories. But there's no drinking on duty."

"Like that ever stopped anyone," Wade called out. The Sergeant grinned and pointed his way. He turned back to Bill.

"Well then, I guess I'm going to have to load my men up and move on down the road," he said. "It's our last tour through the town, anyway. The rest of our platoon is busy dropping tents and packing up."

Dotty was confused. "But why? And what will happen with the meals for the people at the shelter?"

"We've off-loaded all of the remaining MREs, and we suspect there will be another shipment of those in a week or so, from another unit," the Sergeant said. "As to why, we've got orders to pull out. We're moving across the Bay to help guard the nuclear plant at Calvert Cliffs."

"Is someone threatening the power plants?" Seth asked.

The Sergeant blinked at them, brows pulled together. "Wait. You know the power's out for good but you don't know about Michael?"

"We've overheard talk of a Michael," Bill said, "but we're still unsure as to who he is."

The Sergeant looked shocked. "Michael isn't a who. Michael's a *what*." He turned to the soldier behind him and waved his hand. "Get me the tablet."

The soldier sprinted over to the MRAP and dug around in the cab for a minute. He returned with a tablet that looked like it was armored enough to survive a nuclear blast, and the Sergeant tapped and swiped the screen a bit. Finally he turned it around to face them, showing a map of the United States with a long, teardrop-shaped blob stretching from the coast of Texas to Delaware.

"It's just like after the Carrington Event back in the 1800s," the Sergeant said. "Michael's a hurricane, and he's headed straight for us."

PREACHER

Preacher was cold, wet, and angry.

The nights had been dipping down into the fifties, but with the steady light drizzle falling on his head and the wet grass and soaked ground under him, it felt a hell of a lot colder.

The family had gone to bed hours ago. Staying up late was hard to do without lights and televisions. After the Guard had dropped their bomb and left, the group of would-be revolutionaries drifted off to plan preparations for Michael.

They only had about three days, give or take. It depended on how much the terrain slowed the storm. From the way the Sergeant had talked, the thing was a beast and had pretty much leveled Galveston. It was stomping across the south as if it were over water rather than land.

A freaking hurricane.

Dotty had called it Murphy's Law. Preacher just called it more shit to deal with. They'd decided to move things around in the cellar tomorrow to make room, and they'd ride the storm out down there. There wasn't much else they could do. They'd already used up all the plywood they could find, unless they took down the outhouse. No one wanted that pit uncovered. The Millers were going to follow suit. If one cellar got flooded, they could all squeeze into the other, and if both of them flooded out, they could try the one at the Cobbs'.

And after all the work they'd done moving the food, now the kids were dead set on going over there and finding a way to get everything up higher, just in case *that* cellar flooded.

Gotta stop calling them kids. They're only a few years younger than me.

And he still needed to get those doorknobs for Dan in the morning, get started on Teddy's outhouse pit, and keep working on the firewood supply.

So much work to be done.

But right now, his most pressing issue was his wet crotch. He hadn't thought this through when he came creeping out earlier and had tucked himself down in the shadowed corner next to the back porch steps. Wet ground, wet grass, wet crotch.

That asshole better show up tonight.

Three chickens gone and the thief hadn't gotten caught. In Preacher's old world, the thief would chalk that up as good luck and never go back. Too much a tempt of fate. But who knew how desperate *this* thief was. Maybe his or her success would encourage them to try again.

He hoped it would. He had a couple loads of bird shot reserved especially for thieves.

Who'd have thought that he'd be back to teaching bad guys a lesson, here on the outside?

The Outside.

He hadn't admitted it to anyone, but the freedom was actually eating at him. On the inside, everything was so tightly scheduled and controlled that you knew exactly where you were going to be and what you'd be doing any minute of the day, even three months in the future.

Out here, things could change from minute to minute. If you decided you wanted to do something else, you could simply *do* it, and not even give a thought to being tased. While he was in the pen, he'd dreamed of that kind of freedom.

Now that he had it, it was like a low-level itch in the back of his head. He kept catching himself trying to recreate some kind of routine that matched what he'd had inside.

He missed running. Now that he had some shorts, he was going to start that back up. He could run to Teddy's and back tomorrow for the doorknobs; that would be a good warm-up. He'd help install the things, then run back out there. Hell, he might even take a few laps around Teddy's property. At least back there, he wouldn't be attracting attention or scaring some little old ladies seeing him pound by on the sidewalk.

He thought he heard something, but couldn't be sure with the sound of the drizzle. He turned his head extra-slow, so if someone was nearby they wouldn't catch the movement.

Maybe I should've put Jax in the coop, after all.

He'd considered having her out there because if he drifted off and a stranger came into the yard, she'd go nuts and wake him up. But the chances of the thief having a gun and shooting her to shut her up were too high. He wasn't going to be responsible for getting one of Ripley's dogs killed.

Not like I could fall asleep in this cold, anyway.

There it was again. A low rumble, with a tick. A car's engine, creeping by slowly.

He resisted the urge to sprint to the edge of the house and watch. If this was his guy or gal, he couldn't chance being seen until it was too late.

Besides, after sitting here in the cold for so long, sprinting might be out of the question. Just in case though, he quietly lifted himself up into a squat and stifled a groan. His legs weren't happy.

He squatted there for what seemed to be twenty minutes. It was probably just five, but he didn't have a watch.

A tall, thin shadow sprinted down the side of Dotty's yard. It tucked itself behind the fence on Dan's side, crouching down behind what was left of the dead green bean vines.

Preacher barely dared to breathe, watching the shadow from the corner of his eye. If the thief had a flashlight, they hadn't used it yet. He hoped they didn't. One sweep of the backyard and he'd be seen.

After a number of minutes watching the back of the house, the shadow crept back up the fence and came around to Dotty's side. From there it sprinted to the side of the house itself and Preacher lost sight of it. Was it going around the front? Maybe deciding to go for a bigger payoff? Maybe whoever it was had been watching this evening when they'd moved the chickens from the tractor into the house?

The shadow sprinted past him, closer than ten feet, and headed straight for the chicken tractor. Not bothering with the pen, the thief went right for the sleeping quarters and fiddled with the latch. He flipped it out of the way, grabbed the handle, and cussed.

The door would take a little more than a simple tug to open, since Corey had sunk a screw into it.

Preacher lifted the shotgun to his shoulder and took aim. He caught himself aiming for the back of the thief's head and lowered it a bit. They wanted to catch the thief, not kill him.

Or her, Preacher thought. He still couldn't tell.

The thief grabbed the handle with both hands and began yanking on it, putting all their weight into it in rapid tugs. He heard little grunts of air.

To speak, or not to speak?

He let the shotgun speak for him.

BOOM.

The thief let out a distinctly male scream and dropped to the ground, clawing at the back of his head. Preacher racked another shell into the chamber and stood up.

Well, he *tried* to stand up. His cold, cramped legs had other ideas. He fell over.

The thief scrambled to all fours, grabbed at his middle, and pointed a hand Preacher's way.

BOOM.

The orange flash of light from the thief's barrel seared his eyes. He heard something whiz over his head and the sharp splinter of wood as a bullet hit Dotty's porch railing.

He pulled the shotgun's trigger again.

BOOM.

Firing at this angle, it would have been a miracle if he'd hit anything. The thief scrambled to his feet like a runner coming off of the blocks and took off for the street. He flung an arm in Preacher's direction as he went by and fired off three more shots.

BOOM. BOOM. BOOM.

Preacher had no idea where those rounds went; he was too busy hugging the ground. When it seemed there wouldn't be a fourth shot, he looked up.

The thief was gone.

The back door slammed open.

Preacher climbed to his feet as quick as his legs would let him and stumbled for the corner of the house.

"David!" Dotty screamed. "Stop!"

Can't stop. Gotta catch that son of a-

"DAVID! NOW!" Dotty screamed.

His shoulder slammed into the corner of the house but with the rain, he couldn't even see to the street.

A car engine roared and tires spun on the wet pavement.

He'd missed his chance. The thief was gone, and probably would never come back.

He'd failed.

DOTTY

Dotty sat at her kitchen table and stared at Teddy's envelope. She still hadn't opened it. She still didn't want to. It had been days and Teddy hadn't returned. She was starting to wonder if he ever would.

She closed her eyes and said a small prayer for the old coot and his family.

A nice breeze was blowing in from the back porch. It smelled of green things, and rain. Corey and Thomas had been in and out of the cellar all morning, moving things around to make room. They were down there right now, hammering on something. Probably shoring up a loose shelf.

Other than that, it was strangely quiet. Mel and Marco were over at the Cobbs' house trying to raise everything up, and the Millers were all trying to ready their own cellar. Even Jax was missing, and lately she'd been living in Dotty's house more than she lived in her own.

Dotty had gone out this morning, when Preacher had run up

to Teddy's house, and looked at the fresh bullet hole in her porch railing.

People were firing on her family. For nothing more than a *chicken*, for god's sake.

The world had gone crazy. She was glad Nate wasn't here to see it.

She checked her watch. Preacher would be home soon, wanting some lunch. After he'd helped Dan put the new doorknobs in, he'd seemed almost desperate to get out of the house again. Sure, he had that outhouse to dig and he'd promised to do it, but Dotty couldn't help but feel that he felt ashamed about something and just didn't want to risk talking about it.

Maybe he'd talk to her tonight, after it got too dark to work. She didn't want him beating himself up for not catching that chicken thief. He'd done the best he could. They hadn't been able to tell if Preacher had hit the man--he might have just screamed because the blast startled him--but it was a safe bet he wouldn't be coming back. The chickens were safe now and no one here had gotten hurt; that was the important thing.

Said chickens were bumbling around in the bathroom upstairs, talking to each other and trying to make a perch out of the shower curtain rod. It was spring-loaded, and Corey had lowered it for them. At least the floor in there was tile; it would be easy enough to clean up after them.

She reached over and put a hand on the Wonderbag that was keeping Preacher's lunch warm. Ripley had given it to her as a christmas gift a couple years back, so she could stop using her good wool blanket to bundle around her soup pots. She loved it. Get the soup to boiling, put it in the Wonderbag, and a few hours later you had a fully-cooked meal. Today's lunch wasn't that fancy; just a chicken soup stretched with lots of rice, but it would fill the men up.

Something thumped on her front porch, and she stood and put the envelope on the shelf next to her ICOE booklet. Preacher must be back. She pulled down a soup bowl and fished around in the drawer for a spoon.

A knock sounded at the door.

Oh, that's right. He's only got a key for the back door, she thought. She set the bowl and spoon down on the table and hurried to the door.

"You could've just come around the back-" she started, then froze.

Frank Stalls filled her doorway. He had more papers in his hand. There were people behind him, but she couldn't see past him to know who they were.

"Ms. Parker," Frank said. "Is your grandson Thomas Winters home? I need to speak with him."

"What do you want with him?"

Frank sighed. "I *want* to speak with him. Could you call him out here, please?"

"Give me a minute," she said, and shut the door in his face. She flipped the deadbolt and hurried to the window, then nearly cursed when she pulled the curtain aside and could see nothing but plywood.

"Thomas?" she called. "Officer Stalls is here to see you." She went back through the kitchen to the porch and met him as he was emerging from the cellar. "I don't know what he wants-"

She looked up and saw a man standing on the back porch steps, staring through the screen at them. Two more men were in the yard. All three were armed.

"Grams?" Thomas asked. "What's going on?"

"I don't know," she said. "But I'll go with you. I'm right beside you, you hear me?" Then she called down the cellar stairs. "Corey, you stay down there. There's men up here with rifles. We don't know what they want. You stay down there and don't do anything foolish."

They walked back to the front door, holding hands, and Thomas pulled her to a stop.

"Should I go upstairs and get the shotgun?" he whispered.

"Lord, no. You go out there with a gun and they'll shoot first, ask questions later. We'll just see what they want, and we'll deal with it together."

"I can see both of you," the man at the back door called. "I suggest you open the door."

Dotty shot him a glare and reached for the deadbolt. Her hand was shaking.

Frank was still standing there, but turned to the side, and talking to...*Mayor Wilhelm?*

"Officer Stalls, you needed to speak to me?" Thomas said.

"Step out here please, Mr. Winters," Frank said, gesturing to the porch. "I don't want the door shut in my face in the middle of our conversation. It would be a shame if my men and I had to turn this into a forced entry situation."

Thomas looked down at Dotty and then pushed the door open. She followed him out and got an eyeful.

There were more men in the front yard, and over at the Miller's, it looked like the same situation was going on. Seth, Lily, and Ripley were all on the front porch, and they were arguing with a big man in a black shirt.

What in God's name is going on? She thought.

"Mr. Winters, can you tell me of your whereabouts last night, around midnight?" Frank asked.

Thomas looked confused. "I was upstairs, asleep. We've been going to bed early since there's no lights."

Frank nodded and scribbled on a little notepad. "You weren't outside at all at that time?"

"No," Thomas said.

"Is there anyone who can confirm you were inside your home between the time period of eleven PM to about one AM?"

"I can," Dotty said. "I was still awake. I know he was asleep upstairs."

"You saw him go upstairs?"

"I did."

"About what time was that?"

Dotty looked at Thomas and shrugged. "Maybe about nine-thirty? Ten? I didn't look at my watch."

"Mmhmm," Frank said, still writing. "Mr. Winters, did you perhaps fire a shotgun last night?"

Thomas blinked. "No. I was asleep."

"Liar," Mayor Wilhelm spat. "You shot my son! You threatened to shoot him a week ago, and last night you shot him!"

"I'd never shoot Donny," Thomas said. "We go to church with Donny. He's a nice kid, usually."

"Not Donny. Jack! My son Jack!" Wilhelm pointed.

Dotty followed his fingers and her eyes flew wide. There, at the bottom of her steps, stood the same kid who had been messing around with all the trash bins; who'd stood out in the street and tried to get Bill to come fight him.

The one Thomas had threatened to shoot with the shotgun.

He looked like he'd rather be anywhere else. He waffled between staring at the ground and peeking up through long lashes to glare at Thomas. He had fresh, bright pink scores in his closely-shaven scalp. They nearly matched the ones on Ripley's head, but hers were on the side. At the edges of his white tank top, she could see more scores tracing over his shoulders. His whole back must have been covered.

He'd been the thief, and Preacher *had* hit him, after all.

"That's your son?" she gasped. "But he's never been at church-"

"He lives with my ex-wife most of the year," Wilhelm said. "He was on visitation when all of this happened. At first I was grateful, because he's safer here than in Towson. But now your grandson's gone and shot him!"

"I didn't shoot him," Thomas said.

"Bullshit you didn't," Jack said. "Lyin' mother-"

"Jack!" Wilhelm barked. "Stay quiet!"

"Lady and gentlemen," Frank stepped forward and everyone quieted. He turned to Thomas and handed him a piece of paper. "This is an emergency Extreme Risk Protection Order against you, Mr. Winters. It gives us permission to enter your home and seize all of the firearms and ammunition inside."

"What?" Thomas said, shock evident on his face.

"But it's *my* home," Dotty said. "And the shotgun is mine."

"And it's his residence," Frank said. "And by the Maryland Code of Public Safety, Sections 5-601 and 5-602, *all* firearms in the home can be seized, no matter who they belong to." He spoke into a walkie-talkie. "Protection order's been served. Enter and seize the weapons."

Dotty heard her back porch door bang open, and boots thumping through her house.

"Grams?" Corey called. "What's going on?"

Thomas scanned over the paper, lips moving quickly as he read. "Reasonable grounds to believe that the respondent poses an immediate and present danger of causing personal injury to the respondent, the petitioner, or another by possessing a firearm? How am I a danger to anyone?"

"By threatening Jack last week, in front of witnesses, and by shooting him last night!" Wilhelm said.

"But I didn't shoot him!" Thomas said.

Frank held out another piece of paper, this time to Dotty. "This is a warrant for his arrest. Thomas, if you could turn and place your hands behind your back, please?"

"What in the world for?" Dotty gasped, snatching the paper from Frank's hand.

"For attempted murder," Frank said. He grabbed Thomas' shoulder and spun him around. "Thomas Winters, you have the right to remain silent-"

"Grams?" Thomas said, his voice high.

"He didn't do it!" Dotty cried.

Frank gave her a look that said he'd heard that a million times before, and pulled Thomas' wrist behind his back. "Step back please, Ms. Parker."

"But he didn't do it," she said again. "I did it. I shot at a chicken thief last night. Here, in my backyard. And he shot back!"

Frank froze, looking at her with his brows raised.

"Grams, don't-" Thomas started.

"You stay quiet, Thomas Winters," Dotty said, shaking the paper at him. She looked back to Wilhelm. "I'm the one who shot your son, because he's stolen three of my chickens already and he was back to steal another one!"

"You're a liar!" Wilhelm boomed, jabbing a fat finger at her. "He was walking on the sidewalk minding his own business and you shot him out of spite!"

"If he was on the sidewalk then tell me why there's a bullet hole in my back porch railing?" Dotty shot back. "Tell me why we found pistol casings in my backyard!"

"You were probably shooting them yourself, you crazy bitch!" Wilhelm roared. His finger was nearly touching her nose. "How *dare* you shoot at my son? *My* son?"

"Your son's a petty thug!" Dotty said, swatting at his hand.

Frank grabbed her wrist.

"Dorothy Parker, as witnessed here, you've admitted to firing a shotgun at Mr. Jack Wilhelm. Is that correct?"

"Yes," Dotty said. "It wasn't Thomas. It was me. So all of this-" she waved the paper around in her other hand-"is a simple misunderstanding. There's no need to arrest him."

Frank nodded, and twisted her wrist. She yelped and spun, trying to relieve the pain.

Frank pushed her up against her front wall, not overly hard but not gentle, either. He yanked her hand up high behind her back, and she felt something slip around her wrist.

"Dorothy Parker, you're under arrest for the attempted murder of Jack Wilhelm," Frank said. "You have the right to remain silent."

PREACHER

Preacher was feeling pretty good, physically. His legs burned, his arms burned, and the wind he made in his passing was helping to cool him off.

Mentally was another story. He hadn't been able to run that off, yet.

He'd dug in Teddy's back yard until his stomach threatened to start in on his spleen, and then he had run three laps around Teddy's property before heading home. All the work had helped burn off the extra energy he'd woken up with today. Too bad it hadn't touched the guilt.

His first clue that something was wrong was when he got within sight of Dotty's yard and Jax, sitting at the sidewalk, saw him. She ran all the way up the street to meet him and no one called her back. She happily loped along beside him as he closed the distance, tongue lolling and tail wagging.

Maybe I should take her with me the next time I go out, he thought.

He slowed as he reached the yard, and walked all the way into the back to cool down. A quick stop by the rainwater tub to splash some liquid relief on his face gave him a second to take a measure of things.

Jax outside, no one out with her, and it seemed like everyone was inside Dotty's house. Raised voices. They weren't happy.

He sprinted up the back steps and held the door open for Jax. She bounded inside and he followed. In the doorway to the kitchen, Mel turned around to see him, and her eyes were bloodshot and red-rimmed.

"What's wrong?" he asked. "Who am I killing?"

"Grams is gone," she said. "They came and took her."

A feeling of red-hot lava ran down his spine.

"*Who* came and took her?"

Mel's eyes widened, and she took a step back. He took a deep breath and tried to tone it down a little. "Who took her, Mel?"

"Frank and the Mayor," Bill said, stepping into the doorway. "Maybe you should come in and sit down, David."

"Where?"

"Come on in, and let us tell you. There's a lot to-"

He practically growled out the question. "Where did they take her?"

"They took her to their jail," Marco said from the porch steps behind him. He must have been in the outhouse. Preacher hadn't even heard him get close. "They arrested her for attempted murder because she confessed to shooting the Mayor's oldest son."

Attempted murder? Dotty? But she didn't...

"We're going to get her back," Marco said. "Father Bill is insisting that we try it his way, first. If that doesn't work..." he trailed off. "I'll need your help with some planning."

Preacher's mind was reeling, but he latched onto Marco's words and held tight.

"A reckoning?" he asked.

Marco's lips moved a little, and he recognized that smile. It was a killer's smile.

"A reckoning," Marco promised.

Preacher turned back to Bill and moved into the kitchen. The whole family was there.

"Tell me everything," he said.

He was turning it over and over in his head, and while he knew there was nothing he could have done had he been here, he still felt a crushing boulder on his chest that had *Your Fault* chiseled into it.

He was supposed to be here, to protect Dotty. But instead he'd been digging dirt and running laps while she took the fall for *his* actions.

"The church keeps an emergency fund," Bill was saying. "We use it to help people keep their lights on, or keep their car from being repossessed. I'll take all of it down to the Rec Center and offer it as a bond for her release."

"What if they won't even talk to you, because you're not a lawyer?" Lily asked.

Bill tapped the table as he thought. Then he snapped his fingers. "Bishop Sorenson, of the Mormon church, is a criminal lawyer. I can go talk to him. I'm sure he'd help."

"What if they keep her?" Mel asked.

"Officer Stalls said the other day that they don't have access to a proper jail. They're using restrooms. So they can't keep her long-term," Seth said. "It's in their best interest to give her a court date and let her come home."

"One less mouth to feed?" Corey asked.

"That will probably figure into it too, now that the Guard's gone," Seth said, nodding. He leaned back against the sink. "I'll go with you to talk to Sorenson. I did some work for him and his group."

"We'll go see him this afternoon then, and go to the Rec Center in the morning," Bill said.

"The morning?" Preacher asked, then shook his head. "Get her tonight."

Bill held up a hand. "Tempers are high right now. Let's let them cool down a bit. Having Dotty spend the night might put them in a better mood, make them feel like they've won a victory. They'll be easier to work with in the morning."

"What about our weapons?" Ripley asked.

That was another thing eating at him. Both Thomas and Ripley had been served with something Seth called a "Red Flag Law". He'd read the papers. That thieving piece of shit Jack had petitioned against Thomas, and Cathy had petitioned against Ripley, saying she'd witnessed Ripley pointing a pistol at Dotty and a large man last week.

He'd mentally tallied that point in his Fault column, too.

Police Chief Frank had filed an additional witness statement on both petitions, stating he'd witnessed both Ripley and Thomas being "uncooperative" with law enforcement officers, both on Teddy's property and while serving the inventory warrants. Judge Wilhelm's signature was on both petitions.

The officers had taken *every* firearm and piece of ammo out of both houses. They'd even searched both cellars, now that they knew they existed, under the guise of "making sure they hadn't missed additional weapons in the first search."

No weapons made the idea of having a reckoning a little more difficult. Difficult, but not impossible.

Beside him at the table, Marco was bent over a piece of paper, drawing and labeling something. He wasn't finished yet, but from the peeks he'd had, Preacher was pretty sure it was a diagram of a pipe bomb.

He was more of a molotov cocktail kind of guy, but if the kid wanted pipes, Preacher could get him some pipes.

Bill continued to tap the table as he thought. "I'll ask the Bishop about those protection orders, too. He'll probably have to look through his state law books to check the language on that, which gives us another reason to hold off until the morning. It'll give him time to beef up on the subject, so to speak."

"How did they get *all* the weapons?" Preacher said. "We burned the lists."

Mel made a disgusted face. "They had printed pictures with the corners blacked out. Someone who was here the other day took friggin' selfies in front of the '*arsenals*'." That last word was made with air quotes and a distinct note derision.

Thomas stood in the corner next to the kitchen hutch, arms crossed and eyes staring a hole through the back of Preacher's head. He hadn't said a word since Preacher had gotten home.

Home.

Could he really call it his home, if he couldn't even defend it and keep the people inside of it safe?

He had some making up to do, he knew that. But the sheer rage being directed his way from the elder Winters wasn't going to end well if he had to endure it much longer.

Marco slid the paper over to him. "As many as you can get," he muttered.

Preacher swiped the paper from the table and pushed his chair back.

"If you see the Warden, send him to me," he said to Bill. "I'll be at Teddy's. Gotta burn off some steam."

Bill nodded. "That's probably a good idea. We should all find something constructive and labor-intensive to do. Seth, you're with me?"

"Just let me get one of the bikes from the shed," Seth said.

Preacher was out the back door before Bill had even made it out of his chair.

TEDDY HAD a huge old radio in his shop with speakers on both ends, a cassette player in the middle, and a handle on the top. As if you'd actually carry this beast around. It had been plugged in, but with a little fiddling, Preacher was able to get some big-ass D batteries from the shop's inventory and pop them in. It fired up just fine, but of course the stations were all static. He browsed through a wooden cassette rack on the wall next to the workbench.

Lynyrd Skynyrd, Kiss, some old AC/DC, Fleetwood Mac, and the Eagles were some of the bands he recognized. He popped in Fleetwood Mac and started humming along as he dug through the inventory to fill Marco's list.

The six-inch pipes were easy enough. Finding caps to fit them, and a drill bit to go through them, proved harder. He gave up on finding the kerosene lamp wicks. Although he was sure he had seen them when they were packing up the few lamps Teddy had in the shop, he had no idea where Corey and Marco had decided they should go when they were unloading. Plastic tubs of nails and nuts for shrapnel were the easiest to find. Teddy had hundreds upon hundreds of pounds of nails, screws, and the like.

Marco hadn't said if Preacher should shred the note when he was done with it or keep it, so Preacher decided to err on the side of caution. If Marco could draw it once from memory, he could do it again. He shredded the paper and sprinkled it in a puddle in the funky oyster shell drive.

Back inside the shop, he was stuffing a canvas tote with his carefully-stacked materials, singing along with *The Chain*, when the music cut off.

He initially froze, then looked around. There were plenty of stacks of things to hide behind, but if he moved at all, his heavy boots would make noise across the cement floor.

And here I am without a shotgun, again, he thought. *Screw it.*

"Sheriff?" he called. No answer.

He folded the top of the tote closed and scooted it to the back of the pallet of standing fans he'd been using as a table. As quietly as he could, he crept to the door leading into the workshop.

Frank Stalls sat on the workbench, one foot on the floor, his arms casually crossed across his other leg. Four men, all armed, stood in the workshop with him, rifles pointed straight at Preacher.

"Why hello there," Frank said. "We've been all through Teddy's house, and the other end of this barn--thanks for the loud music, by the way--and we've found two interesting things."

Preacher stayed quiet. There'd be nothing to gain by talking to these men. They'd twist anything he had to say.

"Not going to ask? Fine, I'll tell you," Frank said. "We found a big empty spot where our APC should be sitting, and what looks to be a rudimentary grave dug in the backyard."

A grave? You've got to be kidding me, Preacher thought.

Frank waited, and when Preacher still didn't speak, he sighed.

"I've seen you at Dotty Parker's house, and you sure as shit aren't part of her family." He held up a hand and started ticking off his fingers. "I want to know who the hell you are, where you came from, where you took our APC, and what you did with Teddy's body. And then, maybe, if you survive that, I'll take you to a nice clean jail cell. But I have to warn you: my men and I are *very* invested in finding the whereabouts of that APC. So if you don't cooperate, surviving might become a real issue for you."

SIMON

Sheriff Simon Kane's day had started going to hell right around lunch time.

First, he'd fished his bag of protein bars out from under the seat and found he only had one left. He'd thought there were two more. Once he finished that up and was trying to figure out what he should do next, his old CB crackled and a scratchy voice had said "Sheriff? You still monitorin' this thing?"

It was Fish, a long-time guard at the federal prison where he used to be Warden. Seemed a certain someone and his band of merry men had come along the night before and "commandeered" Fish's diesel truck. It had taken Fish most of the morning to dig out his old generator and get it running, then dig out his ancient CB from the attic and get it hooked up. Simon had gone over to pick him up, and they'd started cruising the town looking for Frank.

Simon was aiming to get that truck back.

They'd been at it a while when they came upon Father Bill and Seth Miller flagging him down.

A thief had been shot at Dotty's last night, and late this

morning she'd been arrested for it. Apparently the thief was still
walking free, because he was the Mayor's son.

And boy, did that not surprise him in the least.

Bill and Seth were aiming to get *Dotty* back. Legally.

And now Preacher, one of his inmates, wanted to talk to him.
He had a pretty good idea of what it was Preacher had in
mind...and it probably wasn't going to be legal.

Problem was, he wasn't sure if he'd even be able to talk
Preacher out of whatever he was thinking, because frankly,
Simon's thoughts were rambling down that same path. He'd gone
past the line of patience with Frank Stalls' shit days ago.

They were getting close to Teddy's driveway when Fish held
up a hand.

"Hold on, Warden. Does that door look open to you?"

Simon pulled over and looked. Both Teddy's screen door and
his inner door were hanging wide open.

"Inch it up a bit, so we can see past this tree-line," Fish said,
gesturing. Simon let the car roll forward a bit.

"Well I'll be," Fish said. "Found my truck."

Teddy's house sat a good ways back from the road, and his
drive continued far past that to the big barn-shaped shop near the
rear of his property. Parked right behind the house, where you
couldn't see it if you were directly out in front, was Fish's pickup
and another. If Simon had been cruising by at normal speed, he'd
have missed them completely.

"You think Teddy's okay?" Fish asked.

"Teddy's gone on a road trip," Simon said. "Preacher's
supposed to be in there."

Fish's eyebrows flew up. He looked at the house for a moment,
then back to Simon. "You think Frank's still alive?"

Simon frowned. "Frank doesn't go anywhere these days

without armed backup." He threw the car in reverse and pulled it back to the tree-line. "Feel like a little walk?"

THE HOUSE WAS EMPTY. Neither Simon nor Fish could tell if the trucks had been sitting there long; the sun beating down in a rare bit of cloudless sky foiled the classic method of "feel the hood to see if it's warm". But one of the doors to Teddy's workshop was open, and they could hear some yelling going on.

His pistol was already out and at the ready, as was Fish's. They crept up to the doorway and paused.

"Just tell us what we want to know, and this all stops. Where did you take the APC?"

Yep, that was Frank.

As if in answer, there was the sound of someone spitting, and a yelp from someone else.

"Asshole spit on me! I've got blood on me! You trying to give me a disease?"

Simon didn't recognize that speaker. There was the meaty sound of a fist striking flesh, and a soft grunt.

Annnd that was about enough of that.

Simon turned around the corner and cut the left side of the room, feeling Fish hugging his side and doing the same on the right. They'd run this drill at the federal prison dozens of times; you had to stay prepared for a riot. It had been years, but the old guard slid into position like they'd just practiced it yesterday.

Simon took it all in in a heartbeat: Preacher, in an old wooden chair, hands zip-tied to the back. Black and blue face, swollen. Blood running from a cut by his eye and more from a busted lip. Frank and three men standing around him. They looked to be unarmed. A fourth man in the doorway leading to the barn's side-wing loosely holding an AR-15 pointed at the ground.

"Police! Hands up!" Simon yelled, and all the men jumped. The one with the rifle thrust his hands in the air like that rifle was on fire, leaving it dangling by its strap. Not a professional, then. That was good. Even as pissed as he was, he wasn't looking to kill anyone today.

Beside him, Fish turned to an angle that would let him see the men and the door behind Simon. He was grateful. Having someone sneak up behind him and add some lead to his blood would really be the cherry on his day.

Frank was the only one who didn't raise his hands. He glared around him at the other men. "Put your damn hands down. You're police officers," he growled. The men started to lower their hands.

"Keep them up!" Simon yelled. "Take two steps back from Frank. That's good. Y'all keep this up and we'll all go home happy."

"Simon why do you seem to be wedged head and shoulders up my backside lately?" Frank said.

Simon ignored the question. "What the hell's going on here?"

"What the hell does it look like?" Frank shot back.

"Sure don't look like police business. Looks like you're assaulting a citizen."

"I'm *questioning* a suspect," Frank said.

"With your fists? Is that a new up-close-and-personal form of sign language?"

"He won't talk," Frank said. "Hasn't said a damn word since we got here. And I know he's not mute; he was talking at the Parker house. So we decided to use some incentive."

"Warden, I've got multiple rifles leaning against that rolling toolbox," Fish said, nodding towards them.

Shit. Missed those in my scan. Sloppy, Simon. Sloppy.

He had to get some food. This lack of focus was liable to get him killed.

"Secure them," he said. Fish holstered his pistol and crossed the room, making sure to duck low to keep out of Simon's line of fire. He gathered up the rifles and came back, duck-walking to keep them from slipping out of his arms.

"Pistol...workbench," Preacher croaked.

"*Now* you talk?" One of the men said.

"Fish?" Simon said.

"On it." Fish brought the rifles back and dropped them in a jarring crash of noise, making most of the men wince. Then he went for the workbench.

"You in the doorway," Simon said. "I want you to lift that strap up over your head with one hand, and give it to the deputy when he comes for it."

The man nodded quickly and complied. Fish found the pistol and carefully moved around the men to get the rifle. Once it was in his hands, he came scurrying back. He ducked down behind Simon, and after a minute Simon could hear the clicks and slides of magazines being removed and chambers emptied.

"Stop acting like you might shoot us, Simon. It's a nice show of force, but we're all police officers here. You're not going to shoot a brother in blue."

"These men aren't police officers, as far as I'm concerned," Simon said. He dropped his arm to hang loose by his side. Holding it up for too long built up lactic acid and caused a tremble. If he had to use it, he wanted his aim to be sure.

"I *made* them police officers," Frank said.

"You're not a police officer, either, Frank."

"The City hired me-"

"Police officers don't tie people up and beat the shit out of them until they talk, Stalls!" Simon yelled. "Police officers don't let a thief walk free while they jail little old ladies for defending themselves!"

"That's what this is about? I arrested your friend so now you're getting revenge? She tried to kill a kid, Simon! His back is full of holes! He's lucky she didn't blow his head off!"

Simon shook his head. "The *only* way you could get that woman to fire a gun is if she thought she was in extreme danger. She had a stranger in her yard, with a gun-"

"He claims he wasn't in her yard," Frank said. "And she admitted to shooting him. I'm in the clear here, *Sheriff*."

Simon gestured to Preacher's swollen face. "This is being in the clear?"

Frank rolled his eyes. "Look at this guy, Simon. Really look at him. You think he's some model of good behavior? His arms are covered in tattoos. He's all roided out. Probably some kind of gang member. And he's here in Teddy's workshop, stealing hardware to make pipe bombs, from the looks of it." He pointed to the rolling toolbox, and Simon glanced in that direction. His eyebrows went up. There was a neatly-arranged line of hardware next to a canvas bag. Small pipes, caps, nails and the like.

What the hell are you planning, Preacher?

"Yeah. See?" Frank said. "We caught him gathering the materials. Red-handed."

"Do you have proof that he's not permitted to be here?" Simon asked.

"Well conveniently enough, Teddy isn't here to ask," Frank said. "He's missing. But there's a nice deep grave over on that side of the property ready to be used." He pointed in the general direction of the would-be outhouse and nearly smacked one of his men in the face.

"For god's sake Frank, that's an outhouse. Teddy hired him to dig an outhouse," Simon said. "He's got cause to be here. He's not digging a grave. He's not stealing anything. You, on the other hand..." Simon jabbed his thumb over his shoulder. "That's not your truck."

"I was wondering when we'd get to that," Frank said. "I've legally commandeered that truck."

"No. Only federal agents can commandeer things, Frank. You're not a federal agent."

"The Governor gave Wilhelm emergency powers-"

"You're not Wilhelm, either."

"Jesus christ Simon, stop it! Just stop it! Stop acting like *you* are the law! Friggin' Judge Dredd or Buford Pusser or some shit! We're in an emergency situation, and that requires emergency action!"

"The stealing cars and beating people up kind of emergency action?"

"Like you've never *accidentally* made a suspect face-plant into the concrete? You're not some damned boy scout!"

Simon sighed and looked at Preacher. The big man was watching him carefully.

"You want to press charges?" Simon asked.

"You've got to be kidding me," Frank said.

Preacher spit a wad of blood out of his mouth and cracked his neck. "If I press charges, you put him in a jail cell?"

"Yeah, until we can get a judge to decide on bond," Simon said.

"Then no," Preacher said. He turned to look straight at Frank. "I want him out where I can get to him."

"Is that a threat?" Frank said, his voice high.

The corner of Preacher's mouth lifted a little bit.

"Fish, you want to press charges?"

Fish watched Preacher for a moment, considering. Then he smiled. "No," he said. "I'm happy to just get my truck back unharmed. No need to put him in jail over a misunderstanding of federal law."

Fish gave a nod to Preacher. Preacher dipped his chin once and looked back to Frank. His smirk got a little more pronounced.

"You heard them," Simon said. "You're free to go. And don't touch the weapons; I'll bring them to you later."

"You can't keep my gun," one of the men said, pointing at the pile.

Simon tapped his pistol on his thigh. "I asked the man if he wanted to press charges against Frank. I didn't ask him about you. If I were you, I'd escape while I could and get my gun from Frank some other time."

The men took the hint and filed out, giving Simon and Fish a wide berth. Frank walked up to Simon and fixed him with a hard look.

"You and me, we're going to have to come to some kind of an...*understanding*," Frank said. "One way or another. I'm getting tired of this."

"One way or another," Simon agreed, nodding. "Get the hell out of my sight, Frank, before I make that choice."

He watched them stomp across the yard and pile into the second pickup truck. The tires tore up the grass as they pulled back onto the drive. When he turned around, Fish had cut Preacher's hands free and the big man was standing, rubbing his wrists.

"Did you *have* to come right out and threaten him?" Simon asked, holstering his pistol.

Preacher swiped the back of his hand across his busted lip.

"Yeah," he said. "I want him looking over his shoulder."

Simon sighed and pulled a handkerchief from his pocket, handing it to Preacher. "You must have some plan, if you wanted me to come see you. Let's hear it."

BILL

Bill took a deep breath as he strode to the reception counter at the Rec Center and gave the lady there a big, friendly smile. He didn't recognize this one.

"Can I help you?"

"We're here to see Dorothy Parker. This is Mr. Sorenson, her lawyer," Bill gestured to the smartly-dressed man beside him, "and I'm Pastor Bill Flannigan, her religious counsel."

The woman frowned at him. "If they're in the shelter, I guess you can just go on back and talk to them."

Bishop Sorenson shook his head. "It's our understanding that Dorothy Parker is in your *jail*," he said. Bill nodded.

"Jail?" The woman made a face. "What jail?" She waved a hand. "You know what? Hold on." She slid off of a tall stool and disappeared around the corner. Bill could still hear as she off-loaded her issue onto the clerk.

"Got a couple of guys out here saying they want to see someone in our *jail*? Any idea what they're talking about?"

"They mean the rooms where we've been putting people who

misbehave," the clerk said. "Don't you worry about it. I'll handle it. Stay here." In a moment, she appeared at the corner and crossed over to the counter.

"Oh! Father Bill. I wasn't expecting it to be you." Her smile was genuine. "I thought it would be some of those awful people I've heard about." She leaned forward and lowered her voice. "No one's allowed to go into the *jail*. We've got an actual prisoner in there now and she's not allowed visitors."

"By what law is a prisoner not permitted to discuss their rights with their counsel?" Sorenson asked.

The clerk blinked at Sorenson. "It's...it's just what Mayor Wilhelm said. No visitors."

"That's not going to work for me," Sorenson said, shifting his briefcase to one hand so he could pull a pen from an inner pocket with the other. "Could I have your name, please?"

"Samantha...why?"

"And your last name?" Sorenson produced a small notepad from the same pocket. He dropped the pad on the counter and with a practiced one-handed efficiency, flipped it open to a blank page and started writing. He looked up expectantly.

"You don't need my name," she started, but he held up a finger.

"I need your full name so I can spell it properly on the lawsuit I'll be bringing against you for not allowing me access to my client, which is required by law."

"Lawsuit?"

"Lawsuit. Now. Samantha...?"

"Hold on a minute," she said, and scurried away.

Bill and Sorenson shared a look. Sorenson lifted his briefcase to the counter and with a loud double-snap, flipped the latches and opened it up. "You might want to adjust that phone," he whispered, and pulled out a slim stack of papers.

Bill looked down and saw that the cellphone peeking out of

the top of his shirt pocket had tilted a bit. He straightened it, but it tilted over again.

"Here," Sorenson said, and slid a pen into the pocket, clip side out. The phone leaned against it and stayed.

They heard Wilhelm's voice boom down the hall and a few moments later, the rotund man hustled around the corner. When he saw them, he stopped and blinked in confusion.

"She said there were lawyers out here."

"Nice to see you again, Mayor Wilhelm," Sorenson said, stepping forward and offering a hand. "Although I hear you're a judge now."

"I...I am," Wilhelm said, shaking hands. "Father Bill, what-"

"Excellent," Sorenson said, stepping back and laying a hand on his papers. "Then perhaps you can inform me why legal and religious counsel are being denied to your prisoner, Mrs. Dorothy Parker?"

"Legal and religious counsel?"

Bill smiled and pointed to himself. "Religious counsel." He pointed to Sorenson. "Mr. Sorenson, criminal attorney."

Sorenson nodded and patted his papers. "I trust I really don't need to read all of the myriad laws you'd be breaking if you denied my client her right to an attorney. I brought them along just in case, but I'm expecting with you at the helm, things will be run legally and properly, yes?"

Wilhelm finally seemed to catch up. His eyes narrowed. "This isn't going to change anything," he said. "She confessed."

"I'm not here to argue her guilt or innocence, Your Honor. I just want access to my client so I can advise her of her rights, as the law allows. Now either someone can take us to her, or-" he pulled out a larger stack of paperwork "-I can start filling out the lawsuits right here. Which would you prefer?"

DOTTY DIDN'T LOOK any worse for wear. Bill was thankful for that. Frank had taken her little canvas shoes that she wore in the summertime without socks, and the tiled floor was cold in the air conditioning. She'd been sitting with her feet tucked under her and a thin wool blanket wrapped around her when they came in.

After they'd finished hugging and she'd treated Sorenson to a bone-crushing hug of his own for his willingness to help, Bill had sat down on her cot and taken off his own footwear. He handed her his pair of socks and she took them, her bottom lip trembling.

"Never thought I'd be missing warm socks in the summertime," she said, slipping them on. She visibly relaxed.

Sorenson got right down to business, dragging a second cot over and spreading his papers out on it. He asked rapid-fire questions and took extensive notes on a legal pad.

Bill had hoped that since this wasn't an official jail and Wilhelm wasn't used to actually incarcerating suspects, that they'd have skipped the worst parts of an arrest. Unfortunately, Frank was quite familiar with the process.

They'd made her strip down to her bra and panties in front of Frank and Stella, one of the women that had been present at the inventory search and a member of Bill's church. Then Frank had turned around while she stripped down the rest of the way, and he instructed her through squatting and coughing while Stella watched.

"It was so humiliating," Dotty whispered.

Bill wrapped an arm around her shoulders while Sorenson continued to scratch notes.

Frank had insisted on taking her bra, since it had underwires. They'd taken everything she'd had on her at the time other than her jeans, t-shirt, and underwear. She kept covering her chest with the blanket as she talked.

Bill couldn't explain why, but for some reason the thought of Dotty's bra being somewhere in this facility while she sat here trying to keep herself modestly covered made him seethe.

"They made me fill out a statement and sign it, saying I shot that boy," Dotty said. "Made me sit in front of a cellphone and read it out loud while they video recorded it."

"When they recorded it, did they read you your Miranda rights before they had you start speaking?" Sorenson asked.

Dotty thought for a moment and nodded. "Frank did. He must've repeated those lines to me three or four times, starting at the house."

"Are they feeding you?" Bill asked. "Taking you to the facilities?"

Dotty grimaced. "They gave me one of those MRE things and a bottle of water last night. I haven't had any food yet today. I haven't left this bathroom since they brought me in here." She lowered her voice, as if speaking of something shameful. "There's a garbage bag in the toilet in that last stall. I have to use that."

"What about fingerprints?" Sorenson said.

Dotty held out her hands, and the finger pads were stained with ink. "They found one of those little pads that you press stamps into," she said. "Frank used that and some printer paper."

Sorenson shook his head. "I was hoping this would've been less official. Looks like Chief Stalls was being painstakingly thorough."

"That's not good for us, right?" Dotty said.

"You let me worry about that," Sorenson said. "It might actually help us. They're establishing a precedent that this is going to be by the book, so any attempt at deviating from that saying it's *an emergency* will be harder for them."

He had many more questions, and Dotty answered them as best she could. Bill held her hand through it all. He'd sat through dozens of these sessions with other people, but he'd never been as invested. Sure, he'd felt for the people he was counseling, felt empathy for what they were going through and a certain level of anger on their behalf.

But right now he wanted to smash down Wilhelm's door and beat the man senseless. Then he wanted to go find Frank.

"I'm done with the official interview," Sorenson finally said. "If you two want to talk or anything, I do have to stay here for it. And I'd suggest you not discuss anything you don't want anyone else hearing. I'm supposed to have confidentiality, but I can't guarantee our discussion isn't being listened to or recorded somehow." He pointed to the door and raised his eyebrows.

Dotty looked up at Bill. "How are the children? Are they alright? Is Seth keeping an eye on the boys so they don't do anything foolish?"

"The kids are all fine," Bill reassured her. "They're upset and angry, but they're safe. I've talked to them. Don't you worry about them."

"And the girls?"

Bill smiled a little. "I think they'd be here breaking down that wall if they knew where to find keys to a bulldozer. Mel...err...the shorter one, especially."

Dotty tried to smile. "You tell her that I said to behave, and that her Grams loves her. Tell them all that."

"And..." she looked at the door, then shook her head and traced her finger across the back of her knuckles. "Him. You tell *him* to let this be. I can get through this. I confessed, and even if Frank had come for him instead of Thomas, I'd have still done it."

"I don't have the kind of influence over *him* that Simon does," Bill started.

"You tell him I spoke, and that's all there is to it," she said. "Don't let him get himself into any trouble."

Bill had made it back to Dotty's house before Preacher, and he'd seen the man's injuries when Simon brought him home. There was no use in telling her any of that. He just nodded.

"I'll try," he said. "No promises."

Someone knocked on the door. "Five minutes," Samantha's voice called out.

"Did Teddy come back last night?" Her face was hopeful.

"No," Bill said. "When he shows back up, I'll let you know."

"Okay Mrs. Parker. Here's what I hope will happen: I'm going to go talk to *Judge* Wilhelm and ask him to give you a bond hearing. Bill's brought some money-"

"Bill, you didn't," Dotty said.

"Shush," he said. "It's for emergencies. This is an emergency."

Sorenson held up a finger to get their attention. "It's enough that even if Wilhelm demands a sizeable bond, we should be able to put down ten percent. That's the standard. I'm hoping we'll have you out of here today, with a court date some time in the future. But it might not go that way. So cross your fingers, but try not to get your hopes up too far. We'll know what we know when we know it. I'll keep you informed."

Dotty nodded, and squeezed Bill's hand. He could see tears welling up in her eyes.

"Hey," he said, turning her head. "We're working to get you out of here. And come Hell or high water, I promise we'll do it. You hear me?"

She nodded, looking down. Tears fell on their joined hands.

He kissed her on her forehead, and then led the three of them in a prayer.

When Frank slammed the door open and told them time was up, he kissed her hands and left. She looked so small and alone, curled up with her knees to her chest and staring after him as he walked out.

Frank slammed the door shut and slid the pin back into place.

"You've got a lot of nerve, coming down here and pulling this red tape shit," Frank said. "Religious counsel, my ass."

"Judge Wilhelm allowed it, as he was required to, by law," Sorenson said. "And now we're going to speak with him again. If we could get by?" He moved around Stalls in exaggerated steps and then walked briskly down the hall.

Frank stood glaring at Bill.

Bill stared back for a moment, then stepped closer.

"Officer Stalls-"

"*Chief* Stalls," Frank corrected.

Bill tightened his jaw and smiled. "Frank," he said. "There's something you should remember."

"Yeah? What's that?"

"I wasn't always a man of God," Bill said.

Frank snorted. "What's that supposed to do? Scare me?"

"That depends on how smart you are," Bill said, then stepped around him and headed down the hall, where Sorenson stood waiting outside Wilhelm's office door.

BILL

Bill sat across from Mayor Wilhelm with his hands pressed together between his knees. He was letting Bishop Sorenson do the talking, but it wasn't going well. Wilhelm didn't want to let Dotty go, and was manufacturing excuses as to why he couldn't do a bond hearing.

"You've got your main law enforcement officer right here," Sorenson said, referring to Frank, who was looming in the doorway. "There's no reason why we can't review the charges and set bail."

"I don't even have a Bible to swear everyone in," Wilhelm said. "We'll do it some other-"

"I happen to have one handy," Sorenson said. He flipped his briefcase open on his lap and slid a copy of the LDS Bible onto the desk with a smile. "Never leave home without it."

Wilhelm frowned and looked to Cindy Stalls, who was standing in the corner with her arms crossed. She didn't acknowledge his unspoken plea for help, and he sighed.

"Frank, please bring in the accused. And could you bring in another chair, please?"

Cindy and Frank left.

Sorenson leaned over. "I'll need Mrs. Parker beside me. You can stand or sit in the back."

Bill got up and moved to the back corner of the office.

When Frank walked Dotty through the office door, her hands were zip-tied. Bill bit back a remark.

Cindy produced another chair, sat it on the side of Wilhelm's desk, and promptly sat in it. She dropped a stack of papers on the corner of the desk. Then she pulled out a cellphone, tapped it a few times, and slid it to the center of the desk. It had a large screen on it counting up in seconds. Wilhelm raised an eyebrow at her.

"You'll need someone to represent the State," she said. "I'm the closest thing you have to an attorney, unless you want to go comb through the unwashed masses in the gym. And this needs to be recorded."

Wilhelm looked at Sorenson. "This will be a little unorthodox, but being that these are emergency measures..."

"We'll take that into consideration," Sorenson said. "We're just setting bail, after all."

Wilhelm had both Frank and Dotty swear in, using Sorenson's bible. Wilhelm went over the charges against Dotty aloud. Attempted murder, interfering with a police investigation, and resisting arrest. Bill opened his mouth to object, but Sorenson silenced him with a sharp look over his shoulder. When Wilhelm asked if she understood, Dotty said yes. Cindy smiled.

"Defense?" Wilhelm said.

"Your Honor, my client is an upstanding citizen in this community. She's lived on Washington Street for many years, worked at the local hardware store for most of those, and is currently unemployed. Her family lives here in town. She attends a local church, and donates much of her time and her personal food stores to that church for the needy. Given her work status, which limits her income, as well as the emergency situation we find ourselves in without access to fuel, I believe she is not a flight risk whatsoever. She poses no risk to the community, which she is deeply involved in and cares for as if they're her extended family. She's an excellent candidate for bail."

Wilhelm snorted. He actually snorted. Bill took a deep breath and let it out slowly.

The Mayor tapped a paper in front of him. "Chief Stalls, in the statement I've got here, you claim that Mrs. Parker confessed to these crimes. Could you detail for me the manner in which this occurred?"

"You were standing right there," Dotty said, and Sorenson put his hand over hers.

"Any more outbursts from the Defendant, and she'll be returned to her cell," Wilhelm warned.

Frank detailed everything that had gone on the previous morning. Bill wasn't sure if he elaborated or not, given that he hadn't been there at the time. But it sounded like it meshed with what Thomas had told him.

Then Wilhelm asked Cindy if the State had any objections to releasing Dotty on her own recognizance.

"The State has many, Your Honor," Cindy said. "The Defendant has established a clear pattern that she is unwilling to work with any government or law enforcement official in any capacity. She refused to sign papers that the City presented to her concerning the numerous code violations and federal codes for historical buildings that she is currently breaking. The Defendant refused to fill out the census form that the City provided to all of the residents, forcing the City to issue a warrant for a full search and inventory of her property."

Bill could see Dotty's shoulders tense up. He tried to silently will her to stay quiet, but he was having a hard time with that himself.

"She's encouraged and orchestrated others to act on her behalf to interfere with the City's law enforcement operations," Cindy continued. "I was informed that she even organized a revolutionary meeting on her property-"

"Objection," Sorenson said. "Hearsay."

"Considering the word 'revolutionary', this seems pertinent enough that I'll allow it," Wilhelm said. "Please continue."

Cindy gave Sorenson a withering look before continuing. "A revolutionary meeting on her property where she encouraged fellow residents of her street to not comply with the emergency measures put into place by the Governor and by the City's Council. Also, she is suspected of orchestrating a theft of the City's census forms from this very facility."

"Objection," Sorenson said. "Hearsay, again. Your Honor, we're here to discuss facts, not rumors and speculation."

Cindy didn't wait for Wilhelm's response. "The *facts*," she snarled, "are that Mrs. Parker confessed to this crime not once, not twice, but at least *three* separate times. We have two witnesses who were present at her first confession. She signed a statement confessing, and we have recorded video of yet another confession. There's no question she attempted to kill the victim, and therefore the idea that she poses no threat to the community is preposterous."

"What about flight risk?" Wilhelm asked.

"She's been establishing her own lordship over on Washington Street and spurring an uprising there. It's not out of the realm of reason that she would use that network to procure a means of flight, Your Honor. The State believes that Mrs. Parker should *not* be released on bail."

Bill felt his fists clenching and unclenching, and tried to make them stop. Cindy Stalls was making Dotty sound like some would-be warlord. It was ridiculous. And he couldn't say a thing.

"Well, given the State's position, I'm inclined to deny bail," Wilhelm said.

"Your Honor, Father Bill is willing to deposit a sizable amount of money to assure the Court that he will have Mrs. Parker present for any trial date you might set," Sorenson said. "I can easily produce witnesses that would refute the character assassination occurring here-"

"It's not a character assassination, it's the truth!" Cindy spat, leaning forward and jabbing her finger into the desk. "She's hoarding food when the City and its residents are in need. We've got witnesses that have seen the amount of food she has. Yet when we went to inventory it, it was all gone. She'd rather destroy that food than share it with her community. Is that typical of a caring, sharing, church-going woman? She's a menace who won't comply with government or law enforcement, and openly flaunts that fact and encourages others to do it. She's starting her own lordship over there, and it's my belief that she plans to attempt a coup of the lawfully-elected City Council so that she can install her own leadership. And now she's admitted--*admitted*--to shooting a child!"

"Your Honor," Sorenson said, his voice heavy with patience.

"She needs to be made an example of," Cindy raved on. "If you let her go, you'll just be encouraging others to take the same actions. She needs to be tried and convicted, *immediately*. Michael is coming. We don't have the time or the resources to drag this out."

"Your Honor," Sorenson tried again, but Wilhelm held up a hand.

"The State brings up a number of good points," Wilhelm said.

"The City does not have access to a proper jail, and the county Sheriff refuses to allow us access to his. Our resources are quite limited, given that the National Guard has left town. The longer we keep Mrs. Parker, the less food we have for the other residents in our shelter."

"A perfect reason to allow her to return to her home," Sorenson cut in.

Wilhelm shook his head and looked at his watch, then Frank. "Would the State's witness be available this afternoon? Say, around four?"

Even Frank looked a little shocked by this, Bill noted. Interesting. Apparently this was as off-the-cuff as it appeared to be.

"Yes sir," Frank said. "I can gather up my men who were also there, if necessary."

Wilhelm nodded. "Do that, just in case. I'll make sure the victim is present. Mrs. Stalls, you'll be available?"

"Absolutely," Cindy said. "And I'll also have a witness to the other issues I raised. The hoarding food, and such."

"Those issues don't pertain to the situation that allegedly occurred last night, Your Honor," Sorenson said. "Also, I need significantly more time to prepare. I need copies of statements-"

"It's settled then," Wilhelm said, cutting Sorenson off. "We'll have the trial this afternoon at 4pm. Chief Stalls, escort the accused back to her cell." He banged his fist twice on the desk and stood.

Dotty looked back at Bill, her mouth agape and eyes wide. Frank crossed the room and lifted her bound wrists, and she naturally followed them up.

"Your Honor this is unprecedented," Sorenson argued, leaning forward. "We've got bail money, we can set a more reasonable trial date-"

"I've made my decision," Wilhelm said. "Either be here at 4pm ready to defend your client, or...don't. The trial will be held either way. Good day, gentlemen."

Sorenson snatched his bible from the desk and tucked it away before slamming his briefcase closed. He watched Dotty be led from the room and nodded his head for Bill to follow him out.

In the lobby, Bill stopped. "What the-"

"Not here," Sorenson said, grabbing his arm and pulling him forward. "Hold it in. Not. Here."

They broke out into the late morning sun and walked briskly to Sorenson's car. When the Bishop finally let go of his arm, Bill turned on him and jabbed a finger back towards the building.

"What in God's name was *that*?" He yelled. "I've been to dozens of bail hearings and I have *never* seen such blatant, ridiculous-"

"I know. I *know*," Sorenson said. "But right now he's the elected judge, and his is the highest court we've got. I could file appeals to the state board, but how am I going to get them there? And in a matter of mere hours?"

"How are we supposed to prepare anything by four o'clock?" Bill said, pacing. "We can't! They're not even going to give you the documents you need!"

"Probably not," Sorenson said. "It seems like it's going to be a kangaroo court all the way around."

"Then what the hell do we *do*?" Bill said. "They're sending her up for attempted murder! They could lock her away for the rest of her life!"

"Bill," Sorenson said, his voice suddenly quiet. Bill stopped and looked at him.

"You heard what they both said about not having a jail and the resources to keep her jailed. I don't think we're talking about years, here. I'll have to check my books and look at this Civil Officer title that the Governor conferred to Wilhelm, but it's likely there's nothing we can do to get this extended or fight it given the emergency declarations. I'm going to go home and get right on that."

"And what am I supposed to do?" Bill said.

"You gather everyone together that you can that we might use as character witnesses, and you pray for guidance," Sorenson said. "Pray hard."

DOTTY

The sound of the metal clasp on the restroom door being rattled jerked Dotty alert. She'd gotten lost in thought staring at the unopened MRE packet and bottle of water in her lap. She set them on top of the folded wool blanket at the head of her cot and stood up.

Frank Stalls came through the door, followed by Stella. Stella wouldn't meet her eyes.

Coward, Dotty thought.

"Mrs. Parker, it's time. Hold out your hands, please."

Dotty kept staring at Stella while Frank wound a new set of zip-ties around her wrists and pulled them tight. Stella kept staring at the floor.

"Move over here and face the wall, please," he said, pointing to the space by the sinks where the hand dryer hung, defunct.

Dotty was confused. "We're not leaving?"

"I need to restrain your ankles," he explained.

"It's not as if I can outrun you-"

"Against the wall, Mrs. Parker." He produced a small, boxy

device from his pocket with two silver nubs protruding from the end. With the push of a button, the device gave a low hum and electricity sparked between the two posts. Dotty's eyes flew wide.

"Is that a taser?"

"A personal stun gun, but it'll get the job done. The wall?" He indicated the space again.

Dotty moved over and waited as Frank gave Stella the taser and squatted down to wrap zip-ties around her ankles. She looked down and watched his hands in a disconnected state. It was as if this were happening to someone else.

Frank was quick and efficient. A shorter loop around each ankle, connected by a larger loop in-between. She wouldn't even be able to take a full step; not that her stride was long to begin with. She'd be shuffling like an old woman.

"We're going to exit the restroom, turn left, and head down the hall," Frank said. He took a firm grasp of her upper arm and guided her to the door. Stella still wouldn't meet her eyes. Dotty had an urge to say something spiteful, something that would sting. She pressed it down. Bill had told her what he'd learned talking with the shelter residents: able-bodied people were expected to do whatever was asked of them. The first refusal carried a penalty of no food for the day, for both that person and any members of their family. The second refusal resulted in the family being evicted from the facility.

Stella was nearly as much of a prisoner here as she was.

When they stepped out of the restroom, she could hear raised voices coming from the lobby. For an instant, she thought she heard Corey and turned to look, but his voice was shouted down quickly by someone threatening to throw everyone out if they didn't quiet down. Frank yanked her to the left and got her moving. Stella took up position on her right side.

"Was that my grandson I heard?" she asked.

Neither of them answered.

"Was that my grandson?" she said again.

"They're all out there," Stella said, her words quick. "And they brought other people, too. That's why we're going this way."

"No talking," Frank ordered.

They walked--or shuffled, rather--her past the office where the parody of a bail hearing had been. They passed more doors, some of them open. Some had paper taped to them; hand-written signs in bold marker stating things like "Residence: Wilhelm", "Residence: Stalls", and other names she didn't recognize. She caught glimpses of cork-boards and dry-erase boards on the walls, colorful graphics and motivation posters, and cots like hers. Only these had actual pillows, and were lined with fluffy comforters.

She'd had to borrow the blanket from one of the unused cots in the restroom to use as a pillow. They hadn't even given her that small comfort.

The smell of coffee hit her, and despite her lack of appetite, her stomach growled. She craned her neck to see into the room it seemed to be coming from, but Frank tugged on her and snapped her attention forward again.

There was a pair of large double doors at the end of the hall. Just before them, Cathy emerged from the doorway to another side-room. She pulled the door shut behind her as she looked at her watch, but her head snapped up at the sound of their approach. Her eyes went wide.

"Residence: Cathy Riggs," Dotty read from the sign as they neared. "Well haven't you moved up in the world?"

Cathy sneered and tugged her shirt into place. "Some of us know how to work *with* the system."

"No talking," Frank repeated, and hurried her along. Dotty heard Cathy start walking behind them. Just what she needed: her own personal escort of hate on her way to her life sentence.

Life Sentence.

That had been the phrase Bishop Sorenson had used when he'd come back to see her earlier this afternoon. He'd walked in with a rolling black case stuffed to overflowing with binders and papers, a sports bra from Ripley that had grudgingly gotten Frank's approval after a thorough inspection, and a grim expression that told her none of his news would be good.

In Maryland, a first-degree attempted murder charge carried a maximum sentence of life in jail. Sorenson stressed that it was the State's responsibility to prove that she had actually planned to murder Jack Wilhelm and had sat in wait. He knew they couldn't do it beyond a reasonable doubt.

"They've got no evidence, no witnesses of you setting up a plan," he'd said. "They can't prove that you knew Jack would be walking along that sidewalk."

"He wasn't on the sidewalk," Dotty had told him. "He wasn't even walking - he had a car."

"I know that, and I'm going to try to trip him up on that. But it's the story they're going with, so they'll have to prove it."

Dotty wasn't so sure they'd have to prove anything. Not with Wilhelm presiding over the case. She figured she was in this for the long haul, and that cot was going to be her bed for the rest of her natural life.

The double doors opened up to the big gymnasium where Sheriff Kane had disrupted Wilhelm's town hall. They started walking down the length of it. Rows and rows of cots lined the space, many with people on them. Some sat with their clothes and bags piled next to them, others had tucked their meager belongings underneath. The heat was oppressive and a shock to her system, after staying in that cold tile bathroom all night. When the heavy doors swung shut behind them with a bang, most of the occupants turned to look.

Dotty felt her face flush red. Instinct told her to drop her head and hunch her shoulders so she'd be harder to see, and she started to, before she remembered who she was.

She was the widow of a good, *good* man. She was the proud mother of a Navy sailor. She was grandmother to an entire herd of young people--not all of them by blood, but hers nonetheless--and she was the daughter of the king of kings.

She straightened her spine, lifted her chin and stared straight ahead as Frank paraded her past most of the town. With her hands cuffed and her legs shackled, police pulling her along, she refused to be ashamed.

She had stood up for her innocent grandchild. She had kept her silence and protected a man who did what he did to protect her and her family.

She was proud of those things.

Her bound hands came up to rub the little cross pendant at her throat, and she frowned when she found only cotton there. Frank had taken that, too. Him, and King Kenny, and Cindy...they were trying to take everything she had.

They couldn't, no matter how hard they tried. God was with her, always. She didn't need pretty jewelry to remind her of that.

Someone whistled, and someone else called out "Selfish bitch!"

She kept staring ahead. Even when someone yelled "Good catch, Chief!"

Even when the applause started, and swelled. And when a flip-flop came sailing through the air to strike her directly in the chest. That started a chain reaction, and more strange items started landing around them. More shoes. A rolled-up pair of socks. A wadded MRE packet. Various pieces of trash.

Would this gymnasium never end?

They finally pushed through another pair of double doors into another cool, relatively quiet hall. There were fewer doors dotting the sides of this one, and they were spaced incredibly far apart in comparison.

Must be big rooms, Dotty thought. *Surprised the Council didn't take these for their residences.*

There were a few people standing outside another set of double doors, but it was no one she recognized.

"In here," Frank said, and pushed one of them open. She stepped through to a cafeteria, complete with school-type benches attached to tables. Quite a few people were seated among them. She recognized a few faces from seeing them in passing around town; another few had been occasional customers at Teddy's hardware store. She scanned quickly, looking for her family. None of them were there.

At the head of the room, a long brown table had been set up, and Wilhelm stood behind it, conferring with Cindy. Another two tables sat about ten feet in front of that one, with a generous space between them. Sorenson stood at the one on the right, and smiled sadly as she was brought in. Jack sat at the other, looking sullen. He was wearing a dress shirt that was too big for him and an expensive tie, and she nearly snorted. Someone had gone to a lot of work to make him look like such an innocent, nice young man.

Frank escorted her all the way up to the table, and didn't let go of her arm until she was seated in the chair Sorenson held out for her.

Cathy slipped onto the bench closest to the plaintiff's table.

"Where will my family be seated?" Dotty asked Frank as he started to turn away.

He raised his eyebrows. "They won't. They'll have to wait in the lobby. The judge has determined they'll be too disruptive to the proceedings."

"But all these strangers get to watch?" Dotty said.

"These strangers are here to witness you getting a fair trial, so no one can claim there was any funny business later on," Frank said. He directed this last at Sorenson. "It saves time."

He turned and strode off before she could think of anything else to ask. Stella stood, fidgeting, and finally moved a little behind Dotty's chair.

"It's really not a requirement for you to stand there," Sorenson said. "Attending officers usually stand on the side of the room, or take a seat in the back."

"I was told to stand here," Stella whispered.

"I cannot conduct confidential communications with my client with you directly behind her chair," Sorenson said. "Please find somewhere else to stand."

"I *have* to stand here," Stella whispered again, with more force.

"It's fine, Bishop," Dotty said. He shook his head.

"No, it's not." He stood and motioned to Frank, who had joined Cindy. "Chief Stalls, your officer is violating my client's right to confidentiality. I'd like to request that she be moved."

"Denied," Wilhelm said, without looking up from some papers he was shuffling on his table. "Your client's a dangerous suspect. She needs to be guarded to protect the members of this court."

"But Your Honor-"

"*Denied*," Wilhelm said, fixing Sorenson with a glare. Then he looked around the room and cleared his throat. "Everyone, take your seats please. Let's get this over with."

DOTTY

Dotty quickly started to wish she'd spent more time watching those crime shows on TV, just so she could keep up. There was a lot of procedural mumbo-jumbo narrated by a woman with frizzy red hair, involving everyone rising after they'd just been told to be seated, and then being told to be seated again, and Wilhelm introducing himself and thanking everyone for coming. He read off the charges against Dotty and asked her how she pleaded.

"Your Honor," Sorenson said, standing again and lifting a piece of paper. "Before we begin, I'd like to file this request with the Court. If I may approach the...bench?"

"You may not." Wilhelm looked around and gestured to the redhead. "Samantha, if you would?"

Samantha crossed over and took the paper, and moved quickly to hand it to Wilhelm. He slid his glasses further down his nose and scanned over it.

"What the hell is this?" he asked.

"The Defense requests that Your Honor recuse himself from

this trial, based on his personal association with the alleged victim. This is a clear and blatant conflict of intere-"

"Denied," Wilhelm said, and dropped the paper aside.

"But Your Honor, the alleged victim is your *son*," Sorenson said. "Surely-"

"Are you implying that I'm incapable of being fair and impartial during a court proceeding? Is that really how you want to start this trial? Insulting me?"

"Of course not, Your Honor. The Defense apologizes for any misunderstanding," Sorenson said.

"Good. Now, Mrs. Parker. How do you plead?"

"I'd like to request a trial by jury of my peers," Dotty said.

"Mrs. Parker," Sorenson murmured. "Don't-"

"You're not getting one," Wilhelm said. "We don't have the time or even the manpower to provide you with a jury. Now how do you-"

"You've got all of these people seated here in the cafeteria--err, the courtroom," Dotty said. "Couldn't they stand as a jury?"

Wilhelm removed his glasses and set them down on the table. He made a show of leaning forward and speaking directly to a small handheld recorder that was sitting on the table in front of him. "Let the record show that the Defendant is refusing to enter a plea."

"I'm *not* refusing to enter a plea. I'd just like to do so in front of a jury," Dotty said.

"The Court does not *have* a jury available for you at this time. Your lawyer can feel free to appeal any decisions made by this court, and even demand a re-trial if he'd like. But we're moving forward with this today. Is that understood?"

"Yes, Your Honor," Sorenson said. He gave her a hard look.

"Yes, Your Honor," Dotty echoed. "I plead Not Guilty to all charges."

"Of course you do," Wilhelm muttered, and slipped his glasses back on. "Does the State have any opening arguments?"

"We certainly do, Your Honor," Cindy said, standing. "The State intends to prove, through witness testimony and through signed and recorded statements, that the defendant is guilty of all charges."

"Objection," Sorenson said. "Anything signed and recorded outside of this courtroom is not admissible as evidence."

"Overruled," Wilhelm said.

And it was more of the same, all the way through. Most of it was a blur of indignant outrage for Dotty. Despite Sorenson's many objections, Cindy played the recording of Dotty's confession aloud. Jack made a statement and outright lied. Wilhelm even allowed Cathy to stand up and make a statement about all the food she'd seen in Dotty's house before, and how Dotty had refused to give her any chicken the day she was canning it.

There was one bright spot when Dotty thought they might get the whole thing thrown out.

Jack was testifying. "And that's when she just started shooting at me. I hadn't done nuffin'!"

"So that's when you pulled out the Hi-Point and fired in defense?" Sorenson asked.

Jack's head jerked back and he sneered. "Hi-Point? I ain't carry no Hi-Point trash. I used my Glock."

"Did you empty the magazine?" Sorenson pressed.

"Naw, man. I only fired three o' four shots," Jack said, waving a hand.

"Just enough to get back to the car," Sorenson said affably, nodding and shrugging as if this was the most reasonable thing in the world.

Cindy, who'd been writing something on a legal pad next to Jack, suddenly straightened and her eyes went wide.

Jack shrugged too, unconsciously mimicking Sorenson. "Yeah, man. I was gettin' my ass outta there like she told me to do-" He jabbed his thumb towards Cindy.

"Objection!" Cindy barked.

"On what grounds?" Sorenson said.

"On um, on..."

Sorenson interrupted and tipped his head at Cindy. "Bet she gave you shit about the blood in her car."

"Yeah man, she was *pissed*," Jack started.

"*Objection!*" Cindy shrieked.

"On what grounds?" Sorenson said again.

"I don't know what grounds! But I object to this! All of this!" Cindy said.

"Counsel for the defense will get back to the point," Wilhelm said.

"Defense moves for dismissal of all charges, Your Honor," Sorenson said.

Wilhelm rolled his eyes. "On what grounds?"

"The State witness' testimony has revealed that he was *not* walking in front of Mrs. Parker's house, but *was* in fact *driving*, and that he came to her house armed with a Glock pistol-"

"Inconclusive. Denied," Wilhelm said.

"And that he was definitely aided and possibly instructed in these actions by Mrs. Stalls, who is representing the State-"

"You put words in his mouth!" Cindy said.

"Counsel is *speculating*," Wilhelm said, stressing the last word.

Cindy caught on. "Objection! Speculation!"

"Sustained," Wilhelm said.

"Your Honor, State's counsel has been implicated through testimony. The State's witness has changed his story from his initial statement. There's no way this trial can move forward," Sorenson held out his hands. "Be reasonable-"

"The mere fact that I'm even *having* this trial shows I'm being reasonable," Wilhelm said. "Does counsel have any more questions for the witness?"

"I have plenty of questions, Your Honor, like when did Mrs. Stalls first contact him about going to Mrs. Parker's house-"

"The court acknowledges that counsel for the defense has no more *relevant* questions for the witness," Wilhelm said. "The witness may step down."

There was no podium, no witness box. Jack looked around in confusion. "Step down from where? I'm sittin'."

Wilhelm sighed. "It means you're finished testifying. Chief Stalls, please escort the witness to a waiting room."

And so it went.

Frank Stalls, for his part, didn't outright lie during his testimony. He gave a heavily-overblown rendition of the facts, in Dotty's opinion, but he didn't make anything up. At one point, they brought Jack back in and had him remove his shirt so the judge—meaning, the crowd—could fully see his wounds. Cindy did her best to imply that the pattern of the shot was indicative of someone aiming for Jack's head. When Sorenson pointed out that the majority of the shot was centered on his lower back, Cindy argued that the shotgun was probably too heavy for Dotty to keep pointing in an upward angle. Sorenson pointed out Dotty's relative fitness, and how she'd regularly lifted gallons of paint and heavy tools at the hardware store earlier in the year. The crowd murmured their disagreements here and there during the trial. To Dotty, it seemed that Wilhelm's plan of getting the town to go along with his and Cindy's version of events wasn't working quite the way he planned.

In the end, to no one's surprise, Wilhelm found her guilty of all three charges.

"When would you like to set the date for the sentencing, Your Honor?" Sorenson asked, flipping through his planner.

"I'll set the sentencing right now," Wilhelm said.

"Your Honor, the Defense requests time-"

"Sit down, counsel, before I find you in contempt."

Sorenson's hands were fists when Dotty pulled on his suit sleeve.

"This makes a kangaroo court look like SCOTUS," he muttered as he slipped back into his chair.

The "State" wanted maximum penalties awarded for all of the charges, served consecutively. Cindy actually read from a piece of paper as she requested this. Dotty wondered if those notes were scrawled in Wilhelm's handwriting.

Consecutive sentences meant that Dotty could not file for parole on a particular sentence until all the other sentences were satisfied. With the very first one being life in prison, that meant she'd never see parole.

Wilhelm accepted the State's recommendation and gave her the maximum penalty for all three charges.

Dotty couldn't think. She felt frozen in place. She stared at Wilhelm without really seeing him. The paper he held in his hand while he read the sentencing was in sharp focus, and everything around it seemed blurred out. There was a strange low tone buzzing in her ear, but it was background noise.

The boys. She might never see the boys again. She'd never get to hold her daughter and tell her how proud her mama was for all that she'd sacrificed to see that her children had a good, safe life away from the streets of Baltimore. There'd be no more sitting on the porch swing and drinking a cool glass of iced tea on a warm summer evening. No more talking about the most inconsequential things with Bill, that often turned out to be the most important things of all.

Just a cold cell. Years of cinder block walls and isolation. *All* of the years that were left to her.

It was so incomprehensible. It didn't seem real.

Something squeezed her shoulder and that low buzz repeated. In a daze, she turned her head to see what in the world it could be.

A hand. It was a man's hand. Confused, her gaze followed the hand to its arm, and up to its shoulder.

Sorenson had taken hold of her shoulder, and he was talking intensely to someone else, not looking at her. His other hand was gesturing at the papers in front of him and at her.

She blinked a few times, and tried to focus. The buzz turned into words. It still took a few moments more for her to understand them.

"-Absolutely ridiculous, Your Honor. State law requires at least thirty days so that an appeal may be filed. There are personal papers and affairs to be put to order. This is nothing short of outright murder!"

Dotty blinked again. She didn't understand. Was Sorenson saying she'd committed murder?

Wilhelm sighed. "We simply don't have the resources to incarcerate a criminal-"

"The Governor himself ordered all criminals, even felonious murderers, to be set free, Your Honor," Sorenson said.

"And that was done," Wilhelm said. "This is a *new* case. The Governor's pardon does not apply."

Sorenson released her shoulder and held out his hands in placation. "At the very least, give us twenty-four hours. So that she might visit with her family and say goodbye. *Please*, Your Honor. Show mercy."

The crowd's murmuring rose to a swell.

"Show mercy!" A woman cried out.

"This ain't right!" Said a deep voice.

"She tried to kill the kid! She doesn't deserve any mercy!" Yelled another woman.

"Even prisoners on Death Row get more than twenty-four hours!" Called out a third woman.

Wilhelm scowled at the crowd and looked over to Cindy. Dotty looked, too. What in the world were they arguing about? Letting her see her family before she was sent away?

Cindy shook her head. "In twenty-four hours *Michael* will be here." She raised her eyebrows and made a *move along* motion with her hand.

Sorenson spoke again. "Your Honor, do you want to be known as the Civil Officer who sentenced an old Black woman to death and immediately executed her? That harkens back to the days of mobs and lynchings! What do you think they'll think of that in Annapolis, and in D.C.? They'll never let you near Congress with that on your record."

Executed? What?

"That's a career-killer right there," called a member of the crowd.

Wilhelm glared at Sorenson.

"Your Honor, it's best that this be done immediately, so as to set an example to anyone else who might try to use these same tactics to rise up against the City-" Cindy started.

"We'll hold the execution by firing squad at first light on Monday, assuming the weather's clear," Wilhelm said. "That gives you at least twenty-four hours to seek an emergency appeal from the Governor or to get her affairs in order."

"Execution?" Dotty echoed. Her voice came as barely a whisper.

"Delaying this will only encourage other troublemakers-" Cindy started.

"My ruling is final!" Wilhelm barked at her, and slammed his fist on the table. "Court is adjourned! Chief Stalls, take the prisoner back to her cell." He stood up and stomped from the room.

Dotty turned back to Sorenson. He was still standing, looking down at her with a stricken expression.

"I'm so very sorry, Mrs. Parker," he said softly. "I'll do the best I can. I'll try to get to Annapolis tonight, myself."

"I'm being executed?" Dotty asked. "I didn't...I didn't understand that last bit."

"Stand up please, Mrs. Parker," Frank said from behind her.

Sorenson's face softened and she saw pity there. "The City has nowhere to keep a criminal long-term, so Judge Wilhelm has sentenced you to die by firing squad. Monday morning."

"No," Dotty said. "No, that can't be true. He said life sentence. That means I live out my life in jail-"

"Let's go, Mrs. Parker," Frank said, pulling her chair out from the table. Stella stepped beside her and tugged at her arm.

"I'll try my best, I promise I will," Sorenson said. "I'll pool together all the fuel I can find and leave for Annapolis as soon as I can."

"Firing squad?" This couldn't be happening. She was going to die? In less than two days?

Sorenson nodded.

"Okay, we'll do this the hard way," Frank said, and grabbed the zip-tie between her wrists. He lifted, and she came up out of the chair with her wrists on fire and her feet dangling.She caught a glimpse of Cindy standing to the side watching, her face smug.

Everything snapped into clarity.

She'd been railroaded far further than any of them had

imagined could happen. They weren't just going to remove her, they were going to kill her.

And she'd bet every minute of life she had left to live that after she was taken care of, they'd go for the rest of the family.

"Bishop, tell Seth Miller to take the boys," she said, struggling as Frank dropped her on her feet and started yanking her around by her plastic cuffs. She twisted around and yelled at Sorenson. "He's the closest thing they've got to a father. Tell him I said to take everyone and *leave*, now! Now! Don't wait!"

Sorenson was nodding. "I will. I will."

"She'll come for them!" Dotty called. Frank was practically dragging her down the aisle between the cafeteria benches.Stella followed close behind. "Tell them to get out now!"

Frank slammed through the cafeteria doors and pulled her into the hallway. The doors swung shut with a bang, and he wrapped his arms around her torso and lifted her from the floor.

She struggled, but he was far stronger and taller. He held her in a vice grip all the way back through the gymnasium, past the offices and classrooms-turned-residences, and to the restroom jail.

He dropped her inside and slammed the door shut, and she heard the pin slide into place.

And only then, crumpled on the floor in rage and heartbreak, did she realize she hadn't told Sorenson to tell her family how very much she loved them.

PREACHER

Preacher leaned against one of the brick columns outside the front doors of the Rec Center. He was still under the portico, but it didn't matter. He was soaked through. The rain had been pouring steadily since they'd arrived, and the wind had blown it under the portico and around the columns.

They'd been inside the lobby, for a while. They'd arrived early for the supposed "trial" with all of the supporters that Father Bill had been able to round up trickling in behind them. They'd filled the place.

All of the inmates were there. A plump little woman Father Bill introduced as Betty immediately set about managing people and getting the crowd to make room as others came through the door. A large white man and a much smaller, very pregnant Black woman were there; Ripley hugged and talked with them for a long time. They'd brought two little girls along, who clung to their parents and looked big-eyed at all of the strangers. Most of the neighbors from Dotty's street that had been at the bonfire showed up. Some others came that Bill welcomed warmly and thanked for coming, but Preacher had never seen them before.

Bill must have nearly worn the tires off of his bicycle alerting all of these people. A modern-day Paul Revere.

Sheriff Kane was missing. Preacher hadn't seen him since he and a little man named Fish had taken him home to Dotty's last night. When Preacher had asked Father Bill if he'd seen the Sheriff, Bill had just nodded and said not to worry.

Preacher *was* worried. He'd tossed a few ideas the Sheriff's way, and he wanted to know if the Sheriff had worked out any of the logistics. Plus, it might be useful to have him here with all of the city "police" looking so damn nervous.

No one that had come in support of Dotty had been permitted to sit in on the trial. Too disruptive, the goons with the guns told them. Too dangerous. Anyone in the crowd could be armed and there were no metal detectors now that the Guard had left.. Patting everyone down by hand would take too much time, and the only one of them trained to do it properly was inside the "courtroom".

When four o'clock had come and gone without even Corey and Thomas being permitted to observe the proceedings, the crowd had gotten indignant enough and loud enough that the goons had forced them outside into the rain. Then they'd stood in a line inside the double sets of doors, holding their personal shotguns and rifles like riot police.

Nice and safe and dry behind those glass doors. It made Preacher's blood boil.

The big guy, who looked like a farmer in his worn ball cap and faded overalls, took his girls to his truck and brought back a rain poncho. He slipped it over his little wife and it nearly brushed the ground. He'd tried to get her to sit in the truck too, but she refused.

The inmates formed a line at the back of the crowd, almost

mirroring the goons inside. They had no guns, though. Some members of the crowd tried to get them to come in closer, where there was more protection from the rain, but they politely declined.

The rain had finally tapered off to a light drizzle, so now he was able to hear what people were saying without being right next to them.

Thomas paced in front of the door and checked his watch. "It's nearly five," he said. "You think they've finished and they're just not telling us?"

"If they were finished, Bishop Sorenson would let us know," Seth said. He was busy holding up his own brick column on the other side of the portico. "How about you come over here and stand? You're probably making the guys inside nervous."

"Let 'em be nervous," Thomas said. He turned and glared at the goons. "I've gone into burning buildings beside some of you, and this is what I get? This is how you let me be treated?"

"Thomas," Lily came forward and reached for him. "Come on-"

"No!" he yelled, pulling away from her. He kept eye contact with the men inside, banging his hand on the outer door. "You make me stand out here while my Grams is in there being tried for attempted murder? How many casseroles has she brought to the firehouse? Huh? And you just let us be treated like this? One of you? One of your brothers? Screw you! Screw all of you!"

He was beating the door so hard it rattled in its frame. A few of the guys inside turned their heads, suddenly fascinated with the ground next to their feet.

"Cowards!" Thomas yelled. "You're all cowards!"

"You're not helping her, Thomas," Lily tried again. Thomas spun on her, wild-eyed. Tears tracked down his face.

"What else can I do Mrs. Miller? Tell me what to do! They

won't let me in there to see her!" He spun and slammed his fist against the glass again.

Corey stepped forward and grabbed his brother's hand, pulling him into a fierce hug. They stood like that, rocking a little, with Thomas sobbing into Corey's shoulder and Corey making shushing sounds.

My fault. This is my fault. I came into this family and tore it apart.

All Preacher had wanted was a slim second chance. Something to prove to himself that he wasn't a monster, that he could be a good man.

Dotty had made sure to tell him every day that he was a good man. She'd thanked him for every little thing he'd done.

When he'd shot that thief in her backyard, she'd hugged him and thanked him for that, too. And just before she'd finally gone back to bed, she'd told him he'd done the right thing.

His fingers curled into fists. He'd let her down. He should've been there when the goons came the next day. He should've been the one to confess. He should be the one sitting in there now in front of the judge, not her.

She didn't deserve this. The kids didn't deserve this. And there was no way he could see that he could ever make up for it, even if Dotty was somehow allowed to walk free.

The Sheriff's car pulled into the parking lot and wove around the traffic cones the Guard had left behind. It came to a stop at the end of the walkway, and the Sheriff and Fish got out.

Sheriff Kane was in his full dark grey dress uniform, including his wide-brimmed hat with the red cord on it. Fish was wearing a uniform Preacher was intimately familiar with: that of a Federal Prison guard.

The crowd parted for them and they walked clear up to the doors without a word being said.

"They've locked them," Preacher said just before the Sheriff reached for the handle.

The Sheriff stopped, spread his feet a bit, and crossed his arms. He stared at the men inside. They all started fidgeting.

Beside the Sheriff, Fish put his hands behind his back and stood at parade rest. They looked like they could stand there all day.

Father Bill wove his way through the crowd and turned to lean his back to the entryway. "I was starting to worry," he said, keeping his voice low.

Fish spoke without looking away from the men inside. "Preparations took a little longer than we expected."

"Everything's ready, then?" Bill asked.

The Sheriff gave a tiny, sharp nod. Bill sighed in relief and then spoke. "Let's hope we don't need it."

Preacher had no idea what they had planned. Bill had told him earlier that the further he was away from this, the better. Bill had also wanted him to stay at the house, but there was no way in hell that was happening. The consensus had been that Mel should stay there too, to reduce the risk of someone recognizing her. She'd told them all to just try making her stay; they'd be bleeding by the time she was done. The two of them had walked up here side-by-side.

Preacher looked over the crowd and found Marco. The young man met his eyes and gave a little nod. He'd spent most of the day out by the shed, cooking up something noxious on the Miller's fire pit that he'd dragged back there. When he wasn't stirring the concoction with a rag tied over his mouth and nose, he'd been sitting nearby pounding charred wood into powder.

Preacher liked him, even though Marco had ordered him around earlier as if he didn't expect to be questioned. There hadn't been any insult in it, just efficiency. Preacher could respect that.

"Someone's coming," Ripley said, and everyone's head turned.

The goon squad in the lobby parted, and Frank Stalls escorted Bishop Sorenson to the double doors. He unlocked the first set, and stood in the vestibule for a moment looking over the assembled crowd. Frowning, he took a deep breath, unlocked the outer set, and pushed one open.

The Sheriff didn't wait. "Has she been convicted?"

Frank turned to the side and leaned to keep the door open as Sorenson went by. "Yes, on all three charges. Her attorney will give you all the information-"

"Then I'm here to pick up my prisoner," the Sheriff said.

Preacher could have cheered.

"Your *what*?" Frank helped Sorenson's rolling case over the frame with his foot and straightened to block the doorway.

"She's been convicted of a felony. She's now a federal prisoner. I'm here to escort her to the prison," Kane said.

"No you're not," Frank said. "She's not going anywhere."

"I'm acting Warden of the federal prison. My guard and I are here to safely take the prisoner into custody, as is required by law."

Frank snorted. "So you can take her back to her house and act like nothing's happened? I don't think so, Simon."

"Her cell's been prepared and ready. Guards have been assigned shifts. We're fully prepared to carry out our responsibility *as is required by law*," Simon said, stressing that last bit.

"Let's pretend for a minute that I believe you, that you've actually talked a couple of your old buddies to pony up and go back to work. We both know it's total bullshit, but let's pretend," Frank said. "It was all for nothing. She's not going to prison. She's not getting released. She's going to stay here, in *our* custody, until her sentence is carried out."

The Sheriff cocked his head. "What do you mean, carried out?"

Frank shook his head. "Like I said, her attorney will give you the details. Now if you'll excuse me?" He started to pull the door shut.

"Frank," Simon said, "This isn't small-town stuff anymore. The moment an elected judge convicts a suspect of attempted murder, it becomes a federal matter. You're messing with *federal* laws, here. You sure you want to do this? Or do you want to stand on the right side of the law and release the prisoner into my custody?"

"Simon, take your bullshit and shove it up your ass," Frank said. "You're not impressing anyone, and you're not getting your hands on *my* prisoner. You and all these people have five minutes to get the hell off of this property."

He pulled the door shut and locked it, turned, and disappeared back through his line of men.

"Bishop?" Bill asked.

Sorenson looked out over the crowd. Preacher didn't like the expression on his face.

"If any of you have *any* fuel at all, I need it," he said. "I need enough gas to get to Annapolis and back, as fast as I can do it."

The big farmer spoke up. "What for?"

"Because Mrs. Parker has been sentenced to be executed at the first opportunity Monday morning-"

"*Executed?*" Multiple voices cried out. Everyone started shouting questions.

"Please, *please!*" Sorenson yelled.

"*QUIET,*" Preacher and Simon boomed.

Sorenson spoke quickly into the silence. "Time is of the essence. I need all of you, please, to go get any fuel you have and bring it back here so I can leave immediately. Meanwhile I'll relay as much info as I can to Mrs. Parker's family, and they can pass it on after I've left."

"But what do you mean, executed?" Corey asked.

"I've got the fuel, and I've got a four-wheel drive," the big farmer said. "I'll take you."

Sorenson shook his head. "I can't ask you to go with me-"

"Have you ever driven through an occupied city, sir?" He didn't wait for an answer. "I have. You'll be going through the equivalent of war zones, and you need someone with experience and a gun."

"Are you sure, John, Charlotte?" Father Bill asked. He gestured to the man's little wife. "That's a big risk."

Charlotte lifted her chin. "He knows what he's risking, Father. And I support him in it. If he says he'll get the Bishop there and back, that's what he'll do. There's no one better."

"Then I appreciate it," Sorenson said. "She's got very little time."

"Dotty would do whatever she could to help us," Charlotte said. "We'll do the same."

"John, let me speak to you a minute before you go," the Sheriff said, and when the big man nodded, he lifted his hands and spoke up. "Everyone else, start clearing out. Let's give the family some privacy and get off the property. We don't want more arrests."

The crowd, with the exception of the family and the inmates, started drifting off. The Sheriff murmured something into Father Bill's ear, then walked with John to the back of his car.

"Someone tell me what the hell is going on!" Corey said. "Executed? This is a joke, right? This has to be a joke."

"I'm sorry son," Sorenson said, and seemed to sag as if the tension of finding fuel had been the only thing keeping him upright.

"Don't panic," Father Bill told Corey. "We'll figure something out. The Bishop will ask for a pardon, and given the circumstances, I'm sure he'll get one."

"Folks, we need to move out to the end of the parking lot, at least," Fish said. "The City has sent us a clear message that they're not playing. Let's not tempt fate."

"If someone doesn't start talking-" Thomas shouted, and Bishop Sorenson took him by the arm. "Thomas, Corey, walk with me," he said. "Mr. Miller, you too, please." The four of them moved off, with Father Bill following behind, pulling Sorenson's case.

"This can't be happening," Mel said, her voice soft. "He told us 'life sentence'."

"C'mon honey, let's let them talk," Lily said, wrapping an arm around Mel's shoulders. "And let's move, like they said. Imagine how upset Dotty would be if one of us ended up in there with her."

She put her other arm around Ripley and the ladies moved off. The inmates drifted about halfway down the parking lot and stopped, waiting for the Sheriff to tell them what to do. Preacher watched the Sheriff hand John something from his trunk that looked like a clear plastic case. Then some kind of clothing...a shirt? He couldn't tell.

It didn't matter. The likelihood of getting a pardon was slim. The likelihood of returning from Annapolis in time was slimmer. As if to underscore the implausibility of that idea, the drizzling rain turned into a downpour.

Preacher looked back at Fish, whose face was grim.

"Tell me we've got a backup plan," Preacher said.

"Something involving explosives," Marco added.

Fish raised his eyebrows at Marco. "Explosives might be nice. You know where we can get some of those?"

Marco and Preacher looked at each other and smiled.

PREACHER

Preacher sat on the couch in the Miller's house, with Jax sitting on the floor between his knees and her head in his lap. He rubbed her behind the ears and tried not to look at anyone.

Ripley sat on the floor on the other end of the couch, next to the cast iron stove, curled around King. Across the coffee table, Mel was curled up with her arms around her knees in an overstuffed chair. Marco sat next to her in a matching chair, leaned forward with his elbows on his knees and his thumb tapping a staccato beat on his wrist.

Here in the living room, it was quiet. There was plenty of conversation coming from other parts of the house, though. Seth and Lily were upstairs, arguing. They were trying to do it quietly, but it wasn't working. The hard rain just wasn't enough to mask the more intense parts of their debate.

Seth wanted to pack everyone up and leave, like Dotty had asked them to. He agreed with her, that Cindy would be coming back. He didn't want to be here when Frank and the goons showed up again. Lily was hesitant. While Seth was fired up to just throw everything and everyone into his truck and drive as far as the gas tank would get them, Lily wanted a destination. Going off into the wild without a plan was stupid, she argued. It might just get them killed.

Preacher agreed with them both. And with Dotty laying the safety of Corey and Thomas at Seth's feet, it made both sides of the decision that much harder.

He couldn't escape the guilt he felt about that. About all of this.

In the kitchen, Father Bill talked low with Corey and Thomas. The emotions back there had ranged from despair to rage and back again.

"Christ, I could use a cigarette," Mel muttered. Then she sat up and put her feet down in one quick motion. Everyone else jumped at the movement.

"Cigarettes!" Mel said, and dashed from her chair, streaked across the room, and pounded up the stairs.

They looked at each other, wide-eyed.

"I thought she ran out of those a long time ago," Ripley said. Her voice was hoarse from crying.

"She did," Marco said. "I've been looking for more for her, but haven't found any."

Thumps and footsteps sounded overhead. Then a cry of triumph. Heads swung to the stairs as Mel came pounding back down, holding up a small piece of paper. It looked like a business card.

She slid to a stop in front of Marco and thrust it at him.

"Get me a radio," she said. "You had to have seen a radio in one of those houses."

Marco took the card, confused, and his face fell when he turned it over.

"Melanie," his voice was soft. "This takes a special kind of radio."

"Then find one!" she said. "I'll call Agent Perkins, and he can come down here and stop this."

"HAM radios are rare," Marco said. "I haven't even seen *one*. If I had, I'd have brought it home and found a way to power it up."

"I don't want to hear that, Romeo. You go out, and you find me one." She jabbed a finger at the card.

What the hell is on that card? Preacher thought.

"You can't call Perkins," Ripley said. "If he comes here, he'll take you back to the bunker with the rest of the Senators and families."

"I don't care!" Mel cried, her voice breaking. "If it keeps Grams alive, I don't care! I'll go. I'll put up with my bitch whore of a mother and I'll be happy about it, knowing that Grams is still here and she's safe!"

"If we had a HAM radio, I might be able to get in touch with someone in Norfolk," Corey said from the doorway. "Maybe even contact the base directly. Tell Mom what's going on. Maybe she could stop this." Thomas stood behind him.

"She likely couldn't get here in time, and she'd probably get hurt trying," Bill said from the kitchen.

"She's in the military. They've got all the fuel they need. She's got more of a chance of getting here in time than the Bishop does," Thomas argued.

"Across the mouth of the Bay?" Ripley said. "That guy Marco talked to said the bridge-tunnel was flooded."

"The Navy has boats," Thomas started, but Bill cut him off.

"There's nothing anyone in the Navy can do, Thomas. They have no jurisdiction. And your mother's a nurse, she's not even military police."

"There's got to be *something* we can do," Thomas said. "At

least we can friggin' *try*, instead of just sitting here. The longer we sit here the closer we get to Grams dying!"

"There is something we can do," Preacher said.

Everyone looked at him, and he wished he hadn't said anything. Not yet, anyway. Across the coffee table, Marco gave him a stern look and a barely perceptible shake of his head.

"Well?" Thomas said, stalking towards Preacher. "Speak up! You got us into all this shit, the least you can do is offer up some kind of suggestion."

"That's not fair," Bill said, stepping into the room. "This isn't David's fault."

"Yes, it is," Preacher said.

"Damn right it is," Thomas said, standing over him now. Preacher gave Jax one last pat on the head and pushed her away.

"You wanna give me payback for that?" Preacher asked, sitting up straight.

"Damn right I do."

Preacher nodded, and stood. Thomas, unlike Corey, was average height. But he was built wide, like a football player, and packed with muscle. This would probably hurt.

Preacher stepped out away from the couch and the very breakable coffee table and checked that nothing was behind him. He looked back at Thomas and nodded.

"Go ahead."

The elder brother didn't hesitate. His fist hit Preacher's jaw like a hammer.

"Holy shit! Thomas, stop!" Ripley said. She scrambled up from her spot on the floor.

Preacher straightened his head and wiggled his jaw a bit. It was a nice punch. A straight, quick jab. No telegraphing it with a wide arc. Preacher nodded and met eyes with Thomas.

"Again?" Preacher asked.

The blow came from the other side. Just as quick, just as hard. Then another. And another. Everyone was yelling. Preacher just took the hits, his head rocking a bit with each blow.

At least he's alternating sides, he thought.

Ripley latched onto Thomas' arm, dragging him back. The next swing missed. Marco dove from the chair and Thomas went down, crashing onto the floor with Marco wrapped around his hips. Footsteps thundered down the stairs and suddenly Seth was in front of him, yelling for everyone to stop.

"Enough! Enough!" Seth shouted, holding his hands out. "We can't do this. I know everyone's angry, and we're all upset, but we can't take it out on each other."

"It's *his* fault," Thomas snarled, struggling to get free. Marco had crawled up his body and had him in some complicated, twisted mess. Thomas couldn't move.

"No, it's not," Seth said.

"It is," Preacher said, and rubbed at his jaw. It was going to be sore.

"No, it's *not*," Seth repeated, pointing a finger at him and raising his eyebrows in a way that practically dared Preacher to argue with him.

"If he didn't-" Thomas started, but Lily's voice rang out.

"It's Cathy's fault!" she shouted. When no one spoke, she leaned over the railing and pointed to the front door. "That bitch stood right at that door, on *my* porch, and demanded Dotty let her in. And when Dotty didn't, she got mad, and she went to Cindy. *She* brought the City down on us. *She* reported the historical violations. *She* fed Cindy Stalls all of the information. *She's* the one responsible for this. Not anyone in this family."

Everyone was staring up at her. Preacher had turned to look, too.

Lily swung that finger to point at him. "And when I say *family,* that includes *you*. So quit acting like a dumbass. You're no one's punching bag. You hear me?"

Preacher blinked. "Yes ma'am."

"You'd better. Thomas Winters, do you hear me? He's not your enemy."

"Yes Miss Lily," Thomas said.

"Good," Seth said, and let out a breath. "Good. Now let's sit down, and try to figure out what we're going to do."

A deep voice boomed from the other side of the door. "Well if you'd stop yelling and answer the door, I might could help with that."

SIMON

Simon's footsteps echoed down the empty halls. It was strange being back in the prison, with wide open doors and dark corridors. It was even stranger hearing the laughter coming from the men's wing. The previous tenants didn't laugh much.

He stepped into the space and took it in. Thomas Winters clung to the underside of the metal stairs, doing pull-ups while Preacher watched. His brother Corey sat at one of the few octagonal bench tables in the general area, loading bullets into magazines next to a row of police-issued rifles and pistols, and tossing harmless insults Thomas' way. Far off in the corner, the strange and quiet Marco fellow dipped twine into candle wax, laying the stiffened strands out next to assembled pipe bombs. Coleman lanterns lit both of the tables in use, and provided enough light that Simon could have turned off his headlamp, if his arms weren't full.

"Here we go," he said, dropping his armload of vests onto an empty table. He thumbed the button for his headlamp, then fished a larger vest out of the pile and slid it to the side. "This one's for you, Preacher. It's my backup, so it should fit you."

The big convict straightened and walked over, lifting the body armor and rapping his knuckles on the front. He held it up to his chest and made a face.

"It says *POLICE*," he said.

"They all do. Everyone going with me's getting deputized," Simon answered.

Thomas walked over, wiping sweat from his face with the bottom of his tank top. He dropped the shirt and reached for the vests. "If I put one of these on, you'll let me go?"

"Hell no," Simon said, smacking the young man's hand away. "You, your brother, and the girls stay here. We've been over this."

"It's bullshit. That's *my* grandmother in there," Thomas said.

Corey spoke up from his table. "Drop it, Tom. You know Grams would kill everyone involved if we went over there, even if we came out without a scratch."

"Dotty's main concern was that you kids were safe," Simon said. "We don't know if we'll be able to get her out alive, much less ourselves. I'm not risking you."

"That's what I'm for," Preacher said, dropping his oversized vest on a different table. He jabbed a thumb into his chest. "Expendable."

Corey snorted. "If you think you ain't getting an ass-whooping, you've got another thing coming. Grams gets out of there, she'll string you up right next to the rest of us."

Preacher shrugged. "I'll risk it." He pointed down to the vests. "What's in those?"

"Kevlar vest, polyethylene plates," Simon said. "Should stop most of what they'll be throwing at us."

"I saw shotguns," Marco called out from his seat. "They might have slugs. And those ARs will be packing a punch."

Simon shrugged. "All our guards here had to worry about were knives and maybe handgun rounds if the inmates acquired a weapon. Either way, this is what we've got. It's better than nothing."

Marco frowned, but nodded.

Simon looked around at the empty cells and blew out a breath. Back when he'd pulled the New Home inmates out, he'd thought it might come to this. Either the Mayor's team, or a posse of convicts from another county; either one would seek to take control. The convicts had been his back-up plan. Bringing any civilians into it had never been part of that. Now Father Bill was insisting on coming, and Marco had told him flat-out that either he came along as part of the team or he'd follow behind them. And since neither of them were Dotty's family, all of his words that kept the others sullenly compliant just bounced off the two of them.

"I'm supposed to tell you that the ladies need more victims," Simon said. "They're playing poker, and my mother's just about wiped everyone clean. Fish was holding his own when I passed through, but it's a near thing."

The single men were over here in one of the pods in the men's wing, while the women and families were in the women's wing. The guys had decided this on their own, figuring it would ease everyone's mind. Honestly, Simon thought Preacher had a lot to do with it. He'd headed straight for his old cell when they'd moved the family in, and the guys had just kinda followed along. Now all the "war talk" and activities were happening here, while in the women's wing Charlotte's little girls were running around and the cutthroat game of poker was taking place. Two entirely different atmospheres.

"Penny ante?" Corey asked.

Simon shook his head. "Tongue depressors from the infirmary.

It's the only thing they could find in bulk that didn't have an immediate use."

"Our people. How much longer?" Preacher asked.

"Should be any time now," Simon said. "The wind's really picking up outside. We're in heavy tropical storm conditions, it looks like. The full hurricane will probably be here in a few hours."

"Are any of them former military?" Marco asked. "If not, I'll need enough time to run the group through some basic communication and movement drills."

"You'll need to do it regardless of their status," Simon said. "Just so we're all on the same page."

"I appreciate you letting me take the lead on that, Sheriff," Marco said.

Simon shrugged. "I'm guessing your training is a lot more recent than mine. No skin off my nose."

Footsteps echoed in the hall, and two of the New Home men came through the block's doorway carrying duffel bags wrapped in big trash bags. A few days ago, with new growths of hair and civilian clothing, they'd looked like any other town resident. With dripping wet hair plastered to their skulls, wearing wet tank tops with all of their tattoos showing, they looked every bit the hardened convicts that they were. The men looked around the block with frowns.

"When they said y'all were in the men's wing, I kinda figured I'd be back in my old block," Trench said.

"You can bunk there if you want to, but I'd *prefer* that you all stick together. Get to know each other," Simon said. "The only thing off-limits is the ICE wing. I'll probably have to burn the mattresses in there."

The prison had been one of only two in Maryland that housed illegal immigrants being held for trial and deportation. Most of them came through the door with viruses and lice. Even though they each got a full medical examination and treatment on their intake day, lice took multiple treatments to get rid of. Being that the ICE detainees were "temporary" residents and the prison couldn't shave their heads like they did for their long-term inmates, killing the lice and the eggs was an unending battle. They'd never been able to keep ahead of it when he'd been Warden.

Bringing the families here as a fortified shelter was meant to help protect them from both the storm and Frank's so-called police force. However long they ended up staying, even with each family bringing what food they had and Charlotte's seemingly endless supply of canned chicken, they'd have enough problems keeping everyone fed and setting up better toiletry facilities outside. They didn't need to be dealing with lice, too. He was keeping that cell block locked tight.

More footsteps echoed down the hallway, and Simon gestured at the cells. "Sounds like the others are coming. Best get yourselves settled in." He pointed at Marco. "That's Marco. He needs to see everyone once we're ready to get started. Let everyone know."

Trench cast a look over his shoulder and back, nodding. "Yessir, Warden." He dropped his duffel by the door and held up a fist. Another wet, tattooed arm reached out of the darkness to bump it. Two more men stepped into the pod.

"None of that," Simon said. "Anyone over there hears you call me Warden, they'll catch on pretty quick."

Mumbled agreements from the growing crowd at the doorway made him sigh. He couldn't expect them to change year-long habits overnight.

Father Bill made his way through the human block, shaking hands and greeting each man as he passed. Against one shoulder he carried something long, wrapped in a poncho.

"Sheriff," he said, stepping up and shaking Simon's hand. "I brought Nurse Macy and the doctors Butcher. They've gone to see the infirmary, but I'm sure they'll swing by to say hello. Thank you for offering us this shelter."

"Only makes sense," Simon said. He pointed at the long bundle. "What you got there?"

Bill smiled and patted the poncho. "This is my *other* girl," he said. "She's been with me probably about as long as you've been alive. Where can I lay her out and freshen her up?"

Simon pointed to Corey's table. "Anywhere, really, but all the gun cleaning stuff's over there." He laid a hand on Bill's shoulder. "Father, once you get a minute-"

Bill gave him a kind smile. "Having doubts?"

"Those are townspeople over there," Simon said. "And from what we've learned, they've got no choice."

Bill's face grew serious. "We'll try our best not to engage. But Simon, each of those people *do* have a choice. They might not like the choices, but those choices exist. It's not like they're facing death if they don't go along with Frank's orders; they'll just have a harder time. And if they fire at us, it's pretty clear where their priorities lie."

Simon rubbed a hand over his face. "You sure I'm not just as bad as Frank? As Wilhelm? I could be sending people to their deaths."

Bill lowered his bundle down so it rested on top of his foot, and leaned a hand over the top of it. He flicked his fingers in the direction of the former convicts, who were poking through cells now, deciding where they were going to bunk up.

"If any of these men said they didn't want to go with us tonight, would you make them?" Bill asked.

Simon frowned. "It's what they signed up for when we offered them the New Home deal."

"But would you *make* them?" Bill propped his chin on top of his—well, Simon could only assume it was some sort of long rifle—and raised his eyebrows.

Simon took a deep breath and sighed. "No," he admitted. "But they'd still be helping. I'd find something else for them to do. Guard the front doors. Get up on the roof and cover our return."

Bill smiled and he reached up to pat Simon's shoulder. "Mmhm. Don't worry, Simon. You're nothing like Frank Stalls and Kenny Wilhelm. Now, I've got some preparations to make." He hefted his bundle back to his shoulder and clapped Simon's arm.

Simon watched the little man cross to Corey's table and start unwrapping what turned out to be a beautiful antique sniper's rifle.

"I sure hope you're right," he muttered to himself. People were going to die tonight, and if he had anything to do with it, Mayor Wilhelm would be one of them. Ultimately though, he just hoped they could get Dotty out alive.

A lawman arming and leading lawless men to rescue an innocent woman from a tyrant. You couldn't make this stuff up.

Forget doubting my morality; it's my sanity I should be worried about, he thought.

Shaking his head, he crossed to Corey's table and picked up one of the weapons from the prison's armory.

"All right, gentlemen," he said. "Who has experience with a rifle?"

DOTTY

Dotty had spent a long time after the trial wallowing in her grief. Frank had come in and taken off her plastic cuffs, and was going to give her another MRE for dinner, until he saw her unopened one on the cot.

"Not even grateful enough to use what you've been given," he said, and lightning crackled in a shocking clap.

It got her attention.

Frank left the room and locked her in, and she sat there, sure someone was trying to tell her something.

Use what you've been given.

To do what? To fight her way out of here? To maybe break out?

But what had she been given? She looked around the room, at a loss. The bottle of water? The MRE?

She tore it open in a frenzy. Soft lined packets, a chemical reaction pack, a piece of hard candy and a plastic spork. What could she do with a spork? She wasn't sure she was up to stabbing someone, and even if she did work up the nerve, the darn thing probably wasn't sharp enough.

The grout between the floor tiles was rough and she tried sanding the handle against it, but mostly it just scratched the plastic and made it look chewed-on. Applying more pressure might help, but she was afraid to break it.

Okay, so maybe that wasn't what she'd been given.

Think, Dorothy. Think. Use your head.

And then she started smiling. *That* was what she was supposed to use: her head.

She'd been given this life and this intelligence, and if she just sat here and let these vile people take that away from her without trying to protect those gifts, she wouldn't be showing God how grateful she was for them.

So she focused on her goals: either break out, or be able to fight when they came for her. Focusing on the goal first and working her way backwards had always worked best for her; it kept her from getting tunnel vision. Tunnel vision like trying to figure out how she could use a spork, when what she needed to do was find *any* way to fight or break out.

Fighting was a last resort, as she never saw any of *them* without their guns and she was so much smaller than they. Breaking out was a more likely option.

There was a short, very wide window high in the wall at the end of the stalls. It was far too tall for her to reach even when jumping, and it didn't open anyway. It was just to let in light. It looked to be some sort of hammered glass; probably to obstruct vision. But if she could figure out a way to break it, and a way to get up to it, she was pretty sure she could fit through it.

Each stall had a toilet, a flat stainless steel panel set into the wall behind it with a camera to tell it when to flush, a couple of tube handlebars on either side of the stall, and toilet paper dispensers. The toilet's seat was a flimsy plastic that wouldn't do her any good; it would likely shatter if she hit the window with it. The bars, though...those looked pretty sturdy.

She tried unscrewing one of the bars with the end of the spork. It didn't work. She took off Bill's socks and climbed up on the bars, and pulled herself up to peek over the top of the stall. It was skinny and wobbled a bit under her weight, but if she could get up here, she could possibly jump down onto someone. She filed that under *Last Resort*. Besides, it had taken her so long to do that she'd never accomplish it between the time they started unlocking the door and when they stepped in.

But the height gave her another idea.

She climbed the bar in the last stall--this one screwed right into the cinder wall--and reached for the bare cement edge of the windowsill. She could put all of her fingers on it. She might be able to pull herself up there. But she still needed to break that window.

It had gotten dark enough that she couldn't inspect the room in detail, so she went to her cot and sat to think. She fixed her meal and ate every bite. She'd need that energy. She tucked her spork into the the tube sleeve of the cot to hide it, and fell asleep working the problem over.

She slept better than she thought she would. Morning found her at the mirror, using the spork to dig at the silicone sealant securing the edge of the mirror to the wall. If she could get under the mirror, she could break it. A broken piece of mirror could be a weapon or a tool. Disappointingly, the silicone had been put on well. The spork barely made a dent in it.

She could maybe kick one of the faucets and get it to break off, then use that to break the window. Kicking the faucet would make a lot of noise, though, and she'd risk breaking her foot. She also filed that under *Last Resort* and moved on to the beds.

She squatted down and inspected the military cot she'd been sleeping on. It was made with hollow square aluminum tubes. It wasn't very heavy, but it was far too bulky for her to pick it up and swing it.

She wanted something she could swing.

Everything seemed to be welded together at attachment joints. The crossbar on the end of the cot seemed to be the only exception. She didn't see any pins or screws holding it in place. Screws wouldn't make sense anyway, being as the military liked things that could quickly be put up and broken down without using tools. She tugged on it, and it wiggled a bit. She scooted over to the other side and compared.

Nubs. The crossbars were held in by plastic nubs, and pressure from the canvas. She pulled hard on the end of one, levering it away from the body of the cot. It popped off of the nub and nearly flew out of her hand from the tension of the canvas.

This, she could use.

She popped the other end of the crossbar off of its nub and slid the bar out of its canvas sleeve. A couple feet long, it was lightweight but sturdy. Plastic caps kept the ends from being sharp. She frowned. They might also keep the bar from actually having enough force to break something. The plastic might soften the blow. She wondered if she could work those out.

She swung the bar a couple of times, testing it. Any sweat at all and it would probably slip right out of her hand. If she intended to use it as a weapon, she'd need to wrap it.

She'd already figured out a workable solution for that problem, when she was trying to find a way to break the big mirror over the restroom sinks. Her t-shirt tucked into her pants for a good eight inches or so. That was fabric that she could tear off without anyone noticing. She'd planned to wrap her hand with it and hit the mirror if necessary, but now that she had something resembling a bat, she wouldn't have to.

She hurried back over to her own bed and folded her blanket into a long pillow that stretched the width of the cot. This, she tucked the bar into. Then she moved to the door and looked the room over. You could clearly tell that that third cot was missing its crossbar. The canvas sleeve drooped down and called attention to itself.

Moving back over, she took that cot's blanket and re-folded it also, and laid it carefully across the foot of the cot, tucking the drooping canvas under it. She stepped back and gave it a critical eye.

Good. That concealed the missing bar. Another minute re-folding the blanket for the middle cot, and all three of them matched. Anyone coming in now wouldn't notice anything unless they checked her blanket or tried to sit on it.

Lightning crackled overhead and a few moments later, thunder rolled through the building. She smiled up at the ceiling.

"I'm working on it," she told the storm. "You just hold off a little longer, slow down a bit, and I might have something for you to see when you get here."

By noon, she'd used the spork to tear the bottom of her shirt into strips, she'd tied the fabric onto the crossbar as a grippy handle, and she had the workings of a plan.

Wait until it was dark and everyone was asleep. Climb the handles and use the bar to break the window during a crash of lightning to cover the sound. Use the bar to clear out as much glass as possible. Throw one of the blankets through the window to cover any remaining glass...then hope like crazy that she was strong enough to pull herself up and through it.

There were a lot of other variables that could make this go very wrong. The drop to the ground outside might be further than the one inside. She could break something and not be able to run. There might not even *be* ground; maybe the window opened over a shorter roof. The storm itself might be dangerous enough to hurt her or kill her. Someone might hear her break the window.

But she had to at least *try*.

The pin jiggled in the lock and she hopped up from the cot to draw attention away from it. When the door swung open, she was pacing in front of the mirror.

Frank tossed an MRE at her and she nearly missed catching it.

"Lunch," he said. "And a visitor. You've got two minutes."

Bill stepped into the room, a poncho dripping water over one arm and a legal pad in his hands.

"Bill! You didn't have to come out in this mess," she said, hugging him.

"I came to take your last will and testament, since the Bishop is on his way to Annapolis," he said, then slid a glance at Frank, who had positioned himself in the doorway and was obviously not going to give them privacy.

"In two minutes?" she asked.

"Well I didn't know about that part until I stepped in here," Bill said, and turned to Frank. "The pat-down almost took longer than that. Maybe I can leave the pad and pen? You already looked it over and verified there's nothing written in it." He held up the pad.

Frank scowled.

"There's no way I can take down her will in two minutes, and the Judge gave her this extra time to do exactly that," Bill said.

"Fine. Whatever," Frank said.

Bill walked over and dropped the pad on the cot, along with a cheap pen from his pocket that had the church's name and address printed on it. Then he stood back and looked her over, and screwed his face up.

"It's a shame they haven't given you anything to use as shoes. Quick, take off those filthy socks," he said, dropping the poncho on the floor and bending down. "We'll switch."

Dotty looked down. The bottoms of the socks he'd given her were nearly black from walking around in them, but what did that matter? They were keeping her feet warm.

"No, Bill, that's fine. They don't-"

"Take them off," he insisted. He'd slipped out of his loafers and had one sock off already.

"I didn't say you could give her more socks," Frank said. "I didn't even say you could give her the first pair."

"After patting me down, you're afraid I'm going to give her a pair of tactical socks?" Bill asked. "Maybe she'll use them to shoot a hole through the wall and escape?"

Frank rolled his eyes. "You're down to thirty seconds."

"Quick, Dotty, take them off," Bill said, gesturing at her feet.

She slipped out of them and held them up. "New ones will just get dirty-"

Bill grabbed the socks she held and thrust his into her hands. He shoved the dirty ones into his pocket and reached for her.

She closed her eyes as he kissed her forehead and pulled her into a hug.

"We're coming," he whispered. *"Be ready."*

"What's that?" Frank said.

Bill stepped back and scowled at Frank. "I said 'I love you'. Is nothing private?"

"Not in here, it's not," Frank said. "You're not her lawyer. And time's up."

Bill snatched his loafers and poncho from the floor and walked to the door. "You could've given us more time, considering what's happening in the morning."

Frank lifted a shoulder and smirked. "You got *out-planned*. Deal with it."

They left and she heard the pin slide into the lock.

She stood frozen, waiting to be sure Frank wouldn't come storming back inside.

When a few minutes had passed, she hurried to the cot and pulled the socks out from behind the MRE in her hands, and turned them over.

A slim black device slid from Bill's sock into her hand. It was a tube covered in grippy ridges, had a small flashlight on one end, and a sharp, lethal-looking point on the other. There was a little pair of wings etched into the side, with a *TF* symbol in a circle between them. She pulled on the bottom of the device and the pointy cap came off, revealing a pen. If she kept taking it apart, she'd probably find more goodies.

She'd sold devices like this in Teddy's shop. They were part of the small, impulse-buy items he had in the case at the checkout counter, along with some knives, funny mugs, and interesting keychains.

It was a tactical self-defense pen, the kind policemen carried. The tip was strong enough to break glass or stab someone. This pen probably came from the Sheriff himself, and Bill had risked everything to get it to her. He'd been lucky Frank hadn't made him take off his loafers in the pat-down. He'd have seen the hard line of it running alongside Bill's foot.

Tactical socks, she thought, and slapped a hand over her mouth to cover a nearly hysterical burst of laughter. The laughter turned to tears and hope bloomed bright and hot in her chest.

They're coming for me.

PREACHER

The world sounded like it was being torn apart, with howling winds beating at the roll-up doors of the prison's intake bay and water pushing in under the seal. Pools stretched across the floor and little waves rippled across them. Preacher huddled against the innermost wall with the other members of the suicide squad. They'd been here for nearly an hour, waiting for the hurricane's eyewall to pass over.

Having no idea how large the storm was presented a problem. They'd waited in the men's wing for hours, going stir crazy until the Sheriff finally moved them out here.

Not knowing how small the hurricane's eye was presented an *even bigger* problem. They had no idea how much time they'd have once the winds stopped. It could be thirty minutes. It could be only five.

As if turning a switch, the doors stopped rattling in their frames and the howling dropped off; banshees retreating into the distance.

The next minute, all was deathly quiet.

"Holy *shit*," Trench said. "Sounded like the doors were going to rip off. Is it over?"

"Only for twenty minutes or so, and that's if we're lucky," the Warden said. "Let's move."

"You kids make sure you come back with the same amount of holes you got now," Fish said, following them across the bay with a big squeegee propped on his shoulder. "I don't want blood on my floor."

"That's the goal," the Warden said, and then they were out in the darkness.

Preacher glanced up at the sky as they hurried across the parking lot and out into the grass. The sky was completely clear, and moonlight poured down, painting everything in a silvery light. If it weren't for the slap of their steps in the standing water and the big branches strewn across the lot, you'd never have known there was a hurricane going on just minutes ago.

Or that it was coming back.

The corner of the prison's land butted up against the back corner of the Rec Center's land. Preacher thought it was a strange setup, given the law's insistence that no criminals be anywhere close to where children would be learning or at play. Most felons wouldn't be able to live in a house this close, and here was an entire prison full of them. Then again, the rules never seemed to apply to the government; they did what they wanted.

Not this time.

The prison's drive ran along the Rec Center's property, but since the Guard had been kind enough to take their quick-deploy fence with them, the group was sticking to the grass. A group of men jogging across the asphalt would be too noisy. As they crept across the slim field between the buildings, the gym doors banged open and a few people stepped outside.

In the front, Marco gave an arm signal for everyone to get

down, and the group crouched in the tall grass.

More people stepped outside. A couple lit cigarettes. A few jogged for the porta-potties, yelling back about the smell from those that had been knocked over in the storm. One man walked about ten feet away from the door, faced the prison, and started urinating. He whistled a tune and flipped a finger over his shoulder to someone complaining about how close he was. More men joined the first, as if at a line-up of invisible urinals.

Preacher held his breath. If anyone moved and caught one of these men's eyes, they'd lose the element of surprise.

A woman's voice rang out, calling the urinating men pigs, and the first guy finished up with a happy sigh. Preacher could hear his zipper from here.

"Be glad I only had to piss!" The man called back as he turned and walked back into the gym.

They crouched there, for excruciatingly long minutes, as each of the men finished up, chatted a bit, and made their way back inside.

Preacher heard a low murmur ahead of him and waited for it to be passed back.

Father Bill turned and repeated the message. "Now, to the corner," he said in a soft voice. "Low and slow, like we practiced."

Preacher turned and repeated it to Trench, and so it went down the line.

That was something Marco had pounded into their heads earlier: No whispering. All communications while they were outside were to be done man-to-man, in low conversational tones. A whisper, he explained, turned every word into a hissing sound, and that attracted as much attention as shouting.

Preacher did his best to keep up with the little man in front of him, but waddling was slow going. A man his size wasn't meant to crouch and walk at the same time. He kept his head down and his eyes on Bill's heels. The big pair of bolt cutters he was carrying kept tipping him off-balance. His knees were screaming. This was part of why he'd run so much while he was incarcerated--to keep his muscles flexible. Nearly a decade of only riding motorcycles had done a number on his legs.

One foot in front of the other. Just keep going.

A hand squeezed his shoulder. "We're here," Marco's quiet voice said. "Stand up."

Preacher looked up and found that he'd followed Bill past the Center's solar panel array and right up to the backside of the building. Here, on the opposite side of the gym's exit, there were no doors.

"So much for everyone being asleep," Trench murmured as he stood and stretched.

"It doesn't change anything," the Warden said, looking at the sky. "We still have to go in. Sure would be nice if Teddy showed up to save the day with that APC right about now."

"A Hail Mary like that only happen in the movies," Father Bill murmured.

The moonlight was bright enough that Preacher could see lines at the edges of the Warden's eyes and his mouth set tight with worry. They'd only gone about a football field's distance and had planned on it taking about five minutes, but that was walking at normal speed across the uneven ground. The waiting, and the sneaky crouching thing had eaten time. To Preacher it felt like an hour, but he knew his knees were lying to him.

"Front corner, go," Marco said, and the group set off. They jogged to the corner of the building and crouched down again. Marco peeked his head around the front of the building and back, then looked again. After a few heartbeats, he held up his hand and slipped around the corner.

"We're coming, Dotty," Father Bill murmured. "Lord willing,

we're coming."

A whisper started through the trees near the highway. The wind was picking back up.

"I think we're running out of time," the Warden said.

"We just have to get inside. We can make it back through the storm," Bill said.

"It'll just be a lot harder if we can't see," Trench said.

"We'll make it," Bill insisted.

Marco appeared beside them, low and silent. "There's two guards in the lobby, on the couches. They're both asleep."

"Not for long," Preacher said.

"We know others are awake now. We should use the pipe bombs," Marco said.

The Warden shook his head. "We stick with the plan. Hurt no one that isn't trying to hurt us." He looked at each man, and they nodded. "Alright then. Weapons ready. Preacher, you're in front."

They'd agreed on this beforehand. Preacher's job was to get through the doors while the others covered him. They'd head for the restroom and he'd cut the lock, if necessary. Bill insisted that it was just an old-fashioned pin lock, but the Warden didn't put it past Frank to slap a padlock on it at night. They'd hoped they could get in without waking anyone. Looked like that wasn't going to happen.

Preacher swung around the corner and sprinted to the portico. He saw the sleeping figures inside, shotguns draped loosely across their chests. Footsteps pounded past him. The Warden took position behind a column and aimed his rifle at the sleeping men.

"Ready," the Sheriff said. Five more voices echoed him.

The trees answered back with a sound like a distant waterfall and Preacher felt a gust of wind push at his legs.

"Wakey wakey," he muttered, and swung those bolt cutters for all he was worth.

DOTTY

Voices calling for people to get back inside came faintly through the walls. Dotty heard the heavy gym door swing shut, and tugged harder on the zip-tie connecting her ankle to the baseboard heater. It creaked, but didn't budge.

The door swung open and Cathy came in, muttering something about men being pigs. Her flashlight beam hit Dotty square in the face.

"Wind's picking back up," she said. "Looks like Frank was wrong. He needs to come get you the hell out of my room. You *stink.*"

Crashing glass made them both jump. Cathy dropped the flashlight. Shouts to *stay down* boomed through the hall.

"They're here!" A man yelled. "They're he-"

He abruptly fell silent.

They're here! They came!

Cathy cursed and scrabbled for her flashlight, kicking it across the floor in her hurry. Dotty yanked her leg frantically.

"Quit that!" Cathy yelled. "Frank! Frank! She's tryin' to get free!"

The gym doors slammed open against the wall of Cathy's room and heavy footsteps pounded by. Someone was beating on something. Gunshots fired. A man roared. More gunshots.

"She's not in here!" Dotty heard Preacher shout.

The door crashed open and Wilhelm aimed a pistol at her. "Get up!" he screamed.

"I can't!" she yelled back, holding her hands up. She yanked her leg to show him.

"Get her out of my room!" Cathy yelled. "Get her out before they come in here and shoot *me!*"

More gunshots. Men were screaming orders. Someone howled in pain.

Wilhelm spat a curse and holstered his pistol. He pulled a small folding knife from his pocket and started for her.

Dotty screamed as loud as she could. "Bill! Back here! I'm back *here!*"

Cathy slapped her across the face so hard it knocked Dotty's head into the wall. "Shut the hell up! You're not getting me killed!"

"Pin her," Wilhelm said. "Pin her down."

Cathy stepped on Dotty's wrists and shoved down on her shoulders. Dotty screamed in pain. Cathy hit her again, three times. "Shut up, shut up, shut up!"

Dotty wished, for probably the fiftieth time since Frank had dragged her in here, that she had her makeshift club. He'd come into her restroom cell before it was even dark, almost panic-like in his insistence that she had to be moved *immediately*. It had just occurred to him that her family might use the storm as cover for an attempt a break-out. Neither she nor Cathy had been happy about his decision of where to hide her.

Wilhelm levered his bulk down and sawed at the zip-tie. His knife slipped off and he cut her getting it back into place.

"Tell me again why we needed to have the lights off?" he muttered. The zip-tie popped free and she kicked. She struck something, and he yelped and fell over.

"God damnit!" he barked. "I'll shoot you myself!"

"Simon," Frank's voice boomed from just outside the open door. "You don't want to do this. You're already getting people hurt."

"I *do* want to do this," Bill called back. "Where's Dotty?"

Dotty tried to scramble to her feet, but Wilhelm's bulk pinned her legs. "*Bill!*" she screamed. Cathy clubbed her in the back of the head with the flashlight. Dotty's vision flashed white.

"This is suicide, Father. You're out-planned *and* out-gunned," Frank yelled. "And doesn't your God say something about not killing?"

Dotty felt a meaty hand wrap around her bicep and Wilhelm yanked at her arm. "Get up! Now!"

She got her feet under her and stood, pushing against the wall. The room swam. A cold, hard barrel pressed into her spine and Wilhelm hissed in her ear. "Walk. Walk out there."

She stumbled forward, her legs threatening to buckle.

"You guys okay?" Simon called.

"I'll live," Preacher called back.

"Just surface wounds," Dotty heard Marco call out.

The kids are here? They brought the kids? No. No!

She grabbed hold of the doorframe and leaned her head on her bound wrists. She just needed a second for the dizziness to fade.

"Further!" Wilhelm hissed. "Out in the hall. I want them to see this."

"Kenny what the hell are you doing?" Frank said, and Dotty

looked up to see him in a doorway directly across the hall, pistol at the ready.

How can I see him?

"Ending this," Wilhelm said. He shoved her and she stumbled out into the hall. She blinked hard against a bright light aimed directly at her. That's how she could see him. Someone at the other end of the hall had some type of flood light. She held up her hands to shield her eyes.

"Dotty? Honey, walk to my voice," Bill said.

A thick arm wrapped around her throat. "She's not walking anywhere," Wilhelm said next to her ear. She could smell his fetid breath, feel his sweaty face against her temple. The barrel of his gun pressed into her cheek.

She froze.

I will not *die like this in front of William,* she thought. *I won't.*

She moved her fingers quickly, walking the front of her shirt up free from her jeans. Her knees were trembling.

"Let her go, Kenny," Simon called. "Let her go, and this all ends. You go back to doing your thing, and we go back to doing ours."

"Get the hell out of my way you fat bas-" Cathy hissed, and she must have shoved Wilhelm forward. Dotty dangled for a moment, held up only by his big arm around her throat, and then got her feet back under her.

The gym doors banged open behind them and Dotty heard the sound of running footsteps.

"Your *loyal* friend Cathy just took off," Frank said over his shoulder, and from deeper in the room, Cindy spat a string of curses back at him.

"This is how it's going to go," Wilhelm called out. Thunder boomed overhead as if to stress his words. "You're going to put down your guns and surrender, or I'm going to execute her, right here, right now."

"And then what?" Simon called back from the darkness behind the spotlight. "You put us *all* in front of the firing squad tomorrow?"

"An armed attack on government officials and law enforcement officers? A firing squad is better than you deserve," Wilhelm spat.

Shadows streaked across the light, and Frank's gun jerked in that direction but didn't fire. "Joe? Was that you?" he called.

"I'm in the map room," a man called back. "Someone just ran by the door."

Frank cursed.

"I think the story is more like *Crazed madman attempts dictatorship, citizens correct the problem*," Simon called. "Let her go."

Dotty pulled the tactical pen down from the elastic band of Ripley's sports bra, felt for the tip, and gripped it upright in her fists.

"How many men did you bring with you, Simon?" Frank called. "The minute you came through that door I had men going out the back to circle behind you. You're surrounded."

"Yeah, shame about that," Simon said. "We were hoping not to hurt anyone. But when they came around the corner shooting, my deputies outside had no choice. You sent those men to their deaths."

"He's lying," Frank whispered to Wilhelm. "The last of his deputies took off last week."

"Oh for God's sake!" Cindy yelled. "Just *shoot*! Shoot the light! Shoot *her!*"

"You've got until the count of three-" Wilhelm started.

"Don't do it," Simon interrupted. "You kill her, and we've got no reason to keep from filling you full of lead."

Wilhelm growled. "Put your guns down!" he screamed.

"No," Simon said.

The gym door creaked open and Dotty felt Wilhelm's arm tighten as he turned his head to look.

"What-" Frank started, and then went silent. There was a strange sound, like someone stepping on Rice Krispies. Wilhelm let out a high-pitched screech.

Dotty dropped all of her weight and jabbed the tactical pen as hard as she could into that fat arm squeezing her throat. Wilhelm screeched again. The arm disappeared and she fell to the floor.

A gunshot rang out and a heavy weight landed on her, pinning her down. More gunshots fired as she scrabbled to crawl out from under whatever was on top of her. Her ears were ringing. Shadows raced in front of her and she blinked hard to clear her vision.

The weight rolled off and hands grabbed her shoulders. Someone lifted her up, and she struck out blindly with the pen. She felt it hit something and shoved hard against it, trying to drive it in.

"That really hurts, Miss Dotty," Marco's voice said, but the sound was compressed and far away. "Could you please stop?"

She opened her eyes to find the young man holding her up, her pen sticking into his arm.

"Give her to me," Bill said, suddenly beside her. "Give her to me."

Marco let go and then Bill's arms were wrapped around her, and he squeezed her so tight she couldn't breathe.

"I didn't see Cathy," Preacher said from her other side.

"Cathy ran," Dotty said. She turned her head to look, and gasped. Blood ran down his arm in a sheet, coming from a multitude of shallow wounds in his big bicep. His other hand held a gun.

"Preacher, you're hurt," she said, pushing away from Bill. Even her own voice sounded funny and muffled.

"I've had worse," Preacher said. He turned slightly to move his arm out of her sight.

"Hazards of breaching double doors," Marco said. "By the time you're through the second set, the guys inside are awake and shooting. I wanted to use the pipe bombs, but the Sheriff wouldn't allow it."

"We had to give them a chance," Bill said. "There was a possibility they wouldn't follow orders."

"*Never* count on that," Marco said.

Dotty frowned at the distracting chatter. "Preacher, you've been *shot*. Let me look," she said. She tried to step around the big man to grab his hand, only to have Bill grab hers.

"No, Dotty you don't need to see-" Bill said, but it was too late. Her foot hit something and drew her attention down. She pulled in a sharp breath.

Frank lay crumpled in the doorway, like a rag doll that had been dropped by a careless owner. His head was turned and drooping at an unnatural angle. His mouth hung slack, and vacant eyes stared past her. A large, bloody handprint wrapped around the bottom of his face.

Dotty looked at Preacher's bloody hand, then met his eyes, hard and glinting over his still-bruised cheekbone.

He gave a little nod to her unasked question. "I warned him. He didn't listen."

"And Cindy?" she asked.

Preacher gestured into the room past Frank with the end of his pistol. "Had to," he said, his voice laced with disgust. "She was firing at us."

Wilhelm lay across the hall, a large hole in his forehead barely trickling blood. His face was frozen in an expression of shock.

She swallowed down bile and took a deep breath.

Bill turned her around. "What you did was perfect, Dotty. It was so brave. You gave me the opening I needed."

"Opening? What opening?"

"I couldn't get a clear shot until you made him let go of you," Bill said. "Right up to that second I thought we weren't going to be able to save you."

Dotty blinked. "You...Wilhelm?"

Bill grimaced and nodded.

"It was a beautiful shot," Marco said, cocking his head and poking his fingers into a hole in the gym door. "Wish you hadn't done it with us back here, but it was a beautiful shot."

Simon walked up, casting large shadows over the gruesome scene. "What about the people?"

"Most of them were gone when we went through the gym," Marco said. "I think they ran when the shooting started."

"I should lock both of you in a cell to make sure you don't get yourselves killed. Crossing that light was stupid," Simon said.

"But necessary," Marco countered. "We had to get behind them."

Simon made a noise that could have been reluctant agreement. "We need to get back over to the prison before the townspeople come back," he said. "And it's going to be a bear doing it. Wind's really picked back up."

"What about these?" Preacher asked, pointing at the bodies. Everyone looked down, considering.

"You three figure that out. I'm taking her back," Bill said, and steered her towards the light.

"Tell the other guys to come in here," Simon called after them. "We'll catch up to you."

They made it past the big flashlight and into the relative darkness of the lobby. Bill pulled her to a stop.

"Hold on just a minute. We need to let our eyes adjust," he said.

Wind and rain tore through the remains of the doors. A few men huddled there, rifles aimed out into the maelstrom.

"Fellas," Bill yelled. "The Sheriff needs you."

The men stood and turned on headlamps before making their way across the glass-strewn floor. The light caused the broken shards to glitter, and in the reflected light Dotty glimpsed at least two still, unmoving forms draped across the couches.

So many lives, she thought.

She tried to bring her hand up to wipe tears from her cheeks, and remembered her wrists were still bound. She turned and held them out.

"Get these off of me, please."

"Oh, Dotty, I'm sorry," Bill said. He adjusted a huge rifle hanging over his shoulder and pulled out a pocket knife much like the one Wilhelm had used. He cut through the zip-ties with a quick movement.

She rubbed her wrists and watched him put the knife away. When he reached for her hand, she stepped back. He blinked, clearly confused.

"You shot Kenny Wilhelm," she said. "You *killed* him."

He frowned and dropped his hand. Silently, he nodded.

"Why, Bill? Why you?"

His face hardened. "Because he was about to shoot you."

"But Bill, you're a *preacher. Thou shalt not kill?* You just...for *me*..."

Bill shook his head and held up a hand. "The translations changed over time. The commandment, written in its *original* form, says *Thou shalt not murder.* I didn't commit murder, Dotty. I killed a man, yes. But I did it in defense of an innocent. That's not murder."

"And God's going to be okay with you doing that? With a *preacher* doing that?"

Bill gave her a sad little smile. "He forgave me for all the times I had to in Nam. I think he'll forgive me for saving you. And if he doesn't..." he lifted a shoulder in a little shrug. "It was worth it to me. I'd pay any price for you, Mrs. Parker."

He held out his hand again.

This time, she took it with both of hers.

EPILOGUE

Cathy Riggs had never been the sharpest arrow in her parents' quiver. She realized that early on.

But she was crafty, and she could spot an opportunity the instant it raised its hand to knock on the door.

Those talents had allowed her to be the one who could hand the Lieutenant Mayor a crusade. She'd become the only person who could provide valuable information ensuring success for Cindy Stalls' efforts. She'd wriggled her way into this tiny town's upper echelon and secured herself a spot at the big boy's table.

A spot that would allow her to keep living the nice, comfortable, air-conditioned life she damn well deserved.

When Frank Stalls had dragged Dotty Parker into her room at the Rec Center, her eye for opportunity had told her to get out before it all went to hell.

But she'd stayed, because Frank had gotten paranoid lately and it was just plain stupid to think that anyone would go out in a freaking *hurricane* to get one selfish old woman.

But that's exactly what they'd done.

Now she was soaking wet, walking through the hurricane herself, trying to get home. The wind moved past her face so fast it was difficult to breathe. The moon that had been bright and beautiful when she'd run out of the gym to get away from the shooting had disappeared behind the storm clouds. Her flashlight couldn't show her much past the dark, wet surface of the road five feet in front of her or the dark, wet green of the grass that the wind kept blowing her into.

She was bleeding from a bevy of cuts and scrapes. She'd been knocked down a number of times. At least three times the wind that was a steady, solid force she had to push through had suddenly gusted and thrown her off of the road. Once had been from a half-empty trash can that had come flying out of the dark without warning, and once more from the leafy tip of a big tree branch that had slid down the road almost as fast as a car. It had made a horrendous hissing noise as it approached, swept her feet out from under her, and kept going. The ankle it had hit was swelling up now, and pain lanced through her leg whenever she stepped on that foot. She'd probably sprained it.

Yet another thing she could lay directly at the feet of Dotty Parker.

She passed some strange tipped-over wooden contraption with a garden hose dribbling water onto the sidewalk—as if anyone needed *more* water right now, there was at least an inch of it on the road--and thought she was still a block or so away from her house. When her flashlight fell upon her own mailbox, her first thought wasn't joy that she'd made it there alive, it was anger and indignation that someone would leave that trash out in front of her house.

She limped to the front steps and pulled herself up the railing.

The screen door ripped out of her hand and smashed against the railing on the other side, bending in the process. She'd have Dan fix that tomorrow.

The doorknob didn't turn. Locked. Why the hell would it be locked when she wasn't home? Dan always left the door unlocked so she didn't have to bother with balancing shopping bags while trying to get the key in the door. He'd learned years ago how that put her in a bad mood.

There was no candle light coming through the windows. The useless dolt had probably gone to bed. She banged on the door anyway, and then fought with her wet pants to get her keys out of her pocket.

The wind kept shoving her, knocking her against the screen door as she tried to get her key into the lock. It was throwing her around so much that the key wouldn't go in. She banged harder, and yelled for Dan to wake up. The sound of the wind was too loud; she couldn't tell if he was making his way to the door to let her in. He'd better be.

Hunching into the wind and shining the flashlight directly on the lock, she lined up her key.

That's when she noticed the shiny, gaudy brass of the doorknob.

Her doorknobs were a trendy, sophisticated dark bronze.

Her first thought was that she'd mistaken the mailbox and come to the wrong house. But no, this was definitely her door, in the special-ordered *Rustic Red* with the little arched window at the top.

But it now had a cheap, brass doorknob. So shiny it could have been brand-new.

That weaselly, whimpering, sonofabitch husband of hers had changed the locks while she'd been staying at the Rec Center.

After all these years, *now* was when he finally grew a spine? Over what? One little black eye? No, it couldn't be that. It wasn't as if it were his first. And where in the hell had he gotten new knobs? There weren't any stores open.

She'd bet money Dotty Parker had something to do with it. That meddlesome woman got her nasty brown claws into everything.

Cathy looked at the knob again. The classless brass, mounted on her expensive custom door, enraged her. She beat on the door and screamed for Dan to let her in, but either he was cowering in some corner or he couldn't hear her over the storm.

Wait, weren't Dotty's knobs that awful brass?

Had that woman switched knobs with Dan? That was exactly the kind of thing she'd do.

Well, Dotty wasn't home. Her family was currently in a gun fight with Frank and the boys at the Rec Center trying to save the stupid woman, and it wasn't like any of them were going to survive that. The Parker house was empty, and most likely had her expensive doorknobs on it.

If they'd switched knobs, she could hole up in Dotty's house until the storm blew over. Then she'd come over here and teach Dan a lesson that would make sure he'd never pull this type of stunt again. Maybe she could have Frank arrest him for something. Throw *his* ass in jail. It would serve him right.

Cathy stumbled down the steps and pushed against the wind. She made it past the bushes separating the two yards, and finally butted up against Dotty's porch steps. She half-crawled, half-pulled herself onto the porch. The screen door here was already open, banging hard against the house. On her knees, she leaned against the doorframe and brought the flashlight up, key at the ready.

The doorknob was made of cheap, shiny brass.

She screamed her frustration into the wind and beat her fist against the door.

Wait...the back door. Dotty must have switched her back door knob with Dan.

Cathy tucked her keys inside her shirt and crawled back across the porch. She gripped the bottom of the railing hard as she maneuvered out onto the steps.

The wind blew her clean off the steps and sent her rolling through the grass. The flashlight flew from her hands and lay shining at her about ten feet away, half-submerged in the standing water. She scrambled to it, picked it up, and crawled for the side of the house.

The wind was significantly weaker here. She was able to raise up into a crouch and scurry towards the back. The fury of the storm filled her ears, but as she reached the back corner of the house, she swore she heard a sharp *CRACK*.

Was that a gunshot? Is someone shooting at me?

Ducking low, she ran for the back porch. The screen door was completely gone. The wind must have ripped it off.

As she slid to her knees in front of the back door, she heard it again.

CRACK.

Where the storm had inspired anger, these sounds truly terrified her. She knew a storm wouldn't kill her, but a bullet certainly would.

Who the hell is shooting? And how can they even see to shoot?

The shaking beam of the flashlight revealed yet another brass door knob.

Cathy screamed and beat the flashlight against the door. On the third strike, the beam cut off, leaving her in total darkness.

CRACK.

"Stop shooting at me!" she screamed into the night. "I didn't do anyth-"

King's big old pine tree crashed down through the porch with all of hurricane Michael's force behind it.

BACK OF THE BOOK STUFF

Hey ladies and gents!

Breathing a sigh of relief? Cheering for a tree? I'd love to know your reaction to IMPACT.

I'd also really like to apologize for the length of time that has passed since ADVENT was released. Thank you so, SO much for coming back to re-visit our folks in Snow Hill. I hope it delivered. (*I was cheering for the tree. Seriously. You should've seen me sitting at my desk when I finished writing that scene: arms pumping over my head giving the universal one-finger salute, tongue sticking out, maniacal cackling...I looked spastic.*)

Thank you again, and until next time...watch for falling trees. ;)

Want to know when the next book is coming out? Want to spend more time with your favorite characters?

My newsletter subscribers receive occasional notices about book releases, cover reveals, and free exclusive short stories from the SUNFALL world. Sign up at:

http://eepurl.com/Nx3H5

Please consider leaving a review on Amazon. In this digital age of online stores, authors rely heavily on honest reviews from readers like you. It doesn't have to be a book summary or even a paragraph...just a few simple words will do.

I would greatly appreciate it. :)

I never sell or give away email addresses. I hate spam as much as you do.

ABOUT THE AUTHOR

Drew Gideon spends most of her time arguing with the characters in her head—the characters usually win. She lives with her "I'm an ~~engaineer engeneer enginear~~...I'm good with math!" husband and the three coolest kids in the world in the sweaty armpit of the United States. She's proudly owned by two cats and a dog, all of whom adopted her when she went to the shelter in need of a friend.

Drew longs for a time when she'll have a self-sufficient homestead and cozy writing cabin in the mountains, where she can utilize her own personal shooting range clad in nothing but a good set of cans and her pajamas if she wants. Of course, she'd really prefer to dump the cans and use a nice suppressor.

To see what Drew's up to and find out when the next release is, please visit her at any of the following online hangouts:
www.DrewGideon.com
DrewGideonBooks@gmail.com

Made in the USA
Middletown, DE
10 January 2021